Castle Minerva

CASTLE MINERVA

As I walked, roped between them like some slave,
I could feel my face smarting from the blow. It was
the same hand I thought that had struck at Sophie
and bruised her. George Sarrasin, I thought; full of
strength and vigour, who didn't care whether it was
a man or woman he struck, who breathed 'Beautiful'
when a knife went home ... How I hated him, how
I warmed myself with the hope that one day I should
be free on my feet with a chance to get at him.

VICTOR CANNING

CASTLE MINERVA

SUNDIAL PUBLICATIONS LIMITED

First published in Great Britain in 1955
by Hodder & Stoughton Limited
Reissued by William Heinemann Limited in 1973

This edition published in 1980 by
Sundial Publications Limited
59 Grosvenor Street, London W1

© Victor Canning 1955

ISBN 0 906320 53 4

Printed in Great Britain by
Richard Clay (The Chaucer Press) Ltd,
Bungay, Suffolk

Set in 10/11pt Linotype Pilgrim

TO
MY WIFE

CHAPTER ONE

There was a light cold rain falling as I came down the road out of the pass. It would freeze during the night and I knew that any climbing the next day would have to be handled carefully. Across the wide valley the gentle slope of Moel Siabod rose out of the misty rain like a stranded whale. Moel Siabod, Snowdon, Tryfan, the Carnedds ... the lovely Welsh names and the lovely Welsh hills; just to get up here for a long weekend gave me a lift and a freshening of the spirit. It was a far cry from morning chapels, the smell of chalk and changing rooms, and the trapped look of boys floundering in a morass of French irregular verbs. I like my job. I liked being with boys and watching them develop into young manhood, but by mid-term I was always ready for a break. Up here the wind blew all memory of school away, and the strain of setting my body against the steep rock faces brought that liberation of the spirit which every man needs now and again if he is going to keep on top of his job.

I kept going through the rain, happy, and with that growing tiredness of the body which is a form of contentment. At that moment I wasn't asking for anything. I was over thirty, reasonably ambitious, and interested in my work. I imagined I could see the shape of the future, and I liked what I pictured. One day I'd be a housemaster, perhaps a headmaster. I'd be married, have children and then I'd have to make my vacations more orthodox, bathing and sailing, not trying to feed still the old war-bred appetite for strange places and people. A good future. But right then I should have had the sense not to compliment myself about it. The future maps itself.

Below me the lights of the inn showed up through the rain. I began to anticipate the comforts of getting out of wet clothes, of soaking in a hot bath, of the large whisky before dinner and the leisurely pipe afterwards in front of the bar room fire.

But for me that evening there was more than comfort in store. I got in, bathed and changed, and went down to the bar and there, unexpected, sitting in a corner was the one man in all the world whose company I would have asked for if the gods had given me the choice.

Colonel Francis Drexel, D.S.O., M.C. He got up and came across to me, his movements dancing, brisk, terrier-like; the iron-grey hair crisp, short cut; the lean weather-tanned and worn face smiling; a small, dapper man full of life and still, for all his near sixty years, as hard as nails.

He grabbed my arm and said, 'David ... Well, if this isn't luck!' Apart from us there was only the barman in the place and Drexel's voice echoed about the room joyfully. It was the old voice, the old tone and with it—the grasp of his powerful fingers on my arm—all the old magic.

'When did you get in?' I asked.

'Couple of hours ago.'

'I didn't know you used this place?'

He laughed, called to the barman for a couple of whiskies, and went on, 'David, I was climbing up here before you were born. And I'll still be here when you're dead.' He stood back and looked at me and then with a snort said, 'Still can't get used to you in those damned civilian clothes. You looked better in uniform. You still buried in that damn school?'

'Still there,' I said smiling. 'Happily interred.' And as I spoke I was thinking of the times in the past when this man had scared hell into me, of the times he had forced me to the edge of breaking but never over. He had taken me as a young officer—Captain David Bladen Fraser of the Gordon Highlanders—with the mist of Edinburgh still in my hair and had put me through the rolling mill of the Mediterranean and the Near East. He had helped to turn me into a man, and I knew that after the war he had hated to see me go back to itchy-bottomed schoolboys with minds like colanders.

He tossed his whisky back and ordered two more.

'Tomorrow,' he said, 'we'll climb together. How's the old knee-cap?'

'It's all right as long as I watch it.' As I answered each of us was thinking the same thing I guessed, both of us years back in the past.

He said, 'We'll do the Milestone Buttress or maybe some of Idwal Slabs. I've been in Berlin for three weeks and I want to get the smell of frustration out of my nostrils.'

I didn't ask him what he had been doing in Berlin. I had more sense, but there was an ugly bruise and a few cuts on the side of his face in a pattern that only a knuckle-duster can raise. I knew because I had used one in his service before now. But no questions: Colonel Francis Drexel, a hero to the public, a war-time legend, and still in harness. I wondered if the Foreign Office or M.I.5 ever pensioned off their people.

I said, 'You'll have to go easy with me. I have to pick my climbs these days.'

'Nonsense. For a six-footer you're carrying too much weight. I'll take it off you. The kind of life you lead makes people fat and complacent. How the hell do you stick it?'

'Because I like it. Don't let's begin that all over again.' This was an old argument between us. We lived now in different worlds. I had touched his during the war, but now I was back where I belonged, with the kind of job millions of men have to do, nine till five, boring sometimes, but with a purpose behind it and pleasure in it. Only during my vacations could I slip into something like his kind of life. With me a little excitement went a long way. With Drexel it was food and drink. The world had a place for both of us.

'Wasted,' he said. 'A good man wasted. However ...' He finished his whisky, and then in that abrupt way of his said, 'Married yet?'

I laughed. 'Not yet. No takers.'

'Not surprised. Don't find your kind in vicarage gardens, or at school bun fights. I've tried marriage twice and it doesn't work. Not for me, anyway. Suppose I'm not at home enough.' For a moment I thought I caught the hint of regret in his voice.

He tapped his glass for the barman to fill it again and I think it was then that I noticed the change in him. At first I thought it was something to do wih the way he was drinking. Then I knew it wasn't. He always had drunk hard. It was an all-over something. There was a strain on him. He looked much the same, the hardness, the trim compactness, the tight rebellious mouth of a schoolboy, the restless eyes full of visions and fire ... but something was gone. His laugh was no longer as easy as it had been ... And then I saw it. He was showing his age. Just that. He was being worn down and, because I had no much affection and respect for this man, I was suddenly resentful of the anonymous service which was doing this to him. He had been in harness too long. No man should have to go on being a hero, a colourful public figure, after fifty-eight. It was time he slowed up and took things easy.

But change or no change, the next day on the towering Idwal Slabs, he scared the hell out of me. Ever since my cracked-knee-cap I've had to go carefully, and anyway going carefully is the best bet in climbing. But Drexel climbed as he did everything else, with one hand on death's shoulder for support. And there was a grin on his face which I knew was for my benefit. It was a challenge and I had to take it. It was a bright, clear March day with a freezing cold wind and a thin layer of ice on most of the rocks, and more than once I said to myself, 'Fraser, if you don't want to break your neck put your pride in your pocket and get down below.' But I didn't. Where he went, I went, and that was like the old times.

When we stopped to eat our sandwiches at midday, Drexel passed over his flask and I was glad of the nip

of brandy. We were sitting on a wide ledge, our feet
dangling over space. Reaching out around us was the
great bowl of the purple and green hills, and far below
the thin line of the road running past the tip of Lake
Ogwen, its surface foam-lined with breakers from the
boisterous wind.

Drexel said, 'You still go well.' He waved his hand
at the view. 'Wonderful, isn't it? Free of all the muck
and stink. A man can breathe.'

'You go too fast,' I said. 'You'll break your damned
neck one of these days. This afternoon I lead.'

He tossed a sandwich crust out into space and
watched the wind take it. Then after a little silence he
said quietly, 'You really like being a schoolmaster,
David?'

'Of course I do. The war's over long ago. My kind
have to go back to work.'

'You seem to get about in your vacations if what I
hear is right?'

'That's what holidays are for.'

'What are you doing this Easter vac.?'

I felt in my windbreaker for my cigarettes. 'Flying to
East Africa. Tanzania.'

'Going to wipe up the Mau Mau?' he grinned.

'No. Going to look for some of the lost property of
the Queen of Sheba.'

Even as I spoke I could feel the excitement rise in
me. Drexel had it out of me in no time. Three of us
were going and the school was prepared to give me a
few weeks extra exeat. A thousand years before Christ
all the islands off the coast of East Africa had formed
part of Sheba's great empire of Tharish. We were to
explore the island of Songa Manara, an island so far
untouched, its thick jungle hiding the ruins of great
palaces and traces of a long dead civilization. It was
something I had always wanted to do, something which,
in an odd way, meant a lot to me. Work by itself isn't
enough. A man has got to have a few dreams even if
they never become real. But this dream was going to

come alive. We were taking an old movie camera and everything was being done on a shoe-string. It was something that had been in my mind for years.

Drexel said, 'You talk as though it were pretty important.'

'It is.'

I couldn't go into it more with him. Some things you have to keep to yourself. The whole Songa Manara thing might cause quite a little stir ... the film we should make, the possible discoveries, and the book to be written. Though we were doing it for its own sake, in my profession these things count. They make a difference when a housemaster's job is going, and later ... Well, the competition is keen, but it's no good being a schoolmaster unless somewhere in the future you see yourself running a show of your own.

He didn't ask any more questions. But he was no fool and I think he understood. He stood up, flipped his cigarette into space and said, 'O.K. You lead. Knee all right?'

'Fine.'

We roped up and started again and, frankly, I took the easier pitches. Behind me Drexel was very silent, which was not like him. But it was good to feel him there. Once on a stretch of loose shale my knee gave me a twinge and the pain took me back ... I had a swift picture of myself lying in the desert sand, the flies thick about the wound in my knee, the sun like a brazen gong and my head spinning with fever, and myself knowing that when the sun went down so would I ... And then Drexel coming back, out of nowhere, unexpected, risking himself for me, and never a moment of doubt in him, bullying me into courage and strength, half-carrying, half-dragging me for a couple of days. From that time every second I lived I owed to him. That's the kind of debt a man seldom gets the chance to repay.

When we stopped for a breather, he came up alongside me. He stood there with the wind shrieking over

the ragged edge of the rocks behind us and the sun
making the ice shine on the spurs below. He stared
down into the valley. After a moment he said, 'This
Songa Manara thing could mean a lot to you?'

'Well ... Yes.' His question was quite unexpected.

He nodded. Then suddenly he turned to me. His
eyes were troubled. The lean, ageing face was very
still. He said, 'David. Meeting you up here was no
accident. I came up after you.'

'You did!' I was surprised and my voice showed it.

'Yes. I had to talk with you, David ... I need your
help. I need someone I know, someone I can trust
absolutely.'

I said, 'You know that if there's anything I can do for
you, you've only got to ask.'

'That's why I hate doing it.'

'Rot. Get it off your chest. What is it?'

Then abruptly, he said, 'No, I can't do it. Get moving.' He waved me on and I had to go. But now the
thought that he wanted something from me and
wouldn't ask stirred me up. I tried him once or twice as
we climbed but he waved me on.

Finally we made the top of the climb and unroped
on the short turf. As we started to walk around the
top to find the easy path down to the lake, I swung
round on him.

'If you want something from me, you've a right to ask
for it,' I said, and I heard my voice angry and determined shredding into the wind. 'I'm not moving until
you tell me.'

He was a long time answering and I could sense the
struggle in him.

'I don't want you to go to Songa Manara,' he said at
last. It was so unexpected that for a second a voice
inside me cried out against it. But only for a second.

'Why not?' My voice showed nothing except curiosity.

'Because I want you to do a job for me during the
Easter vacation. Not such a colourful job, though it

may have its excitements. But it's a job that means a hell of a lot to me.'

In that moment as I faced him I knew that if I put off my Songa Manara trip now the chance would never come again. That's the way life goes. I stood there and if I hesitated it was not because there was any doubt in my mind, but because one wants a few seconds to kiss a dream goodbye. No, for me the choice was never in question. I owed this man my life. I admired and respected him and I knew his qualities. So up there on the Welsh hills I let the Queen of Sheba go out of my life. Drexel wanted me and that was enough.

I said, 'I'll do it.'

'Thank you, David. I knew I could rely on you.' He started to move on round the shoulder of the hill. On the valley road below a green bus moved slowly like a shining beetle.

As I walked beside him, I said, 'But why have you picked me?'

'There aren't so many people in the world you can trust absolutely, David. This is your job.'

'What is it?'

'Private tutor, companion. In a villa I've taken near Banyuls-sur-Mer on the French coast close to the Spanish border. A month on the Mediterranean this April.'

It sounded dull compared with Africa.

'Tutor to whom?' I asked.

'You'll know him when you meet him. You speak his language. That's another reason for it being you.'

'I speak five languages, including a little Welsh.'

He grinned. 'You won't have to brush up your Welsh.'

'What questions am I allowed to ask?'

'Any you like. Though I may not answer some. Everything is confidential at this moment.'

'A large Foreign Office seal on it?'

'In a way.'

'Where do you stand in all this?'

'I'm on the Army retired list. A private citizen. But

the F.O. will come in at a point and then I shall be their agent. I can't go into that now. As far as you're concerned I employ you privately. Five hundred quid for a month's work.'

'I don't want any money.'

He shook his head. 'I know what you're giving up. Don't tell me you couldn't use five hundred.'

I didn't argue with him.

CHAPTER TWO

The place the Colonel had taken was called the Villa Maruba. Calling it a villa did nothing for it. It was a largish, square building with the stucco flaking off it. The green window shutters were blistered and weathered pale by the salt wind and all the rooms smelled as though their only inhabitants had been penitents in damp sack-cloth. Moving about the place, whenever I came upon a gleam of sunshine I used to walk around it as though it were a hole in the floor. Outside, day after day, there was plenty of sunshine. In the house it became something alien and suspect.

But I could see why the Colonel had picked the house. It stood just off the road between Port-Vendres and Banyulssur-Mer. A tall wall ran along the road face and down to the sea on either side of the garden. Along the top of the wall was a *cheval-de-frise*. The only way to look into the grounds was by climbing the vine-covered slopes on the far side of the road. The wall, I was sure, had settled it for the Colonel. The garden was a wilderness of tamarisk and oleander bushes, weed-grown paths and, at the sea-edge by the boat-house, a clump of pines whose shade was patrolled by red ants. Close to the house was a dry concrete pool with a fountain in the middle. The leaf-littered bowl was the haunt of lizards which fed on the flies that were attracted by the hot concrete. Coming up from the sea I used to see the house through a great shimmering wave of heat haze from the pool.

For the first week I stuck fairly close to the place, bathing, reading and letting the sun work into me. Brindle looked after me. Brindle had been Drexel's batman and then servant for years. 'A moon-faced yokel from the leafy lanes of Kent', was how the Colonel had described the Brindle who had first come to him thirty years before. He was no longer moon-faced. He was a square, solid-looking man in whom the blood seemed to have thickened sluggishly. Every movement he took made me think that he was fighting against the onset of immobility, and what had been yokel in him was now shaped to a close, silent nature and a dog-like devotion to Drexel.

The first time I had any real conversation with Brindle was about a week after I'd arrived at the villa. I was down by the boathouse watching the sea. A large, wolf-hound kind of dog was with me, lying in the lee of the low wall below the pines. This one, a bitch, was free all day. Two others were let out at night. After a week of the wall and the dogs and the waiting I was beginning to get curious. During the war, when I had worked with Drexel, there had been some things I never had understood. Maybe because Drexel himself never had the the full truth. But always the Colonel had given me and the others enough to soothe our natural itch for information, enough to make it easy for us to close our minds to demands for more. Since Wales I'd seen him twice in London at his Grosvenor Square flat, but so far he had given me no more than that I was to be companion to someone and was to keep my mouth shut about it.

Brindle came down the path to me, carrying a tea tray, his slippers making lazy conversation with the loose gravel and fallen pine needles.

As he poured the tea for me, I said, 'Is the mail in yet?'

'Yes, sir.'

'Nothing from the Colonel?'

'No, sir.'

I chipped away at his hard mahogany. 'Do you know where the Colonel is?'

'No sir.'

'Do you know what all this is about, Brindle?'

Brindle took a deep, slow breath and just saved himself from turning to wood and then said, 'The Colonel's affairs is the Colonel's affairs, sir.' If there was any emotion in his voice it was of reproach.

I ignored the reproach. 'Do you know when he's due to arrive here?'

Brindle handed me my cup and then holding the sugar basin said, 'One or two lumps, sir?'

'One. And don't be so po-faced, Brindle. You know a damned sight more about this whole affair than I do, don't you?'

He put sugar in my tea and then, straightening up carefully so as not to crack the bark that was growing on him, said, 'At the moment, yes, sir.'

I knew I wouldn't get any more than that from him.

I said, 'I think I'll walk to Banyuls after tea. Can I bring anything back?' Brindle did all the catering and cooking and I used to see him going off in the morning on a bicycle to do the marketing.

'No thank you, sir.'

He went off and I sat there and finished my tea. It was hot, wonderfully hot for the beginning of April and a little way up the coast I could see part of a private beach that belonged to some holiday orphanage home. Children in funny red bloomers and straw hats were shouting and running about, and a covey of black and white nuns looking like magpies were fussing around them. It was a good feeling, sitting there in the sun, facing the sea with the grey and gold coast line spread out on either side of me and the white-topped crests of the Pyrenees behind me. I didn't even think about Songa Manara much. Time slipped by without making a ripple.

I walked into Banyuls along the road, carrying my light jacket over my arm. This strip of coast reminded me of Cornwall, sparse and bare. There was no great height to the cliffs until you got down past Banyuls and on to the Cerbère and the Spanish border. The afternoon had a bright, hard, metallic ring. I liked the neat rows of vines with rags of young leaf showing, the stone walls and the twisted blades of the tall cactus clumps. Some *Ponts et Chausées* man were working on the road just before Banyuls, hard, dark-skinned fellows, and one of them was singing in sudden lusty snatches as though his blood were too hot for his body and his spirits hard to hold down.

I left the road just before it began to curl down into Banyuls. I went out on to the level spread of headland, past tiny patches of garden with dried bamboo fences that protected the rows of lettuce, beans and arum lilies, and then came down through the old part of the town. Banyuls was two towns. The first part was like Clovelly; little cottages clinging to the sides of stepped and cobbled streets. But it had a lot of things not found in Clovelly; a warm smell of garlic, fennel and charcoal, enormous geranium growths and foaming cascades of petunia and bougainvillea washing down over the high garden walls on which hung cages of pigeons, bantams and rabbits. There was a smell of fish and wine, of poverty laid out under a sun which took the mildew and despair out of it. The women sitting at the open doors were mostly old and the men with their backs against the walls mostly asleep. They looked as though they had been sitting and sleeping for a hundred years.

Coming down through this part I could see the sweep of the bay ahead, the long curve of sand, broken by the Banyuls stream where it snaked out of a growth of tall bamboos and under an iron bridge to find the sea. Along the curve, facing the dusty road, was the other town, pure Mediterranean Margate, cheap cafés and bars, two or three hotels, a *rond-point* for dancing, a couple of garages and over it all, at this time of the year, an air of waiting for the season to begin. At the far end of the bay there was a pinkish looking hotel and the tall block of the Arago Aquarium.

About a dozen women in black dresses were scraping up the dead seaweed from the sands and burning it. The smoke went up in brown columns and then the off-shore wind took it and spread it in a fine canopy. Along the road between the dancing platform and the bridge long, tan-coloured lengths of sardine nets were

spread. The men and women mending them looked up
at me curiously as I passed. A young man with a suit-
case came up to me and said he would be delighted
to sell me a pair of espadrilles. I said he wouldn't and
passed on. But I knew he would be waiting for me
when I came back, and I knew that if I came here often
enough he would end up by selling me a pair.

I walked right along the length of the sands. I knew
where I was going and, as I got nearer to it, I felt the
return of an old and familiar excitement. It's a thing
aquariums do for me. Plymouth, Brighton, the London
Zoo, Naples, Monte Carlo ... Since I was a boy I've
never lost the joy that comes from the first movement
into those shadowed vaults where great green panels
let me stare into another world.

This place was something to do with the Marine
Biology Department of the University of Paris. Some of
the building was still under construction. As I went up
the steps a party of students came out; young men, in
brief shorts, with long legs and heavy boots, festooned
with nets and specimen tins, and girls in thick skirts,
stout, workmanlike jumpers and gay head-scarves. I
stood aside to let them pass. There were so many of
them that I pressed back against a dusty run of boarding
above which rose scaffolding where workmen in paper
caps were plastering the face of the building. They
rushed out into the road, shouting at a blue bus which
had drawn up outside the pink-faced hotel. One of the
youths put an empty specimen bucket on his head,
couched his long-handled net and charged at the bus,
defying it to move until they were all aboard. Their
laughter went sailing up into the air and I grinned. In
every class there is a buffoon. I watched the loaded bus
grind around the corner and away towards Cerbère.

I paid my money and went in. The well-known company greeted me with a green silence. The moray eels,
the spider crabs, the starfish and anemones; the shoals of
brill and bream like drifting clouds of birch leaves, the
surly jewfish and the fastidious golden dories. I wan-

dered round, feeling about twelve years old. And come
to think of it, maybe that was why I liked such places.
They took me back to a state of suspended, innocent
tranquillity.

After about half an hour I became aware of the
other people in the place. There were five of them; an
elderly couple, then two men who must have been
officials since they were standing by a door at the far
end of the aquarium discussing some alteration to a
partition, and lastly a woman. There was a large, open
pool in the centre of the place and she was sitting on
the low concrete wall that surrounded it. There were
under-water lights in the pool and as she was immediately above one I could only see her in silhouette.
There was something about the way she sat, as though
she were posing, yet bored and longing to be free, that
interested me. Maybe that fact that I couldn't see her
very well made me want to have a clearer view. I
moved round, and as I did so she, too, moved. Not
much and that was her trouble ... not enough to be
casual, but just enough to keep me in sight. Years in
the army in Drexel's special jobs had grafted into me
the anemone-instinct which contracts when other eyes
watch every movement. I tested her: changing position
and waiting for her reaction. She was still nothing but
a shape, but after each move of mine I saw the pale
frame of her face turn in my direction. I walked so far
round the tanks that she had to change position so
that she could keep me in sight. After a time I went
over to the open pool and stood there, about three
yards from her. There were a couple of turtles and
some dogfish moving sluggishly about the water. The
woman turned away from me. I still couldn't see her
very clearly in the gloom. She wore some kind of loose
coat. The twist of her body brought her legs out towards me and they looked strong and well formed.
Her hair was dark and fell loosely back into a gentle
curl about her coat collar. But her face was hidden
now. She sat there, and something about her stance,

as she leaned on one hand and stared at the pool reminded me of an illustration in an old fairy-story book
of mine. I could imagine she was waiting for one of the
dogfish—though in the story it had been a carp—to
come to the surface holding in its mouth a golden
mirror. And that was odd, for until this moment it had
been her covert interest in me which had made me come
to the pool. Now, I forgot that, and was interested in
her. I pulled out a cigarette and lit it, risking the sign
at the door which said—*Défense de Fumer*. And I
stared at her back and all the time my mind was wondering what there was in the twist of a woman's
shoulders and legs that could evoke such a clear desire
as the one that was running through me. I wanted to
go and sit beside her and say, 'You'll never get your
mirror back. Come with me and forget it. You can
look at yourself in my eyes ...' Then I took a smart
kick at the compassion that was leaping up in me like
a dog anxious for a walk. What do you do to cure yourself of always inventing happiness for people who
probably are quite content with their lot?

The two men went out of the door at the far end of
the aquarium and slammed it loudly behind them. The
noise was like a pistol shot in the long, dark stretch of
room. The woman started and her hand moving away
from the concrete pool wall knocked to the floor a
black handbag which had rested there. It burst open
and a scattering of small objects rolled over the floor
towards my feet.

I squatted down and began to gather some of them
up. And now I was smiling to myself for, despite the
noise of the door, the action had been transparent. She
had even had to move her hand well out of its normal
line of withdrawal to knock the bag over. I didn't look
at her, but she was there, crouching opposite me collect-
ing her things. I picked up a lipstick, a cigarette lighter,
a small bill clip which was empty and two loose keys.
There were also five or six of those wrapped sugar
lumps they give you in French cafés with your coffee,

but she got to those before I did. Why should a woman carry sugar in her handbag?

I stood up and handed the things to her.

She said, '*Merci bien, monsieur.*'

I told her it was a pleasure and wondered where she would go from there.

Speaking in French, and fiddling with her bag, she said, 'There is something wrong with the clip. Whenever I drop it—it goes off like a bomb.'

'Maybe I can fix it?' I reached for the bag.

'Oh, no, no, no ... !'

I smiled at the way she said it and also the movement, the bag drawn up in both hands against her breast. My bet was that the clip was perfectly good but had been left open deliberately. I could see her better now; a long, not unattractive face, solemn until she spoke and then full of a wonderful animation and, unless it was the gloom, she had the largest, darkest eyes I'd ever seen. But it wasn't the way she looked that held me. It wasn't in her voice, soft but touched with a faint hoarseness, or in the way she held herself. It was the way she was; playing a part, and not very well, and under that something else. I didn't get it then. Though I tried to put a word to it. Frightened? No, it wasn't fear. It was something else. A forcing of herself towards some point she hoped never to reach ... In a few seconds a jumble of sensations flashed through me and none of them really rang a bell but I could feel that many of them came close to doing it. And because she did that to me I suddenly didn't want her to go. It suddenly seemed important that I should know more about her. Never before in my life had any woman raised this kind of feeling in me. None of them. This was new.

But she went, and that puzzled me like hell. Why knock her bag over, start something with me, and then go away?

She said, 'Thank you again. You've been very kind.'

She turned. I saw the loose coat swing back, had a glimpse of a white blouse and she was walking away. I

stood there watching her move to the door. And then I
realized something. When she moved she was sure of
herself as though all thought and emotion went from
her and the body took over, strong, and with a beautifully controlled grace. But when she stood still something came sweeping back into the mind and she was
near to grieving for her lost mirror.

I sat on the pool wall and finished my cigarette. A
small boy came in with his mother and, tiring soon
of the fish, began to run round the pool pretending he
was a jet plane. The noise he made echoed through the
place madly. Since the war I'd lived with boys and I
knew that once they got the wind up their tails there
was nothing to do but avoid them. I stood up to go and
my foot hit something on the floor by the pool wall. I
bent down and picked it up. It was a small silver flask,
no bigger than a lighter, and what used to be called a
vinaigrette. I flicked the top open. There was a wisp of
scent in the air. I put it in my pocket and went towards
the door. It had been in her bag. She couldn't have gone
far and I could easily catch her up. I didn't know why
but I was glad that I had an excuse to go after her. I
didn't even ask myself whether the thing had been left
there to give me just that excuse.

When I got outside, at the top of the steps, I saw
her. She was coming back, moving quickly up the rough
path by the scaffolding. When she saw me she hesitated. I raised a hand in signal and she stopped, waiting
for me to come down.

Even without the pure accident that waited ten
seconds ahead, it would have been just the same. Everything was written into that moment. With some people,
I guess, these things are like taking a correspondence
course; six months or a year before you know your
way around. Sometimes you never get anywhere. Hell,
who can say how it happens with other people? You
just know about yourself. You drift into a green cavern,
not caring much about anything, not even unhappy
... you just drift in and all you see is the line of a back

and shoulders, the curve of a woman's legs as she stares at nothing in a pool and something begins to fight for life inside you. And then you come out into the sunshine, with the wind taking the dust from the road and making it dance in tiny wraiths, and the woman is still there. She stands with the wind against her body and her face is raised towards you and her black hair is loose and soft and you don't even see her as a human being but just as the thing, the point, a thin, trembling note you've never heard before, and like an explosion inside your breast the something fighting for life has broken out, free and mad with the tingling of new blood.

I went down towards her and, as I did so, I heard the men on the scaffolding above suddenly shout, a wild, desperate noise and with it a growing, grating sound. I looked up and saw the bucket and rope, a great bucket full of plaster that they had been hauling up, and the two of them grabbing at the slipping rope, and then the whole thing out of their control and the bucket plunging downwards straight for her.

I jumped and my hands found her shoulders and the impetus of my body took us both crashing into a small recess under the scaffolding. The bucket smashed into the ground a couple of yards from us, the plaster spurting up in a great brown fan. I felt the wet flick of its spray on my hands and neck.

I was pressed against her, my arms round her. Her face was close to mine and I could smell the scent from her and knew it was something I would never forget. She was scared. So was I. One always is after a thing like that. We stood close together while the men shouted and flapped above us like a couple of hoarse crows. The fear went from her face and she smiled, not needing to say anything, each of us feeling the other's heart racing, and she worked a hand gently upwards against my breast and with an infinitely slow, gentle touch she rubbed at a plaster mark on my cheek. And with the movement her lips came close to mine and I kissed her as gently and slowly as her fingers had touched me. But it was like no kiss I had ever known, no anguish of body or mind behind it : just a drawing together in recognition and then as she moved away the sound of her breath like the faint sigh that comes as a page of a new book is turned.

The foreman came down and apologized. He and his man fussed around, brushed us, offered wine and cigarettes, told us how it happened and then told each other how it had happened, and then said how good we were to take it so well. Monsieur was English, of course, which explained it and Mademoiselle was *trés courageuse*, and in the middle of it all the blue bus came rattling down the hill to the pink hotel and before I could do anything she had put her hand in mine, looked at me and then was running towards it. She swung aboard just as it began to pull out. She stood on the step and gave me a wave and I waved back, but I made no attempt to follow her. I didn't have to. I knew I wasn't going to lose her. Both of us would come back because the moment when she had been in my arms and our lips had touched carried inevitability with it. It was from this moment that I began to think less and less of Songa Manara and the Queen of Sheba.

CHAPTER THREE

There was reaction of course. The greater the fantasy the harder common sense will come shouldering its way back at some point. The point with me that day was just after I had been tackled about buying espadrilles again as I had come out of the chemist's shop where I'd bought myself some razor blades. Going up the hill out of the old town common sense came back with a rush, and from there on until I reached the villa I did everything to knock it all out of myself. It was rather like playing squash rackets with myself. The racket was common sense and the hard, black ball was fancy ... call it what you like I smacked at the ball and it came back to me. I knocked and slammed it around and waited to see what would happen, but always it came right back at me.

Things don't happen like this, I told myself. You're bored with being cooped in the villa, and you're subconsciously angry because you don't know why you're here. Arguing with yourself is the most exhausting thing I know. The mind frames question and answer, accusation and defence at the same time. I must have walked that length of road like a man in his sleep. I didn't know the woman. There was nothing special about her. She talked as though she were just getting over a sore throat and, if she did move well, she was in fact a little short in the body. And her hair wasn't as soft as I had first thought. There was a suggestion of thready strength in it. I tried to kick her out—and was even a little angry that she should seem important enough to warrant all this effort. I could push her away so far, but then she stopped and nothing would move her. So then I thought about the handbag and the clumsy acting. Maybe I could scare her off with that. What was behind all that? Something to do with the Colonel—or some other ploy of her own? For a time

I favoured the Colonel angle and thinking about this I
began to find common sense taking more room in me.
I had something in trust from Drexel and it was important to me not to fail him. I knew only too well that
when one entered the circle at whose centre the
Colonel sat, then an automatic readjustment had to be
made in one's assessment of the smallest trivia, the
casualest meetings and words. Drexel was no fool, no
matter how melodramatically he seemed to act. He used
mystery and anonymity stripped of all zest or idle play-
acting because that was the surest way to keep alive.
Other men dealt in potatoes and ready made suits, filed
correspondence and totted figures. Drexel's life was
just as precise and regulated. Only in his world if a
bird sang it was almost bound to be in code ... Was
she part of that world? If she were I could mistrust
her and my feelings about her. For the time being I was
back in that world and I had to obey its rules. I got
some comfort from this. I could push her away, but
I still had the feeling that I could not keep her away
for long. Even in Drexel's world—the world which,
tough as he was, had begun to wear him down—there
was room for ... I knew the word, but at the moment
there was a taboo in me against saying it.

It was beginning to get dark as I went into the villa
grounds. The three dogs came rushing up to eat me. I
stood fast and let them see they were wrong but I still
found nothing warming in this last-minute-recognition
act of theirs.

Brindle served dinner and it did something to offset
the damp and gloom of the dining-room. There was
nothing yokel about his cooking. There's a talent buried
in each man somewhere. Brindle had found his in cooking. No matter where he was or what food he had he
would produce something that no one else could. The
first time I'd known him work a miracle was in Yugo-
slavia, high on the grey *karst* above Spoleta, when all
he had was a handful of walnuts, flour, water and a
chunk of fat bacon. Drexel had always refused to eat

rough soldier fashion and he had wasted no sympathy on Brindle because he had had to do the cooking flat on his stomach to avoid sniper's bullets.

I finished a bottle of Montrachet with my cheese and then as the Sèvres clock on the mantelpiece struck ten when it should have struck nine, Brindle brought in the coffee on a tray. As he set it down, he slipped a crumpled envelope over to me.

'The Colonel asked me to give you this, sir.'

I picked up the envelope and began to work the flap loose.

'And I'll bet he said today and at nine o'clock precisely.'

'Yes, sir. Will you have black or white?'

'Black.' He knew I took black but he always asked. When he was gone I pulled one of the table candles towards me and read the note. It was in the Colonel's neat, renaissance-like script.

There is a motor launch in the boat house. Brindle has the key. Within the next four or five days you will receive a telephone call from the British Consul at Marseilles. If he says 'Go ahead' you will that same evening rendezvous cargo-boat *Roi Bleu* three miles due East of Cap Cerbère at 22.30 hours. Signal three torch flashes, five-second interval between groups If no message from Consul await my arrival.

I read it through twice and then burnt the paper in the candle flame, dropping the ashes into my coffee cup.

Early the next morning I got the key of the boat-house from Brindle and went to have a look at the launch. It was a beautiful arrangement of mahogany and chromium plating. I took her out and the song her powerful engine made was specially composed for those in the upper-income brackets. She was fast and, although there was only a smooth swell running, I could feel that she would be seaworthy. I went down past

Banyuls until I could see Cap Cerbère edging out of the
low shore mist. Inland the great sweep of the snow-
capped Pyrenees shouldered roughly against a pale blue
sky. And now that I had had some word from the
Colonel I was content to let my curiosity ride. He had
left England two weeks before I did and he might be
anywhere.

I came back faster than I had gone out, giving the
launch full throttle and singing to myself at the whip of
wind and spray in my face. In the boat-house I filled
up the tank and then handed the key back to Brindle.
He didn't say a word.

Later I walked into Banyuls. In the confusion of the
falling plaster bucket I had forgotten to give the girl
back her silver flask. I wanted to return it, but more
than that I wanted to see her again.

I went and had a coffee at a small café called *Aux
Bons Enfants*. It was in the Place Mairie, well back from
the dancing platform, and shadowed by three tall plane
trees. There were a few green tables and chairs on a
strip of concrete outside. A tall three-ply cut-out of a
man in chef's clothing holding in one hand a large fish
and in the other a card with a list of sea-food stood by
the door which led into a low bar and dining-room.
It was a sad, slightly crumbling place and the proprietor
seemed to have no help, perhaps because the season
had not yet started. He was a big, pulpy man who
looked as though he had been left out in the rain and
at any moment would collapse into a heap of shapeless
cloth and cardboard. He sat on a chair by the door
and read a tattered copy of *Paris Soir* and now and again
he raised his head and stared at the sea indignantly as
though it had just made some offensive remark to him.

After a time my friend of the espadrilles found me.
He came up cheerfully, carrying his battered brown suit-
case and insisted on showing his wares. He covered the
table with coloured, rope-soled shoes and chattered
away, not trying to force a sale, because he knew in
the end he would get me. I gave him a cigarette and he

told me that his name was Jean Cagou and that in a couple of seasons he hoped to have enough to open a shop either here or at Port-Vendres a little further up the coast. He was about twenty-two, brisk and glossy as an olive-fed starling. He said that, in addition to espadrilles, if there was anything else I wanted he could get it for me.

'N'importe quoi, m'sieur—je peux le trouver.'

I told him there was nothing I wanted and quite rightly he didn't believe me.

As we talked a motor-cycle drew up alongside the café. It was a Norton and had a GB plate. A plumpish, elderly man in a cloth cap and a light raincoat got off it and sat down by the door. The proprietor gathered himself up from his chair and went to take his order. He was English, but he ordered breakfast in French, a hard, stiff, badly-accented French as though each word was being dragged unwillingly from his memory.

Jean Cagou at once gathered up his samples. As I left I could hear his cheerful, excited voice going into its sales talk with the new arrival.

For the next two days I walked into Banyuls, morning and afternoon, hoping to see the girl. But I never did. I saw Jean Cagou and I became quite friendly in a monosyllabic way with the proprietor of the *Aux Bons Enfants*. The Englishman was there, too, in the mornings having his breakfast. I think he knew that I was English but he never tried to make my acquaintance. The most he ever did was to look up at me as I sat down, stare for a moment, nod, and then turn back to his food. He was a man with a good appetite.

Although I still hadn't got to the point of admitting to myself that my intuition that I should see the girl again was wrong, I did on the third morning rebel against the thought of going into Banyuls. I went and sat by the dried-up fountain in the villa garden and read. It was some French novel I'd found in the house. But I remember nothing about it except that I got more and more annoyed with it. The old bitch wolf-hound came and lay in the dust by me and scratched away at her fleas, and gradually for no reason that I could think of I began to get depressed. It seemed as though I had been washed into some backwater of time and nothing was ever going to happen to me again. There was only the ugly villa, gloomy and echoing as a tomb, and outside this fierce, unseasonable heat that pressed down over everything. I got up and chucked a stone at a lizard on the edge of the fountain pool and missed it.

And then I was out on the road, walking towards Banyuls. My feet had to go somewhere. I had to create for myself the illusion of progress.

I'd gone half a mile, I suppose, when I heard a motor-horn behind me, I stopped and turned. An old army jeep painted a dark blue, battered and very dusty, drew up alongside me. Sitting in front were two men and behind, alone, was the girl.

The two men looked at me and, while they did not smile, it was clear that they knew about me. She smiled, and I saw her teeth, small and very white, against the warm tan of her skin.

'You are going to Banyuls?' she asked.

I nodded.

She patted the empty seat beside her.

'We will take you. I am glad we have found you.'

I climbed into the jeep and sat at her side and we went off with a quick spin of the rear wheels that sent a cloud of dust up behind us. It was only a short ride and not more than a dozen words passed between us. I sat there feeling a little embarrassed, not because of her but because of the two men. They gave me the impression of having picked me up and dumped me aboard as though I were a crate or package of merchandise.

In the bottom of the jeep were a couple of harpoon fishing guns, a face mask with a breathing tube and a pair of rubber webbed feet. The girl, seeing me look at them, nodded towards the man who was driving and said, 'George is mad about under-water fishing.'

The depression that had been with me was gone. I felt neither lonely nor lost and it was nothing to do with the men. It was her. Just sitting beside me. The way she sat and let her body sway to the movement of the jeep seemed to say something to me. She wore a green summer frock with thin white stripes and her hair was caught back with some kind of clasp at the back. Her arms and legs were bare and she wore white sandals. Most of the time she stared straight ahead of her and I could see her profile, strong and thoughtful; but at the same time I didn't feel she was at ease. Her hands were clasped over one knee and I could see the long fingers moving with a slow restlessness.

We pulled up outside the *Café aux Bons Enfants* and the four of us sat down at a table. It was then that she introduced me to the two men and I got a good look at them. I don't know whether it was anything to do with my feeling for her, some touch of jealousy starting early, but I didn't like either of them. Perhaps like and dislike weren't the right words. The men were wrong with her.

It was the one she had called George who made the most impression on me. His other name was Sarrasin. I'm tall and fairly well built, but he made me feel small. He was well over six feet tall and with a body that was all bulk and muscle; hard, but not ungainly. He wore his short, dark hair *en brosse* and he had a large face, deeply and pugnaciously cut, a rough, unfinished face like a sculpture's first block with all the power of the original material still harshly apparent. His voice was slow and heavy and all his movements, though they had grace, showed economy. He was full of strength but, I guessed, never wasted it. He wore a pair of faded, blue canvas trousers, a yellow singlet and a loose grey jacket. His shoes were no more than a flat leather sole with a toe-piece and thongs that were tied around his ankle.

He ordered the thick dark Banyuls wine for us all and,

while we waited for it, made a little speech of thanks to me for the service I had rendered Sophie. Sophie Orbais was her name.

I pulled the scent flask from my pocket and handed it across to Sophie. 'You left this in the aquarium.'

'Ah, yes. I was coming back to look for it when ... it all happened.'

I wondered whether the moment of hesitation and then the last three words meant to her what I felt they meant to me.

The proprietor came up to us with the wine. Whenever I saw him with a tray and glasses I felt that the weight would tear his limp hands from his arms. We drank to each other politely and while she and George and myself just sipped at the syrupy wine, the other man, Astar Paviot, finished his glass in one movement and sighed. He was small, mean-looking and seedy. One could have collected a hundred of his type from the *bistros* of Marseilles in an evening. He had thin brown hair with a touch of grey over the ears, an unhealthy looking face, the chin too pointed and the eyes a little red as though they were weary of the weight of the pouchy skin beneath them. He didn't look too clean. His suit had once been a smart grey with a fancy stripe and, I felt, had been made for another man. He was a man it would be very hard to like; a man with a shabby spirit, and nothing immediately wholesome about him except his hands which were strong and lean, the fingers full of an unexpected grace and beauty, the nails astonishingly well kept.

The talk didn't flow very easily between us. They puzzled me because they didn't seem to fit together properly; the girl and these two. Sophie said very little. George Sarrasin complimented me on my French and Paviot said I reminded him of a British officer he had worked with in the Resistance. We talked about this officer and the war years, but though I was alive to the possibility I don't think he was pumping me for any information. I'd told them I was staying for a holiday here. Over all I couldn't detect in anything they said the slightest sign that they had any real interest in me except that I had done Sophie a service. And that, since I was sure she had knocked her handbag over by design, made everything seem odder.

We sat there under the shabby plane trees. There was a large circus poster plastered around the trunk of one of them and I could see Jean Cagou, case at his feet, sitting with his back against it. The Englishman, who had been at the café when we arrived, finished his meal and went off on his motor-cycle. And suddenly all conversation died between us. It didn't last long, maybe half a minute, but there was a weight and deliberateness in it which made me feel that it came from design. This was no pause while angels walked over somebody's grave, but a point reached and then a silent gathering of forces for the new move. I looked at Sophie. She was watching the women burning seaweed on the beach. Then she turned a little and saw me. She smiled but so absently that I knew her thoughts were remote and, from the swift tremor about her mouth as she looked away, I fancied the thoughts were unpleasant. Astar Paviot was tipped back in his chair, his face up to the sun, half a cigarette dropping at the corner of his mouth. He seemed to have gone into a trance. George Sarrasin had taken a penknife from his pocket and was shaping a piece of cork for a fishing float. I was on the point of making an excuse to go when he stood up. The movement brought Paviot's chair tipping back to earth and Paviot was at his side.

'All right, Sophie. See you at four?'

George put his hand on her shoulder and squeezed it and then with a look at me, said, *'Au revoir, monsieur.'*

Paviot echoed him. *'Au revoir, monsieur.'*

And there they were the two of them walking towards the jeep and I was left with Sophie. I saw them gather up their fishing gear from the car and then cross the road and disappear among the beached fishing boats on the pebbles of the little cove below the old town.

I said, 'Where are they going?'

She said, watching them, 'They take a row-boat out to fish. It will be this afternoon before they return.'

'What about you?'

'I do not like to fish. Sometimes I have been sick, even when there is no sea.'

'They just leave you to amuse yourself?'

'Generally. I go for a walk. I read.' And then, unpectedly, she turned and smiled at me and said, 'You sound a little angry about it. Don't be. I prefer not to go.' And the smile was the warm, natural smile that she had given me under the scaffolding. It was as though the moment they had gone some new life, new personality had come back to her.

Bluntly, out of a protective affection which was strong in me, I said, 'Who are they?'

She had a right to resent this, but she said quietly, 'They are my friends ... good friends. We are at Argelès for a holiday but they prefer the fishing here.'

Argelès-sur-Mer was a resort about half-way between Banyuls and Perpignan.

We spent the rest of the day until four o'clock together.

I didn't arrange it and I'm sure she didn't. We just drifted into it without ever acknowledging that it was going to happen. We didn't talk a great deal. She was one of those comfortable people whose silences are happy and restful, and, for myself, I was glad just to be with her. We bought ourselves a bottle of cheap Roussillon wine, a length of salami and a loaf and walked down past the Arago Aquarium and then up the twisting road towards Cerbère. After a time we went down across a barren cliff-head, close carpeted with thyme, marjoram and silvery-leaved rock roses, to a steeply enclosed cave. We found a flat rock above a deep pool of jade and turquoise water and sat there talking about

small, unimportant things. If you'd taken each moment
of the afternoon apart and examined it there would
have been nothing special about it, nothing that somewhere in the past could not have been matched, but
altogether it was like no afternoon I had ever spent.

After lunch the wine made me drowsy and quite un-
ashamedly I went to sleep. I think she did, too. When I
woke up she was sitting close to me, looking down at
me. I blinked my eyes to cut down the sun glare. She
smiled at me and her eyes were deeper and darker than
ever. I put up a hand. I don't know whether I meant to
take hers, but her hand was in mine, a firm, strong
hand but with a warm gentleness to it that seemed to
reach right into me and I heard myself saying, 'When I
came and stood by you in the aquarium do you know
what you made me think about?'

She shook her head and the sun through her loose
hair was broken into a thousand bright points of light.

'A fairy story. You were the princess who'd dropped
her favourite mirror into the pond and in a moment a
magic carp was going to bring it up to you.'

She was silent for a moment. Then she said, 'You've
got the story wrong. It wasn't a mirror. It was a golden
ball. The princess had lost her golden ball.'

'Mirror or ball. It doesn't matter. I just wanted you
to have it back.'

She didn't answer at once. She looked down at me and
I felt her fingers escape from mine and then touch the
back of my hand and finally close softly around my
wrist. And then she said very deliberately—

'You are a very kind man, aren't you? A very good
man?'

It was said almost simply, almost childishly, and
came from her with a sincerity and meaning that had
the curious effect of shock in me. At once I seemed to
have acquired a responsibility for which I was completely unworthy.

I was embarrassed and I laughed and then seeing the
watch on my wrist, said, 'Hullo, it's nearly four. We

must be getting back to your friends.'

She changed at once, and I wished to hell that I hadn't said it. With a few words I'd brought her back into another world and it wasn't a world she liked. I knew it and I hated it without understanding it.

We walked into Banyuls and George Sarrasin and Paviot were waiting by the jeep. I refused a lift from them. I made no arrangements to meet her again, but as they drove off she half-turned in her seat and waved to me and I knew she would be back. I walked along the cliffs to the villa, remembering the change which had come over her face.

I was having a drink before dinner when the telephone went. It was from Marseilles giving me the go-ahead to rendezvous the *Roi Bleu* that evening.

CHAPTER FOUR

It was nine o'clock when I went into the kitchen and got the boat-house key from Brindle. He was drinking cocoa and listening to the B.B.C. on a portable radio. As he gave me the key he also handed over a small silver-plated flask.

'What's this?'

'Whisky, sir. Just in case you have to wait longer than you think.'

It was a mark of affection. It is also proved that, at this moment, he knew more than I did of this business. I had an idea that Drexel probably told Brindle everything. The man was a drawer into which he stuffed all his secrets for safe keeping.

I went out into the garden and stood there for a moment while the dogs came up and inspected me. It was a warm close night with little wind and I felt hot in the sweater I had pulled on. The dogs followed me down to the boat-house and the bitch whined a little as I went aboard. I think she was getting fond of me.

I took the launch out, the engine well throttled down so that it made only a gentle bubbling sound, and kept the lubber line of the compass running East and West. I had worked out that if I made five miles due easting and then turned south and ran down ten miles I should be in the position the Colonel wanted me. Fifteen miles and well over an hour to do it was easy for the launch. When I made my rendezvous I should be outside the International limit and practically dead on the Spanish-French border. The only light I allowed myself was from the panel board, so that I could check the patent log and the compass. There was a fair bit of smuggling along this piece of coast and there might be a customs patrol boat. I didn't want to attract attention.

The night was like rotten velvet, a soft, unresisting fabric which fell away before the sharp bows of the launch. Away on the starboard side, down towards Banyuls I could see the little red navigation light that stood on a tripod in the middle of the bay. There were other lights too; a firefly cluster where the Banyuls fishing boats were making out to sea, acetylene lamps flaring at their bows, and a light from the rocky point by the Arago Aquarium. And all along the coast there were the bead-strung lights of the various towns and then the scattered sharp points from individual houses and farms on the hills behind. But the night itself had swallowed sky, land and sea. There was only this amorphous velvet pricked haphazardly with yellow, silver and red.

After a time, away to the left, I picked up the flash from the lighthouse which stood at the entrance to Port-Vendres harbour and I saw that the log read two miles. I sat there with my hands gently on the wheel. In the old days this kind of thing had carried excitement and danger, a heightening of instinct and senses that reached back into the primitive hinterland of one's ancestry. War, a world at war, flags, sacrifice, backs to the wall, *dulce et decorum est pro patria mori* ... In those days it had all meant something. But not now. There was no true excitement in me. Each generation grows out of its own war, turning away gladly to the rows of potato plants and the piles of exercise books. But the war went on just the same, carried on by people like Drexel. I thought of the book he had written just after the war. He had a surprisingly mature and sensitive way of writing. Ethiopia, Arabia, Persia and the Mediterranean and Adriatic areas ... an Odyssey into which now and again I had come. Some of his acid comments had raised questions in the House of Commons but the whole thing had blown over. He was the hero-type, the kind the public had to have to make their morning papers palatable and their comfortable lives bearable. I knew because I was the public and I loved him. Perhaps my love was prejudiced, knowing the man personally and owing him so much. I remembered him coming back over the long sand drifts, myself quiet with the final despair and not even roused by the bullying, vigorous cheerfulness of the man. The bullet had cracked my right knee-cap and he'd dragged and carried me for three days, given up his water and his strength to me, cursed me and insulted me, but had kept me going. I owed him everything from that moment of return. The only way to repay that kind of debt that I knew was with love. I loved the man and was unashamed to use the word to myself. In a little while I was going to see him again and, if there was any excitement in me, it came from that thought.

I made the rendezvous by a quarter past ten. I set the wheel so that the launch just eased around in a slow, gigantic circle. At half past ten I began to work the torch, keeping the flashes seaward. Three flashes and then a five-second interval. Each flash made a little gold shaft across the velvet and the monotony of counting the seconds to myself made me a little drowsy. On this kind of job I knew it was no good worrying about time. It was an element to be ignored.

I thought about a lot of things while I circled round, leaving just enough of my attention on the job, and the rest of me wandering about, having what my brother would have called 'a good old think.' His 'good old thinks' had come to an end on the Normandy beaches. Eventually I found myself thinking about other women I had known and then comparing them with Sophie. Why was it that when they had touched my hand it had been warm and friendly but without any magic? Magic was the only word I could put to Sophie and it was a poor word because it wasn't what I meant. There had been times in the past when I had told myself I was in love. But telling myself so and even believing it hadn't made any difference. I wondered if I was in love with Sophie, and immediately I knew I wasn't going to answer that because there wasn't any answer. The question itself was inadequate. The poor, tired old phrase seemed to have no meaning against the reality that had sprung into existence inside me. Love, as I knew it, was a literary sensation and a sunlit tableau; maybe that was the result of being a schoolmaster with English Literature as a first subject, potted biographies of Shelley and Byron spooned out to a row of healthy little savages who were listening more intently to the buzz of a blue-bottle on the window or the quiet snigger following some inky note making its rounds of the desks. Love; pastoral, lyric, shepherds and shepherdesses, *When as in silks my Julia goes*, resin-flavoured Greek wines ... But now I was beginning to feel that the real thing, which demanded another name, was harsher, more sudden, like the sear of fusing metals. I sat there thinking about Sophie and after a time the warmth of my thoughts was chilled by an insistent question. I began to ask myself what Sophie could be doing spending a holiday with two men like George Sarrasin and Astar Paviot. Who was she, what was she and what was her real interest in me? The men were wrong and she did not seem to fit any life they had. The next time I saw her, I decided, I would be less vague and diffident about these things. There should be question and answer.

My thoughts were broken by the distant thud of a boat's screws. *Chump, chump, chump* it came across the water, like the muffled beating of a hand on a door. A green navigation light swayed low down away on my port side and then, faintly below it, came an answering flash to my torch.

I headed the launch towards the light. After a time, almost over my head, a deck flood-light came on and the high-clumsy bows of a tramp steamer rose sheer before me. I swept down past her, turned and came up again under the stern. It dipped and rolled and I saw the words, *Roi Bleu, Marseille*. As I came alongside and threw out a couple of fenders, a rope ladder was dropped from the deck and lay banging and swinging against the rusty plates. A rope came down, hitting the foredeck with a smack and I hung on to it. Voices shouted above and in the dim light I saw faces peering down. A small figure in a raincoat and beret came down the ladder and jumped past me, moving to the stern of the launch. Then I saw Colonel Drexel. He came down the ladder rather slowly, dressed in an old army great-coat and wearing a white cloth cap I noticed that his left hand was bandaged, though he seemed to have the use of it.

He dropped into the launch at my side, put his arm round my shoulder and grinned.

'David.'

That was all he said. But it was enough. The word and the touch and everything that meant anything between us wrapped up in them. His breath smelt of whisky, a strong, masculine smell that fitted the night and the movement of the boats and the massed faces peering down. Someone shouted and two pigskin cases were lowered. Drexel took them and passed them astern to our other passenger.

The deck flood-light went off and in the darkness a heavy voice called down—

'*Au revoir, Colonel. Nous finisserons la bouteille un autre jour.*'

'*Au revoir, Didi,*' Drexel called up.

And then as I swung the launch away into the darkness the heavy voice came faintly across to us—

'*Bonne chance . . .*'

I said to the Colonel, 'Speed, or gently does it?'

'Speed.'

I opened the launch up and she tore through the velvet with an angry ripping sound and behind us a great curve of phosphorescent wake flared against the darkness.

Drexel ducked behind the wind shield and lit himself a cigarette and, as he came up, he shouted against the wind—

'Everything all right at the villa?'

'Yes. What's the matter with your hand?'

'Just a graze. Messy but not serious.'

'Anyone seen it?'

'Yes. In Cairo. It's all right.'

I glanced back. 'Who's our friend?' I shouted

'Later. Let's get home. Can't talk with my mouth full of wind and spray.'

We were about half-way back when I heard the sound of a mouth-organ behind me. I turned. Our passenger had moved up closer in the well of the launch and was playing gently to himself. He looked up and smiled at me over the instrument. I saw his face touched by the light from the dash panel. Anyway, I knew now what language I was supposed to speak. A young face, dark-skinned, a hawk-like nose, high cheek bones and deep-set, steady eyes.

The Colonel seeing me turn shouted—

'Know him?'

'No.'

'Should do. You went to his father's funeral.'

I began to have an idea then, but I still wasn't sure.

No more was said, but our friend played dance music softly all the way in.

Brindle was waiting at the boat-house for us. He took the cases. I stayed to lock up the launch and when I got up to the house, past the dogs who were barking themselves crazy over the newcomers, there was no one about. I went into the stuffy, uncomfortable lounge and poured myself a whisky. The Colonel joined me after a while and got a drink for himself. As he turned back to me he tossed a key across.

'Here.'

I caught it.

'It's the key of his bedroom—next to yours. I've got a key as well. He's locked in at night and during the day one of us must always have an eye on him.'

'Is he likely to give us the slip?'

'No. But other people would like to get their hands on him.'

I sat down, took a drink and waited. I knew he was
going to enjoy this moment and I had no wish to
spoil it for him. A walled villa, dogs loose at night,
keys, a wounded hand ... it was all the Drexel tradition;
cloak and dagger stuff for most people, but for Drexel,
I knew, it would make sense, hard common sense.

The Colonel, relaxed now, rubbing one thumb over
the curve of his whisky glass, said, 'Remember Saraj?'

'I do.'

The room was suddenly full of hot strong smells, of
bright sunlight on a dusty square noisy with Arabs
crowding around stalls, and I saw a grey plug of a
harbour fort at the entrance to a blue-water bay and
the shark-fin sails of dhows beating in from the sea.
Saraj was the seaport capital of Ramaut, a small, independent Arab state on the Trucial coast where the
Persian Gulf met the Indian Ocean. The Colonel and I
had spent six months there as members of a British
mission during the war, an interesting but uncomfortable
time. It was there that I had improved my knowledge
of the Arab language. I had an easy, almost glib talent
for picking up languages which impressed people.

'Have you been keeping your finger on Arab politics?'

'A little.' I knew the funeral he meant now, and
went on, 'This is one of the sons of King Akhdar who
was assassinated just before we reached Saraj?'

'The elder son. Prince Jabal Akhdar. He's not quite
sixteen. The only other brother is nearly fifteen. Until
Jabal is eighteen the state is being run by a Regent.'

'I remember him. Sheik Ahmed ben Fa'id. A first-
class louse.' It had been one of those goodwill missions
dictated by strategy. Saraj would have made a good
refuelling point for the German raiders in the Indian
Ocean and that was the way Sheik Ahmed ben Fa'id saw
it until we arrived and Drexel got to work on him.
Even then goodwill had not prevailed until we had a
destroyer in Saraj Bay.

'A louse, but a clever one. When Jabal's eighteen he
can take over the country. That's the constitution. But

when he's sixteen then by tribal law he's no longer a minor. He becomes head of the family. It's a nice distinction—and an important one for a lot of people.'

'When is he sixteen?'

'At the end of this month That's why Ahmed ben Fa'id didn't want him to go back to school in England. He wanted him in the country at that date.'

'Why?'

'Because he wanted to make sure that Jabal, as head of the family, didn't sign an important document. As long as he had his hands on Jabal he was safe.'

'And Jabal?'

'He wanted to come back to school. He wants also to sign the paper. But he knew what would happen to him if he stayed there and tried to sign it. The boy's got his head screwed on. He has an idea who was behind the assassination of his father. It could happen to him. That would have left his brother—who is entirely under the influence of the Regent—to become head of the family in a year. His brother would have refused to sign the paper.'

It was not hard to understand. It was the kind of situation that was fairly common in most of the Arab states from time to time. But I wasn't deluding myself that Drexel and the Foreign Office were breaking their hearts over the injustice and savagery. Any reason they had for interference would have a cash or military answer. Goodwill, protection, spheres of influence ... nice phrases with no altruism behind them.

I said, 'What is it? Oil?'

Drexel finished his whisky, and as he levered himself up to go and refill his glass, he said, 'Yes. The original concession was granted by the Akhdar family in 1933 for twenty-one years. It's purely a family affair. Nothing to do with the State, though the whole population of Ramaut lives by it. Just the same as in many of the other Trucial states. The concession is due for renewal next month. Jabal wants to renew it. Sheik ben Fa'id thinks otherwise. He has ideas about nationalization. It's a kind of bug going round the Persian Gulf just now. Maybe they caught it from us. Anyway, his real reason'—he turned back to his chair and his mouth had a sarcastic twist,—'is decently capitalistic. Ben Fa'id feels he could shovel more money into his own pocket if he had nationalization. Not that he isn't doing pretty well for himself as it is.'

'Who's got the concession?'

'Anglo-Media.'

'And you've got Jabal.'

'Sure. I've put up with that damned mouth-organ for over a week.'

I looked at Drexel's bandaged hand.

'Was it an Ahmed ben Fa'id bullet that mucked up your hand?'

He shrugged his shoulders.

'Always some little thing goes wrong.'

Something about the way he said this marked an uneasiness in him. Instead of sitting down he began to move around the room, restless, touching a piece of furniture, an ornament. He was worried and I saw no reason why he should be at this stage.

'What about the Government, the Foreign Office? They're behind you, aren't they?' I said it with some idea of easing the strain in him, but it had the opposite effect. He swung round and the lean, lined face was full of contempt.

'At the moment they know nothing—officially—about it. You've no idea how it goes, David. Sometimes I feel absolutely played out by this kind of thing ...' It was almost a cry and it went straight to my heart because it was so unlike him, revealed that in him which until now I had never suspected was there. There is a weakness in us all which time and trial slowly weathers free of our surrounding strength, the bare, crumbling rock that comes up through the turf as the years wash away the top-soil. I think he caught something of my feeling, my shock, for he went on quickly, angry now rather than pathetic, 'I've no official standing. Nothing

in writing. No firm promises. Just hints, hints, hints
and everyone knows damned well what is meant, and
everyone knows damned well that the last thing any
Whitehall stooge is going to do is to commit himself
even unofficially until it's absolutely safe. I'm the game-
cock that's shoved into the ring.'

'But they know you've whipped this boy out of
Saraj so that he can sign the concession in London?'

'Yes. The cipher people should be decoding the message about now. But the point is that if anything went
wrong while I was about it—then it would be my responsibility. I'd just be a common kidnapper. But once
here—then they take over. Prince Jabal is in France
on his way back to school.'

'You've got no worry then. You're here.'

'Oh, the innocence of the man! It'll take 'em at least
four or five days to take over.'

'I see. I suppose they'll want to get Sheik Ahmed ben
Fa'id's reaction first?'

'He's no fool. He'll see right through the scheme, but
he'll fall in with the diplomatic game. Or pretend to.
But he'll start thinking and acting. That's why until
the F.O. boys take it up officially we have to keep
Jabal's presence here a secret.'

'I don't see that anything could go wrong. And, anyway, the Government and the oil company are going
to be very grateful to you.'

Drexel laughed. 'The gratitude of governments has
never kept down the size of my overdraft. As for the
oil company, they think I'm a public servant. I save
them thousands and may be they'll send me a couple
of cases of whisky at Christmas. And later on I shall
have to fight like hell to get expenses from the Treasury.
Hire of a launch, they'll say. Why not swim? Watch
dogs? What is all this? Five hundred for this Fraser
chap? Really, couldn't you have got him for two?
Termites, that's what they are.'

There was a silence between us for a while. If we'd
still been in the army; if I'd still been under discipline,

a captain who just took orders, I don't think he would have shown himself to me so clearly. But things were different now. I was hired by him, it was true, but the real bond between us was friendship and perhaps a touch of reverence on my side and because of that he could let himself go, knowing that anything spoken in this room would never be uttered again outside it. He was doing a job and like any clerk or shophand he had a right to blow off steam. He could do it safely with me, and perhaps with no one else. I sat there and I was angry for his sake, bitter against the strain in the man, resenting the dark moments he had to live through. I could imagine what had gone on in Saraj, imagine the patient organization that had gone to getting Jabal out; the plane in the desert, the dhow in the Red Sea, the long, hot camel marches and then the quick furtive move into Cairo and so on to the *Roi Bleu* ... and Drexel was nearly sixty.

I said impulsively, 'Why the hell do you go on doing this kind of thing?'

'Why? Because there's nothing else.'

'You could retire. Raise chicken.'

'On what I've saved?' He laughed suddenly and sat down. I could see that his mood had changed swiftly. He was back with himself. 'No, no, David. You know why I do it, and I know. I suppose I bloody well like it. But I do wish these poops in Whitehall had some little idea of what it all means.'

I said, glad that he was over the peak of his resentment, 'Why couldn't they handle it differently? If Jabal wants to sign the concession and the Regent has shown he would go to the lengths of killing him to stop it, then why the devil doesn't the Government step in and kick the Regent out of Saraj?'

Drexel roared with laughter. 'David, you're preposterous! This isn't the war or 1901. The Persian Gulf's no longer a British lake. Trouble? Send a cruiser and a detachment of marines? I wish they would. But the new diplomacy doesn't know how to kick the arses of people like ben Fa'id. Interfere openly in the affairs of an independent state that owes everything it has to British capital? Protect our own interests by open force?'

'Well, if I were ben Fa'id I'd scream through the Press that Jabal had been kidnapped.'

'He won't do that. He's much too clever.'

'Why won't he?'

'Because if he admitted Jabal had been kidnapped from Saraj, it would be admitting that Jabal wasn't safe there. He doesn't want anything out in the open. Least of all does he want to show his hand over this oil business. There's quite an opposition party out there ... you might call it a Jabal party.'

'They helped you get the boy out?'

'Of course. But that's all we need from them. In time the oil concession will be renewed in London and Jabal will go back as ruler. We don't want to start a civil war out there. Neither does ben Fa'id. That's why he will pretend the prince is on his way back to school and make no mention of kidnapping.'

'But that won't mean he's given up.'

'Not on your life. He'll do all he can to get hold of Jabal before he gets a chance to renew the oil concession. That's why you and I have to move carefully. If we lose Jabal now—we'll never get him back.'

'Well, what's your next move?'

'Have another whisky and then go to bed. Tomorrow I shall drive to Marseilles and get things moving through the British Consul. He's been briefed. He'll look po-faced and pretend he hasn't, and within twenty-four hours we shall have Benson down here.'

'Who's Benson?'

'A Foreign Office poop who envies me my exciting life and has a bank balance that's always in the black. Lucky man.'

He had the whisky and went to bed. I sat there for a while after he had gone, and I was wishing that he hadn't had the whisky. He'd always been a hard drinker but his strenuous living had offset it. I had the impression now that he was drinking, not to relax his abundant energy, but to dull some pain in his spirit.

CHAPTER FIVE

I had breakfast with the Colonel the next morning. Brindle took Jabal's breakfast up to his room. The Colonel was a different person, relaxed and cheerful, and eating like a horse. It was a thing I'd forgotten about him; his enormous appetite. He even alluded to his mood of the previous evening.

'Take no notice of it, David. It's a reaction after I've carried a thing off. Just feel I want to raise the roof. Does me good, I suppose.'

I saw him off. He drove an old Bentley with an open tonneau. The car had been locked in the garage by the villa gates. When he saw my eyes going over it, he said, 'I've had this fifteen years. Usually keep it in Paris. Brindle drove it down.' It was just his sort of car, open, splendidly shabby and powerful.

When he was gone, Jabal and I went out in the launch. We took her seawards a couple of miles and then anchored while we bathed. I liked him at once; a lean, finely-built youth with short, slightly curly black hair, and he had that assurance and quiet reserve which was pure Arab. Inside him, I felt, there was already a man, and a man, I was sure of this, who could be ruthless not only because the pattern of his life demanded it, but because it was there already in his nature. He joked and laughed, swam and played his mouth-organ. We talked about his school and the orchestra he had organized there and how he played also the drums and the saxophone (I had met this passion for jazz in the Eastern breast before, as though it were a kind of short-cut, an easy way into the mood of Western life), but, although no reference was made to the real nature of his presence here, there were moments when he was silent and brooding. I knew then that he was back in Saraj. One day Sheik Ahmed ben Fa'id was going to regret the trouble he had given Jabal.

We talked sometimes in Arabic and sometimes in English, but his English was good and I realized that Drexel had not offered me this job because I could speak Arabic. It was good to think that he had wanted me for myself, wanted someone whom he liked as well as trusted.

After lunch Jabal went up to his room to sleep. I went with him to lock him in. I felt a bit like a jailer and to shed my own embarrassment, I said, 'I'm sorry about this.'

He smiled at me. 'It is necessary.' Then the smile going, leaving his face suddenly grave, he went on, 'You are a good friend of Colonel Drexel?'

'I like to think so.'

'Such a friendship is an honour. He is a man.'

I locked him in and went down to Brindle. I told him I was going for a walk. The Colonel had left his key with Brindle and I asked him to keep an eye on Jabal when he let him out.

I did not go into Banyuls. I turned off the road and went across a field of vines to the sea. I found a little dip in the low cliffs, a hollow full of a tall, flowering rush-like plant which I thought was amaryllis. It was common in the district, but maybe it wasn't amaryllis. I lay down with my hands behind my head and stared up at the sky.

I must have dozed off and been in a light sleep. Something wakened me and for a moment I rested with my eyes shut, my lids a red curtain between me and the sun. Then the redness darkened and I felt the movement of a shadow across my face. I opened my eyes slowly.

Sophie was above me, standing between me and the sun so that I could see the outline of her body through the silk dress she wore. It was a firm, beautiful silhouette, and the sight of her there, immobile, looking down at me seemed right and expected for in my light sleep I had been, not dreaming, but thinking about her in wide, lazy splashes of thought which had little definition. Seeing her now, definite and steady above me, carried the mood and thoughts into a warmer, more cogent existence.

I said, 'Hullo, how did you get here?' and my voice was lazy with sleep still as I reached up a hand to her. She came down, kneeling beside me and the light airs playing over the amaryllis brought me the scent of her perfume.

She said, 'You were asleep and you were frowning. Why?'

I laughed gently, playing with her hand. 'Maybe because I was dreaming or thinking about you and I wanted the real person.' I remember that I hesitated over the French, making a decision between saying 'la vraie chose' or 'la vraie personne' and finally, swiftly deciding for 'personne'.

And then she said something which I was beginning to realize was characteristic of her. She had little small talk, at least not with me. She gave me the impression that she already knew all the trivial facts that were to be known about us and that somewhere time was running out and each word and sentence had to count. Or perhaps that was my impression and I credited her with it, too.

'The real person? The real thing? How do you tell? Can you touch it? See it? And when you find it ... how do you keep it?' She laughed and then went on quickly so that it was almost as though she hadn't spoken, 'There's a beetle crawling over your collar.'

She leaned forward and picked it off and her face was very close to mine so that I could see the small creases of her lips and how the line of lipstick near one corner of her mouth was delicately blurred, and her eyes were deep and still like a polished, smoky marble, only there was none of the coldness of marble in them and the depth was not darkness but light in the way that a summer night can be luminous.

I said, 'You know it because you know it.' And I knew what I meant and I knew that she knew. 'And you don't have to try to keep it because it's not a thing that can be taken away from you.'

She may have said more and I may have answered her. I don't know because from that moment neither words nor time had any meaning because the thing that was between us, and then was us, was outside words, outside English literature or any other literature, unrelated to any space or dimension I had known. I knew only that now it was here I recognized it as the fire recognizes flame, the snow recognizes cold ... the element without which we are never ourselves.

She lay in my arms with her face against my neck and her body under my hands was trembling gently and then still, and all I could see was the line of her shoulder and part of the pattern of her silk dress, a green leaf spray with a red berry against a yellow background and I saw how the overprinting of the red berry and the green leaf colours was offset a fraction of an inch from the pattern outline. Perhaps because this said to me that the material was cheap ... I don't know ... it raised a great tenderness in me. I wanted to gather her up in my arms, to walk away with her, away from Banyuls, away from whatever it was that brought the look into her eyes when I said it was time to go back to George Sarrasin and Astar Paviot ... to carry her away from everything she and I knew. Maybe this was love, maybe this was what a lot of people possessed, but the protection and tenderness in me raised an arrogance that said this was ours and for us alone and that it had never been before and could never be again with anyone else.

For a long time I held her, my Sophie with the dark, unravelled hair. The sun was hot upon us and the bees and flies noisy in the amaryllis blooms around us and, perhaps, the beetle that had been on my collar watching from the shade of some granite chip, black, green and irridescent and never to be forgotten by me though I had never seen it.

When she did move and lay back, shielding her eyes
from the sun, the movement brought the opening of
her dress apart where the top button was undone and
I saw the smoothness of her right breast. Above it,
just under the shoulder was a dark bruise. I put my
finger tips to it and kissed it and then, as I sat up, I
was angry in a way I had never been before.

'Somebody hit you,' I said.

She shook her head.

'Somebody hit you.'

I'd been bruised often enough myself. I'd fought
often enough, given and taken bruises, and I knew the
mark of a fist on flesh.

She sat up. The trapped, apprehensive look was in
her eyes again, the wanting and the not wanting.

'Who was it?'

I waited and eventually she said, 'George.'

I kept my anger down now, but I was going to have
it all.

'Why?'

'He wanted me to do something I didn't want to do.
He has a quick temper, but it means nothing.'

'A bruise like that. What the hell did he want?' And
then I saw it. 'Was it something to do with me?'

'Yes.'

She was making no defence. Just answering, her
voice without any shades of feeling.

I didn't have to have finesse. I wanted the truth and
meant to have it, and I knew that she could take anything I had to say.

I said, 'Is there anything between you and George or
Astar?'

'Only business.'

'You knocked over your bag on purpose in the
aquarium?'

'Yes.'

'To get to know me.'

'Yes.'

'Why?'

'They told me to. They want something from you. At first I didn't mind ... but later it was different. You know why.'

'What do they want from me?'

'It is difficult to explain. They live ... we all live ... from one day to another. They because they like it, and I ... because it is something that has happened to me and I cannot yet shake it off. Around Banyuls, you must have heard, there is smuggling. Things coming over from Africa and then up and down the coast between here and Spain. And you, you have just what George wants. I was to get to know you and to ask you to do this for them. This morning I tried to refuse ...'

'They're in that racket, are they? What do they want?'

'They would pay you ... At the villa where you stay there is a launch. All you have to do is to leave the key in the boat-house door one evening and take it back the next morning. I do not ask you to do this. I am telling you what they want.' She was silent for a moment then she put out her hand and took mine. 'David ...'

It was the first time she had used my name and with it all my anger went.

'They're a lot of bastards. I've got to get you away from them.'

She said nothing to that. She didn't have to say anything; but her hand held mine tighter.

'What do I tell them?'

'Tell them I said they can go to hell. They won't take that as a final answer. But I want time to think ... about us.'

I was thinking, too, about Drexel and Jabal. I was in no position to charge off and square up to George Sarrasin. For the moment I was tied to the Villa Maruba.

I stood up and pulled her up with me and put my arms around her.

'They know nothing about us?'

'No.'

'Then don't let them, Sophie. In a little while I can
fix it ... a little while.'

'I can wait ... waiting is no longer important.'

I kissed her and we walked to the road together. She
went back towards Banyuls and I went on to the villa.
But before we parted I said, 'You can tell me what it is,
the thing that holds you to them?'

'Yes, but not now. After this afternoon, I am not
ready. If you had not seen the bruise I would not have
asked you about the launch today. There is only one
thing I want to remember today ...'

I didn't force her, though I felt I could have done. I
didn't want to because I was wishing, too, that I had
not seen the bruise. But I walked back to the villa
promising myself that sometime I would have the
pleasure of leaving my mark on George Sarrasin.

On the way to the villa I thought the whole thing
over and, though I now knew what they were after,
there were certain aspects which worried me. I could
see that if they were smuggling then to hire a launch
publicly would be to draw attention to themselves, par-
ticularly if they were people in whom the police were
likely to take an interest. Our launch would be ideal
for them. I saw clearly, too, that I was under obligation
to tell Drexel all about it. I didn't think it had anything to do with Jabal—but it might. And not to tell
him would have been stupid. My decision to do this
was strengthened by a small core of suspicion which I
could not disperse that somewhere, somehow, the
whole thing was a little too pat and convenient. The
only thing which was natural and unplanned was my
relationship with Sophie. That stood apart from everything else.

I meant to tell him that evening. I had dinner with
Jabal and afterwards we played a game of chess which
ended in a stalemate. It was midnight before we went
to bed and the Colonel had not returned. Brindle sat
up for him. I heard his car come in and the dogs barking

about three, but it was too late then to get up and
bother him.

I was up at six the next morning for I had promised
to take Jabal out for an early morning swim. I pulled
a towelling dressing-gown over my swim-pants and then
turned to get the key of Jabal's room among the stuff
from my pockets which I had emptied on to the dressing-
table. I couldn't find the key. I had a moment of panic
as I ran along to his room, but he was there. The door
was locked and I could hear him playing his mouth-
organ softly, waiting to be released.

I went along to the Colonel's room. He was still thick
with sleep and when I asked to borrow his key of
Jabal's room he slipped his hand under his pillow and
flicked it across to me and was back in sleep before I
had left the room.

Jabal and I had our swim about a mile off shore. The
water was as smooth as treacle with faint trails of
morning mist curling lazily over it and the surface was
marked with a wonderful pattern of slow currents and
colours. Its beauty was lost on me. Most of the time I
was worrying about my key.

Back in the villa as I went along to my room, the
Colonel called to me. The door of his bedroom was half-
open and he was standing before his dressing-table,
brushing his hair.

'David . . . I was half-asleep when you came in. What's
all this about your key?'

I crossed to him and put his key down on the dressing-
table.

'It seems to have disappeared.'

'What?' He turned round quietly, at once alert. 'When
did you have it last?' There was the beginning of crisp-
ness in his voice.

'As far as I know late yesterday afternoon.'

'Who locked him up last night?'

'Brindle. He came up with us and while I was fumb-
ling for my key he got out yours. I've looked every-

where in my room for the damned thing but I can't find it. I must have dropped it somewhere ...'

He was looking fixedly at me and I could see his eyes had begun to take on a touch of the God-damn-you expression.

'You're not the kind of man who drops things.'

'I didn't think I was ...' I could feel the hesitation in myself and a kind of stupid, schoolboy guilt which made me wish I had sat up for him last night and told him what I had wanted to have him know. He saw that, too, for he knew me, knew the shades that could take a man's voice and face.

'Cough it up, David. Something's on your mind.'

I told him then, about Sophie and the two men: everything except the real thing that lay between Sophie and myself because that, at the moment, wasn't something I wanted to share with anyone.

At first I thought he was going to take it calmly.

'No one knows we are here,' he said. 'There's not even been a news release about Jabal leaving Saraj. I don't know ... Maybe you're right. This coast is thick with smugglers. Maybe it's just a coincidence.'

Then he paused and his face went hard and I saw the quick flick of his eyelids as he went on thinking, his mind surveying the whole panorama of possibilities and not liking the view. When he spoke his voice was a familiar echo from the past, the voice of the man who drove hard and demanded obedience to the point of fanaticism. 'You're a bloody fool, David. I'm not paying you five hundred pounds for a picnic. You should have known you had to keep to yourself. You should have known we can't afford to take any risk.'

I didn't mind being reprimanded. I'd asked for it.

'I'm sorry,' I said and, if there's any phrase more inadequate than that one I don't know it.

He exploded. 'Sorry! I don't care a damn about that! Jabal's dynamite. He could blow up in our faces any moment. Don't you see—until the F.O. take him over—everything's got to go right. It's got to go right!'

And then, though I was to blame, I couldn't help but see the difference in him. In the old days he didn't blast you to hell. He looked and said a few words and there was gall and wormwood, contempt and yet understanding in them, and then he left you to sort out your own punishment while he went on to a consideration of practical measures to put things right. But this cry ... *It's got to go right* ... was full of strain. It was an old man complaining that he couldn't carry the same load, the hero losing his vigour to uncertainty. Hearing it, I hated myself for bringing it on him. I wanted everything to go right for him. And, although I was the immediate cause of his distress, I had the odd feeling then that our positions were now reversed. No matter how inadequate I was, I was now responsible for him. I had to protect him and see that this thing he had started came through without any hitch. He was a name and a power in the public mind. He was the principle of valour and adventure which men and women had to have displayed for them to make them forget their own smallness; a hero who could not afford to fail. So I didn't mind when he said—

'What about this woman? Could she have lifted the key from you?'

'It could be. But I don't think so.'

He looked at me queerly and I wondered if he had detected anything in my voice.

'All right,' he said, turning away and slipping into his linen jacket. 'Benson from the Foreign Office should be here today sometime. We'll check on these people just to be sure. I can't afford to neglect anything. Ben Fa'id would pay a fortune to get Jabal back and cut his throat. I don't care a fig about the oil side of it— that's an F.O. business and just my job. But I like the boy. And you do, too. Nothing must happen to him.'

And then he did the thing which he always could do with me, lift me out of purgatory and take me back into the sunlight and warmth of his own friendship. He put his hand on my arm and squeezed it. 'Don't be such a casual, friendly bastard, David—not when you're working for me. You should have given that trio a wide berth the moment you saw they were interested in you. However,' he laughed, 'who am I to tell someone to steer clear of a pretty girl. I still have that kind of trouble.'

We all had breakfast together and the thing was not mentioned again. But afterwards he kept Jabal company and I think he did so because he knew what I would want to do. I went off, along my old route of the previous day, looking for the key. I searched around in the little dip where Sophie and I had been but I couldn't find it. I asked myself frankly, kicking out all emotion, whether I thought Sophie had taken it. But I couldn't accept that. I went down into Banyuls in the hope of seeing her. I was unlucky. I had a drink in the *Café aux Bons Enfants* and when Jean Cagou came and chatted to me, I asked him about the three of them. He should have known anything there was to know about anyone in this district who had anything to hide. He knew nothing about them. I borrowed an old copy of the *Guide du Pneu Michelin* from the café proprietor and telephoned the only three hotels listed for Argelès-sur-mer, *Plage des Pins*, *Commerce* and the *Lido*. There was no one of the names Orbais, Sarrasin or Paviot staying at any of them. But that proved nothing much. There would be plenty of small *pensions* not listed.

I walked back along the road so far and then, still worried about the key, I went over the vineyards to the dip again and had another look. But there was no key. Instead of going back by the road I kept along the coast track towards the villa and, about a quarter of a mile before I reached it, I dropped down between a break in the low cliffs and found myself in a small valley through which ran a dried-up stream bed. One side of the stream was lined by a narrow, sandy patch of cultivated ground laid out with melon plants and young tomatoes. The runnels of sand between the plants were still wet after the morning irrigation from a stone well which stood at the head of the patch. There was a plot of marguerites over which a cloud of yellow and black butterflies lifted and danced. Beyond the stream was a small clump of pines, the bottom of the trunks hidden in a growth of myrtle and broom bushes. The cliff path went up by the pines and as I passed them I heard someone groaning from the direction of the bushes.

I forced my way through the bushes and found myself in a little hollow. A small tent had been pitched under the trees and alongside the tent stood a dusty Norton motor-cycle with a GB plate. A piece of string, tied to the kickstart of the motor-cycle, ran across the ground and then into the tent. As I stood there another groan came from the tent.

I moved round to the front and looked in. The Englishman whom I had seen in the *Café aux Bons Enfants* was inside. He was in a sleeping bag and sat up as he saw me. Although he looked doleful and un-happy I had to smile. His pyjama jacket was open and his hands were clasped across his stomach. He was plump, not very big, and at first sight gave the impres-sion of coming to pieces, of being scattered in parts around the untidy tent. His false teeth were in a glass at the head of the tent. He wore a soft, light brown toupee with a curl and central parting that reminded me of a chairman of an old-time music hall. The toupee was cocked a little to one side as though he had slap-ped it on carelessly as he heard me coming. His clothes were scattered all over the place.

'You in trouble?' I asked.

'Yes. Crab.' Despite his condition his voice had a boom in it, a kind of public-house voice, the voice which is uplifted in withering sarcasm above all others at a football match.

'Crab?'

'Yes. Shouldn't eat it but I do.' His voice sounded miserable, but I couldn't believe he was. There was an incorrigible twinkle in his eyes, a beaming, good-

tempered air about him that seemed to suggest that he
found life a joke, even when its kicks were turned
against himself. He reached out for his dentures, slipped them home, and then, eyeing me up and down,
went on 'Seen you at the *Bons Enfants*, haven't I? You
English?'

'Yes, I am. Can I do anything for you?'

'A nice cup of tea might save me from dyin'. What I
really need is a new stomach.' He belched loudly and
then, as he raised a hand to thump his chest, I saw that
the string from the motor-cycle was attached to his wrist.
He saw me look at it, and went on, 'Safety precaution.
Don't trust these foreigners.'

I laughed and began to sort out his methylated stove
and tin kettle to make him some tea. I wanted to help
him because there was no doubt of his distress but also
I was interested in him. I felt I had already let the
Colonel down once. Nothing was going to pass me now.
This man—as I prepared the tea he told me his name
was Dunwoody, Leslie Dunwoody, from Walthamstow,
London—had chosen himself a spot quite close to the
villa. He might be a genuine camper, but he might
not.

'Have you been here long?' I asked.

'Nearly a week.'

'You enjoy camping?' He didn't seem the type at all
to me.

'Not bloody likely! But it's all I can afford. Travel is
the thing I like. You live in Walthamstow mate, and
you could understand that. Travel—broadens the mind.
Wish it would leave the stomach alone, though. Very
nice of you to do all this.'

I handed him a mug of tea. He sipped at it and then
said, 'I was headin' for Spain, but if I start having these
turns I don't think I will.' He belched again more gently
and went on, 'The 'eat from tea is very mollifying. I'm
grateful to you, real grateful.' He closed his eyes and
became a picture of comic bliss.

'You'll be all right,' I said. 'There's nothing wrong

with you that tea or bicarbonate won't cure.'

He nodded.

'Crab. Any kind of shell-fish. Also oil. Can't stand anything cooked in oil. Limits you, you know, when you're abroad.'

We talked a little more and then I left him. I got back to the villa in time for lunch and I told the Colonel about him. As far as I could judge there was nothing wrong with the man, nothing to arouse suspicion, except one thing and that could easily have been put down to his condition. He hadn't asked me my name, though he had given his own, and neither had he asked me what I was doing here. When I put this point to the Colonel he said—

'I'll wander over and have a look at him.'

He did that afternoon. I was in the garden with Jabal when he returned. We were lying sun-bathing by the boathouse. As he came down by the pines I thought his face looked reflective, almost care-worn. But seeing us he smiled.

'He was asleep, David. What a mess that tent was! Never been in the army that's clear. But he looks harmless to me.'

He sat down and smoked a cigarette, and then after a while he said, 'I've had a phone call from Benson. He's at Perpignan and wants me to go up and see him. He thinks it wiser if he doesn't come here. I shall go off after tea.'

CHAPTER SIX

Colonel Drexel left in his car just after four o'clock. Perpignan was about an hour's drive away, and he told me that he did not anticipate that he would be late back.

I was having a drink before dinner, waiting for Jabal to come down, when the telephone in the hall began to ring. I didn't do anything about it, expecting Brindle to answer it. But he must have been in the garden, for it went on ringing and eventually, grumbling to myself, I got up and went out.

A voice speaking in French said, 'Is that Mr Fraser?'

I said, 'Yes. Who is it?'

My question was ignored and the voice went on, 'Sophie tells us that you are not happy about our suggestion.'

'What Sophie tells you is right.'

It was Sarrasin, and I saw no need to let any friendliness into my words.

Sarrasin laughed.

'Naturally, you have to be cautious. I understand. However, you need not worry. Just leave the key in the boat-house door tonight. No one will ever know anything. And you will have made some very easy money.'

I said, 'Go to hell!'

The door from the kitchen quarters to the hall opened at this point and Brindle's head and shoulders appeared. He raised his eyebrows stiffly and I waved him away. He drew back like a tortoise into its shell.

On the other end of the line Sarrasin was saying: 'About the money. Of course in a few days we shall make a deposit in your name at any Crédit Lyonnaise you name. Say at Perpignan?'

'You say what you like. But keep away from this place. Tonight, or any night!'

'You sound angry.'

'You pick things up fast.'

He laughed and went on quickly, 'Such a small thing to do. Tonight, then? No other night will do. You understand these things—'

The man was taking no notice of me.

I said fiercely, 'Look, Sarrasin—get this fixed in that wooden head of yours—'

There was a laugh, followed by the words, 'Tonight . . .' and then the receiver was replaced.

I slammed the phone down, and I didn't understand the thing at all. I might have been talking to a stranger on a crossed-line.

I went back to the lounge. Why the devil should they think I would help them? Why persist when I made it clear that I wouldn't? And why give me warning that they meant to come? They could come along secretly any night and break into the boat-house. Their only risk would have been from the dogs. There was an oddness in their behaviour which confused me. It was like trying to untangle a mass of thread and knowing somewhere there was the one loose end which needed only a jerk to make the whole thing come unravelled. I spent half an hour trying to find the loose end and couldn't. Jabal came down and switched on the radio. He sat with a glass of orange juice listening to a talk on bell-ringing from some British station. He was absorbed enough to make me think that his great hobby was campanology. In a way, I was irritated that he could sit there so placidly while I became more and more convinced that subtle forces were gathering around him, that somewhere something was going wrong.

In the end I went out into the hallway and got on the telephone to the British Consul in Marseilles. The Consul, of course, was not in. It took me five angry minutes to convince whoever it was on the line that there was such a person as Drexel—though I knew damned well that he knew all about the Colonel—and another two minutes of exasperation to get it into his thick head that the Colonel was meeting Benson in Perpignan, that I didn't know how or where to reach him but if Marseilles could do this I wanted the Colonel to ring me at once. In the end I got a promise that this would be done if possible and the last word I heard was ... 'irregular'. It was a situation I knew well. Secrecy and pretending not to know things you know damned well, and the anonymity of the telephone are all very well so long as things go to plan. Let anything slip, and then it takes ages to get into another gear and another frame of mind. I knew perfectly well what would happen. In fifteen minutes Marseilles would ring back the villa and ask for me. They would then ask me if I had just spoken to them. I was rather looking forward to that moment.

From the telephone I went into the kitchen. Brindle had the radio on, too. But his choice was dance music, very soft and sweet. I surprised him humming to himself but he went wooden the moment he saw me. He was gutting and cleaning fish for dinner.

I said, 'Are there any arms in the house?'

He looked at me and there wasn't even a flicker of surprise in him. 'You mean guns, sir?'

'That's it.'

He cut the head off a bream and flicked it into a pail at the side of the table.

'Two sir.'

'Let's have one.'

I think then for the first time in his life he wanted to step outside his part and ask 'Why?' He looked at me steadily for a moment and then he slowly bent down and drew open the table drawer. He handed me an old service Colt .45, but before he did so he wiped his hands on his apron, broke the gun and spun the chamber.

I took it and saw that it was unloaded. Holding the gun gave me a queer sensation, not the old feeling of being an inch bigger all round and better prepared for what might happen, but another feeling ... of going back and not wanting to go, of myself this time stepping outside the part I'd picked for myself.

The revolver was beautifully kept ... cleaned, oiled. I wondered how Brindle got it through the Customs when he came abroad. Drexel probably arranged that.

'Ammunition,' I said.

Brindle put his hand into his back trouser pocket and then tipped six bullets on to the table. I picked them up.

'You was always inclined to pull a little bit to the left, if I remember, sir.'

'I was.'

I tossed the Colonel's key of Jabal's bedroom—the only key left now—over to him.

'You'll lock our friend in tonight. Then we'll take turns to sit outside the bedroom until the Colonel gets back.'

'Are we expecting trouble, sir?'

'Maybe. You'll want the other gun. You don't know how I could get hold of the Colonel in Perpignan?'

'No, sir.'

'I don't want Jabal to hear about this.'

'Quite, sir.'

At that moment the telephone went. It was from Marseilles. When I confirmed that I had indeed telephoned before, the voice was instantly helpful, passing smoothly into the next gear. If the Colonel could be found it would be done. In the meantime was there anything that could be done that end. I had to say no. I wasn't even sure what I was going to do myself or whether there was any need for anything.

For dinner Brindle gave us the bream grilled, a beautiful côtelette de veau, a cheese soufflé and a bottle of Chateau Margaux 1949. I ate well but I hated to leave the wine practically untouched.

I started a game of chess with Jabal as Brindle brought the coffee. My mind was not on the game and he beat me easily. I think he knew then, from the wine and his victory, that something was in the air, but he asked no questions and I liked him for that. He was a good boy, happy to be by himself or with other people, never demanding but with no false modesty. It's a thing you find in people who inherit dark destinies and learn how to live with them ... this powerful reserve and force, a mixture of patience and strength which marks them with a rare dignity. Even with his few years he had it ... and it had made a man of him already.

He went up to his room at ten and, with Brindle, I saw him locked in. I left Brindle up there, squatting on a cushion, his gun resting on his legs. Anyone else might have brought a book to read, or a pipe to smoke, but not Brindle. He sat down, gave me a look and a nod, and that was it. He would sit there now, unsleeping, until he was relieved. As I left him, I said, 'I shall be in the garden. If there's any trouble you'll hear the dogs bark.'

I put on a sweater and went out into the garden and sat in the shadows on the edge of the fountain. It was a point from which I could watch the front of the house and also the landing steps before the boat-house.

I sat there thinking of George Sarrasin and Astar Paviot. They might well be small-time, bungling smugglers ... but they might not. I had to guard against that risk. And from them I began to think of Sophie, wondering what had brought her into their lives, no matter what they were. She was no innocent raw girl. I had never imagined her like that. There must be a lot of things behind her ... but what they were had little importance for me. She was the thing. She and the life which had flashed into flame between us.

It was a lovely night. Warm and soft and an occasional current of air as though somewhere a curtain was swinging gently. The stars were so bright that I almost expected them to blow their filaments. And sitting there it all became a little unreal ... and I distrusted that at once, because I knew it was nerve tension, the hair rising on the back of the neck. From the far side of the house where there was a gum tree, a nightingale began to sing too theatrically to be true. And the waves down by the landing steps lapped musically until the sound became words, a tune ... a chorus of sweet-voiced peasant children I had heard somewhere performing at Christmas for *Monsieur le Curé*:

> *Mon beau sapin,*
> *Roi des forêts ...*

A late lizard scuttled among the dry leaves of the fountain. I sat there for an hour. And then, the noise growing slowly, I heard the unmistakable sound of oars knuckling against wooden rowlocks. A few moments later I saw the boat; a dark shape about fifty yards offshore and coming up from the direction of Banyuls. I got up and, keeping to the shadows, went down to the landing stage.

As I went the dogs which had been wandering around the garden came padding up to me and followed me down growling softly. Just as I reached the landing stage the boat turned towards the shore. By the light of the stars and a pale crescent of moon which had just begun to lift itself clear of the mauve stretch of sea, I could pick out the people in the boat.

George Sarrasin was rowing. He was dressed in something that looked like a dark-coloured track suit. In the stern was a man I had never seen before, a short, non-descript-looking creature in a light raincoat and a beret. When the boat was a couple of yards from the steps George pulled round and it rested there, swaying gently. George's white, slab-like face turned full towards me and I saw him throw a leg across the thwart so that he now sat comfortably astride it.

'*Bonsoir, monsieur,*' he said.

I said, 'Sarrasin—this is private property. Keep off it.'

He nodded a little, as though he were considering this point. Then he said, 'It is very hard to do business with you.'

'Not hard. Impossible.'

As I spoke I brought the Colt from behind my back and the faint moonlight slid in an oily ripple along its barrel. The boat drifted a little further inshore.

George looked from the revolver to me and again he shook his head. 'You would use that?'

He sounded a little sad as though we were friends and I had affronted him. And I was hating every moment because everything was wrong and out of place. I had the feeling that he wasn't caring a damn about me, that he was absolutely sure of himself. It was a feeling that I'd known before; the fine sense which tells you that your adversary has a card up his sleeve and doesn't care if you know it.

'I'll use it,' I replied, 'if you make it necessary.' And I meant it. Behind me was a powerful backing, Drexel, the Anglo-Media Oil Company, and eventually the Foreign Office and possibly the French *Bureau des Affaires Etrangères*. A bullet in George Sarrasin would cut no ice with them if he were interested in Jabal ... and I was becoming more and more convinced that he was.

George said, 'You are making a great mistake. However, since you are determined ...' He leaned forward to take up his oars. And then, a fraction of a second too late, I realized that this was the moment of the trump card. I had been waiting for it, wondering how it would come, trying to foresee it, and the mistake I made was anticipating subtlety. There was a whisper of noise behind me and I swung round towards the shadow of the boat-house. Part of the shadow moved, crowded in on me and something smashed at my head. I went down like a log and the last thing with me was the sound of my own breath, forced from me in a sob of angry futility.

It must have been a good hour later before I came round. I felt stupid and muzzy and I lay for a while staring up at the stars through the pine branches, not really aware of myself or of what had happened. The bitch wolf-hound came and whined about me. Slowly I pulled myself up. My legs felt like rubber, and, the

moment I was upright, I was sick, I felt better after
that, but light-headed still and I had the extraordinary
sensation of being divorced from my body, of watching
it move erratically up the path to the house and of
wanting desperately to get back into it and communi-
cate urgency and concise understanding to it.

In the house the lights were burning in the hall and
up the stairs. At the top of the stairs lay Brindle. He
was sprawled out with his automatic close to his hand
and was groaning gently to himself. I went past him
and along to Jabal's room. The door was open and the
room was empty. It was then that I came back to
myself, my outside self overlapping and then fitting
itself to my stumbling body in the way the images are
brought into focus in a camera.

I went back to Brindle but he was still out and I
could see that he'd taken a crack over the head too. I
turned him over and loosened his collar and was about
to go to the bathroom to get some water for him when
the telephone in the hall began to ring.

Going down the stairs to it as quickly as I could the
movement made my head swim and I must have taken
longer than I imagined. The incessant *ring, ring, ring*
made me irritable. I picked it up to hear the Colonel's
voice.

'David? Why did you want me? Has anything happened?'

I said, 'Where are you?'

'Perpignan.'

'Then get back here, Jabal's gone . . .'

At the other end I heard him swear, not with anger,
but with a note of sick despair, and then came his
questions and I told him as well as I could what had
happened.

I said, 'What do you want me to do?'

Crisply, taking control now, pushing down whatever
he was feeling, and I could guess even in my state at
the anxiety that was with him, he said, 'Stick there
and wait for me.'

I went up to Brindle again, hauled him along to his room and put him on his bed. It seemed to take me ages. I bathed his face with water and made him comfortable but he was still out. Then I went down to the lounge and got myself a drink. I gave myself ten minutes with it and then I could rest there no longer. I was beginning to be myself now and a lot of questions were hammering away in my mind. I got up and went down to the boat-house. The launch was in its place and there was no sign of the row-boat. I made my way up the path to the road-gate in the villa wall. It was wide open. As I came back to the house the dogs joined me and, thinking of Brindle upstairs, Brindle who must have been taken by surprise, I suddenly realized that the dogs hadn't given him any warning. It was something I didn't understand at all. Even when I had gone down to Sarrasin the dogs had only growled softly.

In the lounge I fixed myself another drink and sat there trying to sort things out. Jabal was gone, and the conviction beat in my mind that it was my fault. I seemed to have done everything I could, taken every precaution, but the whole thing had gone wrong. I was confused and sick at heart because I knew what this was going to mean to Drexel. He'd picked me, relied on me and I'd let him down.

I must have dropped off to sleep. When I woke it was two o'clock and Drexel was standing in front of me with another man whom I soon learned was Benson. Outside the dogs were barking and I guessed that there were other people about.

Drexel was grim and efficient, as I expected him to be. Whatever he was feeling underneath he was not showing it. Benson was a tall, shadow-like creature behind him who said hardly anything.

Drexel fixed my head. Whatever had hit me had been blunt, not making much of a cut. While he did it he made me go through my story, asking a question now and again. When it was over he said, 'All right. Now you get some sleep.'

He came up to the bedroom with me and I wanted to say something but there was nothing I could say. Inside I was dried-up and miserable and, although he hadn't said a word of censure, I had the feeling that he was gone from me; that something between us had been broken.

I dropped off to sleep, hearing the telephone ringing and the sound of movement and voices throughout the house.

CHAPTER SEVEN

I was awake by nine o'clock the next morning. I went along to the bathroom and shaved and showered. I wasn't feeling too bad physically, no worse than having a bad hangover. It was a fine morning, calm, bright and not yet hot. Through the open window I could see the wall gate. There was a *garde mobile* standing by it and I could see his motor-cycle parked on the path. By the garage was a long, low Citroën car.

When I got back to my room Brindle was just leaving. He had set a breakfast tray on the table by the window. He looked all right except for a wad of plaster just behind his right ear.

I said, 'How are you, Brindle?'

'All right, sir.'

'We both bought it, didn't we?'

He grunted something, but it was just a noise. Nothing in it for me.

It was then that I got my first suspicion that something new was in the wind for, despite his usual dourness, his manner carried no recognition that we had shared anything the previous night. If two people get cracked over the head they have something in common. Brindle was miles from me and, before I had time to say anything more, he made it clear that he was only the instrument of a new influence.

'The Colonel's compliments, sir, and he would appreciate it if you kept to your room until he calls for you.'

He was gone before I could question him and I was left wondering what the hell all this was about.

It was an hour before Brindle appeared again and said the Colonel would like to see me. Drexel was in the lounge. When I went in he was standing by the window and there was another man sitting at a small table close to the fireplace. Drexel asked me how I

was, and then introduced me to the other man. He was
a Monsieur Didier, a Commissioner of Police from Marseilles or it may have been Perpignan because at that
moment I wasn't really listening. I was watching Drexel.
He had changed since last night. The strain was on him
clearly now. He looked older and there was a greyness
about his skin which I had never seen before. As a boy
I had known my mother to be worried by things outside my comprehension or kept from me (our finances
had never been very sound and she had had a brother
who had caused her constant trouble) but, even so, a
child, recognizing anxiety in an adult, is distressed by
his own ignorance. I felt like that with Drexel now. I
could not say he was avoiding me but he was making no
movement towards me.

I said, 'Is there any news?'

'No. Not so far. Though we've got things moving.'
He came across the room, one hand rubbing his chin,
his eyes on the ground and he might have been talking
to himself. 'There's been a Press release from Saraj
that Jabal left a week ago for London via France. That's
Sheik Ahmed ben Fa'id playing ball, of course.'

'Do you think he's got hold of Jabal?'

'Possibly. But there's still a chance to find him. Benson and I have decided that the Press must know about
this. It'll help the police in their work. But we've got
to get agreement from London and Paris first. I only
hope it doesn't take long.'

He halted suddenly and beat a fist into his palm and
said, 'I can't understand how anyone could have got
on to us so quickly. There's been a leak somewhere.'
As he finished speaking he raised his hand and looked
at me and I knew then what he was trying not to think.
It was like being hit in the face. I took the shock hard,
and heard my inner self saying 'He can't think that! He
can't!' But I knew damned well that he did, or was
coming to it.

I was going to say something but he forestalled me.
'David. I've told Didier all you told me, but he's got

some questions to ask you.' He paused and momentarily he smiled, for the first time, and I knew it was to cover his embarrassment. 'Didier's a policeman and he's got his job to do. Don't get your rag out if you don't like some of the questions.'

He did not have to warn me. I knew what was coming and had already told myself that it wouldn't help me or Drexel to get angry.

I sat down and looked at Didier and said, 'Go ahead, monsieur.'

Elbows on the table Monsieur Didier rested his chin on tented fingers and stared at me. His friendly, brown eyes were troubled now and again by a nervous flutter of the eyelids. He had short, stubby fingers, not too well kept, as though he did a lot of gardening. In fact his whole appearance made me think of a gardener, solid and middle-aged. His bearing was slow and patient as though he knew that neither the seasons nor human beings were to be forced if you wanted good results. He had a trick, too, of cocking his right cheek forward, possibly to conceal the hearing aid he wore in his left ear.

He said, 'The three people you have described—you say they made your acquaintance by design?'

'They did.'

'You told the Colonel nothing about them until you lost your key?'

'I was going to tell him.' It sounded weak and made me angry with myself.

'It strikes me as odd that, after your refusal to co-operate, they so conveniently warned you they were coming.'

'I think it's odd, too.'

'We agree. In fact I don't think there is any truth in the story.'

'In *their* story,' I corrected and I was beginning to see how difficult it might be to hold my temper. For all his friendly brown eyes this man did not have any interests of mine at heart.

In their story. Or—could it be in yours?'

'They damned well came for the launch, didn't they? They also cracked me on the head—and Brindle.'

'I was coming to that. How do we know they came for the launch?'

'I saw them.'

'But no one else.'

'Brindle?'

'He saw no one. He heard a noise from the stairs and going to investigate was hit from behind.'

'Someone hit him and me.'

'True. At the moment I find the whole thing very confusing. Can you explain, for instance, why they should come for a launch which you had already refused them, and why they should conveniently telephone you and tell you they were coming?'

'It sounds absurd.'

'I'm glad you agree.'

'But it's damned well true.'

'Maybe, but we have only your word for it.'

'Brindle heard the telephone go.'

'He heard the telephone, but that might have been anything. A wrong number or a different message from the one you have told us you received.'

I stood up and looked at Drexel.

'Look, Colonel, why don't you both come out into the open and say what you think.' I couldn't keep the bitterness from my voice.

'Take it easy, David. See it from our point of view. The whole thing's a muddle and we're trying to get it straight.'

Didier ignored the passage and went on—

'Can you explain why the dogs shouldn't have barked when these strangers entered the grounds? That at least would have given Brindle some warning.'

'I don't know. I've been puzzled by that.' I had a fresh hold on myself. I wanted to help Drexel and if this would get us anywhere I was prepared to force under my own feelings. But it wasn't easy.

Didier blinked at the ceiling for a moment, then said, 'The key you lost. Do you think it could have been stolen?'

'Well I suppose it could have been.'

'It was—or else fortunately found, for it was used to unlock Jabal's door last night.'

'Didn't they take a key from Brindle?'

'No. After you left him he hid his in the cistern of the water closet in the bathroom. It was there this morning.'

'Well, I know nothing about that. I can see what you're driving at. You think I may have helped these people in some way. Or even arranged this. I don't blame you for examining that angle—but it's just too bloody fantastic for words. I took every precaution I could. I tried to get in touch with the Colonel. I phoned Marseilles. I armed myself and I put Brindle on guard.'

'And despite all that—Jabal was taken.'

I could have kicked him in the face; he said it in such an unctuous manner, the petty triumph of an official.

'Maybe Brindle's in the thing with me, too,' I said sarcastically. 'We knocked one another over the head to give ourselves good alibis.'

'You could have done.' There was no shaking him and I suddenly wanted to laugh at the absurdity of the situation. But he went on quickly, 'What I would like to know is which of you washed up the coffee cups. Brindle says he didn't.'

'Coffee cups?'

'Yes. There is no sign of struggle in Jabal's room. He may have been drugged before his room was entered. The coffee cups you both used after dinner were in the kitchen washed.'

I turned to Drexel. This was getting beyond anything I had expected and I wanted to see the same recognition of its absurdity in him as there was in me. 'Colonel—are you with him in this?'

He came over to me slowly, biting his lower lip and he put his hand on my shoulder.

'David. I'm not anywhere. I've got a bomb in my hands which is about to go up unless I act quickly. I'm not interested in anything but the truth and, by God, I'm not accepting anybody's word unless it can be proved. Do you think I like standing by and listening to this? But I'm not stopping it, not if it gets me an inch nearer the truth.'

For the first time in my life—and then it was only for a fraction of time and left me ashamed—I found myself against him. With anyone else he could be like this, but not with me. I owed him my life. He was my friend. If I gave him my word then he was in honour bound to accept it. God, it sounds old fashioned, but there's all truth in it. I was angry with him, and sorry for him because he was letting me down. And then it was gone and there was only compassion. He was old and his career was shredding before his eyes, and I loved him for his weakness as in the past I had loved him for his strength; and I knew I would do anything for him—even put up with this.

There was worse to come.

Monsieur Didier blinked, wrote a few notes and then, without looking up, said, 'Last year while you were in Turkey you spent five days in gaol?'

'What's that to do with anything? I was on holiday. It was a passport mix-up.'

'You do some very odd things in your holidays, Mr Fraser?'

'Why not? We all need a change from our work.'

'You are not a rich man, Mr Fraser?'

'Of course not. I'm a schoolmaster.'

'Maybe you'd like to be something different. Maybe you'd like to have money?'

'Who wouldn't?' I was very weary of him now, but not angry, and I let all the life go from my voice. 'Monsieur Didier—you're chasing the wrong hare. I'm a schoolmaster. Not a kidnapper. I can't stop you thinking what you like. But don't think I don't understand what's in your mind. Maybe I should help you.' I heard

my voice taking on a strange bitterness. 'I speak French
fluently. I worked for a short while in the French
Resistance movement which you know had many crooks
in it. Some of them I still know. Some of them, no
doubt, live in and around Marseilles or Perpignan or
who-cares-where. Give me ten minutes and I could
make a stronger case against myself than you could.
But give me ten centuries and I'm still fool enough to
think that nothing could ever make me betray Colonel
Drexel!'

I didn't look at Drexel. I didn't want to. I kept my
eyes on Didier and very quietly the bastard replied,
'Your dossier which Mr Benson of the Foreign Office
has supplied states that at Oxford you were an active
member of the O.U.D.S. Even the police can be fooled
by a good actor.'

But not even that could touch me.

I said calmly, 'Why don't you get out and look for
Jabal instead of sitting on your backside wasting time
with me?' And I said it in the same tone that I might
have remarked on the weather, not caring a damn how
he would take it. To his credit, he took it well.

He gave me a little nod, and said, '*Touché.*'

He got up and looked towards the Colonel who was
standing staring at both of us as though he were
watching some scene from a play, something that
wasn't touching him, his mind busy and far away.

'Colonel Drexel, maybe Mr Fraser is right. We are
wasting time with him at the moment.' Then he turned
to me. 'You will oblige me by staying in this room.
Later today I should like you to come to headquarters
with me. From our photographs you may be able to
identify some of these people with whom you are
acquainted. Also ...' and now for the first time the
edge of a threat crept in, 'we shall be able to go on
with our talk and possibly reduce the confusion a
little.'

He went out and the opening door showed that there
was a *gendarme* outside. Drexel lingered for a moment.

He came close to me and then, unexpectedly, his face cleared and he smiled, really for me this time, and said, 'No hard feelings, David. It's just that the whole thing is slipping through my hands like sand.'

'Forget it. Didier doesn't understand. Don't worry about me.'

I think he wanted to say something else, but it wouldn't come. He punched my shoulder affectionately and then left me.

I sat there alone in the room and it seemed damper and gloomier than it had ever been. For once I was almost in a mood to enjoy it. I turned my back on the sunshine outside and stared at the fireplace which was covered with a great spread of a cheap paper fan. I had a lot to think about. I could see how a fairly good case could be made against me for carelessness, though even so I couldn't really accept this myself. And, in a way, I could see that Didier might have the beginnings of a half-baked case against me on the score of aiding or even planning Jabal's abduction. But, however he was going to look at it, I could not feel any real apprehension and after a time I found that my thoughts had gone to Sophie. Just where she stood in all this confusion I wanted to know more than anything. She had told me that Sarrasin and company were smugglers and wanted the launch. This was a lie. They had come for Jabal. But did she know it was a lie? I wanted the answer to that desperately and I knew why. If the thing which had come to life between us was what I thought it was, then I knew it had no place in it for a lie. If she had known they were going to take Jabal then all she had brought to me was false. And this I was not going to believe unless she herself proved it to be so. Drexel could make a mistake about me, even begin to give credence to an absurd suspicion, but I could not find it in myself to be suspicious of Sophie. I could just not do it. There had to be an explanation. The only one I could think of was that Sarrasin and company had started off as smugglers and then in some way had learned about Jabal and had seen the rich possibilities of kidnapping. They could make a deal with either side—with the Regent, though this would mean the end of Jabal, or with the oil company and British interests. Drexel had been forced to use other people in getting Jabal out of Saraj. He had travelled up through Cairo. There was the crew of the *Roi Bleu*. There must have been fifty opportunities for leakage of information.

I sat there mulling it all over, and outside in the hall I heard the telephone go constantly and a parade of different voices. Brindle brought me some lunch but there were few words between us. After lunch I was allowed to go for a stroll in the garden, but I can't say I enjoyed it with an *agent de police* keeping a strict two yards behind me. A wind had got up, a fierce, whippy touch of tramontane blowing out of a clear sky and raising the dust in my face. I was glad to go back to the lounge.

The hours went by. I read all the magazines in the place and finally finished up with a tattered cookery book which had found it way in there. I remember reading a recipe for *escargots à la bourguignonne*. I shut my eyes and repeated it to myself, knowing I would never forget it. Maybe that's why I was good at languages. I have a facile, visual memory. I can look at a railway time-table and remember the details months later. And if anyone asked me what was I wearing on July 4th two years ago I could go right through the list. Recipes, trains, clothes, useless junk ... *Faites d'égorger des escargots en les faisant boullir dans l'eau où l'on a mis deux poignées de cendre de bois* ... 9.21 a.m. from Tunbridge Wells Central station for Charing Cross: Saturdays only; arrive Charing Cross 10.23 a.m. ... A Donegal tweed jacket, blue shirt, collar a little frayed, blue tie, grey flannel trousers ...

I must have gone off to sleep. When I woke it was dark outside and Drexel and Didier had just come into the room. Drexel was fixing himself a whisky and he brought one over for me.

I took it and stood to drink it.

I said, 'Well?'

'No news. We've combed Argelès-sur-Mer for your three birds. No one knows them. Your espadrille seller—Jean Cagou—remembers you with them but he doesn't know them. Nobody knows them. Also nobody hired a row-boat from Banyuls last night and none is missing.'

'And Jabal?'

'Not a trace.'

Didier, carrying a black brief case, came forward. I could see he was not approving of this conversation.

'Colonel Drexel ... I must get back. There is much to be done.'

Drexel nodded and he held out my light raincoat to me.

'Better put this on, David. This wind's making it a bit chilly.'

I had the feeling that he was sorry for what had happened that morning; that he was trying to make it up to me, reaching out again to draw me closer to him. But he knew and I knew that it could never be the same. We had both taken a step forward and away from each other. I would still go to hell for him. But now, instead of worship, there was understanding; instead of faith a compassionate logic.

As I slipped into the coat, I said, 'What do I do about getting back?'

He hesitated too long before he answered, 'Benson and I will be coming in later. We'll see to you.'

It was as good as saying, 'I don't know how long you'll be kept by Didier. I don't know what's going to happen to you.'

Outside the wind was blowing strongly and the sky was suddy with little clouds. I got into the Citroën, which was driven by an *agent de police*, and sat in the back with Didier. A *garde mobile* on a motor-cycle went ahead of us along the road to Port-Vendres. He must have been an impatient man for he was soon far ahead of us and then eventually lost to sight.

I said to Didier, 'Where are we going?'

'Perpignan.' His tone was clear enough, and I did not have to be hit over the head to make it obvious that he was in no mood for conversation with me. The talk, I knew, would come later. And maybe the hit over the head. I sat there, disliking him more and more.

We went down the steep drop into Port-Vendres, and along the quay front. One of the North African steamers was in, her decks a blaze of light. She was white and beautiful and stirred something inside me, the thing which was always moved at the sight of a boat. With a bitter irony I thought then of Songa Manara. I had given all that up—for this. I kept my eyes on the boat, staring past the stolid Didier. I suddenly thought how good it would be to get aboard her or any other ship and watch Europe sink over the stern ... the desire to get away was strong in me that instant for I felt too much caught up and involved and—to be honest—uncertain of myself. Only one thing I would have asked and that was that Sophie should come with me. I didn't want to be alone any longer.

I sat there as we swept down on to the long straight bamboo-fringed road to Perpignan and thought about Sophie. And I found running in my head a phrase of poetry which though it came straight out of Eng. Lit. third year syllabus—God what ages away the school and the feel of chalk on my fingers seemed!—had in it a great deal of what I felt for Sophie.

> *What I do*
> *And what I dream include thee, as the wine*
> *Must taste of its own grapes*

Parse it, take it apart, write it in paraphrases ... but it wouldn't mean a damn thing unless once in your

life that high note of recognition had vibrated in and
around and through you.

I don't know where we were on the road when I
saw the torch flash from ahead. Beyond Argelès-sur-
Mer, I think, but not as far up as the point where the
road crosses the River Tech on its way to the sea.

Didier muttered something to the driver and the
man slowed. I think he thought as I did that it might be
our *garde mobile* signalling. Then the headlights picked
up the figure of a man in the road centre, the torch
swinging in slow arcs from his hand.

'*Qu'est-ce qu'il y a?*'

There was no answer, not in words; only an incredible
swiftness of movement and manoeuvre that left both
Didier and myself helpless. The nearest I got to doing
anything was a half-move of my arm towards my door
handle and the word, shouted in surprise. 'Paviot!'

The driving door was jerked open and the *agent de
police* was pulled out. As he was dragged into the road
I saw Paviot's arm go up and then down and, although
the darkness hid it from me, I could tell he held a knife.
The driver sighed and then gave a scream that died into
a whimper. Paviot let him drop to the ground and slid
into the driving seat. At the same moment, the doors
on either side of Didier and myself were jerked open.
George Sarrasin, the lower part of his face masked, slid
in and forced me over, his hand holding a gun against
my ribs. On the other side of me a small figure in raincoat and beret, his face masked, too, held a gun on
Didier and a rasping voice said:

'Out!'

Didier was grabbed by the arm, pulled out, and then
forced by the gun in his back to move to the side of
the road. He stood there with his hands raised. Above
the wind I heard his voice.

'Fraser ... you won't get away with this!'

I did not get his meaning then, and I was given no
chance to reply. Paviot turned the car in the road
with two long backing and filling movements. When

he was round, the man with Didier gave him a push that sent him over the road bank into the ditch, and then came running to the car. He jumped in alongside Paviot.

The car drove off at top speed back along the road it had just travelled. There was nothing I could have done. Not a thing. It had been a dark pantomime with no part in it for me except to watch. Behind us I knew there was an *agent de police* who would be lucky if he were not mortally wounded. Before us was the white ribbon of road and around me these three.

Sarrasin relaxed the pressure of the gun on my side. Almost to himself I heard him say, 'Beautiful.' It was a sigh more than a word, a lingering breath of pleasure.

Angrily I said, 'What the flaming hell do you three think you're doing?'

Sarrasin turned his great face towards me, an unsmiling solemn slab of flesh and then heavily he said, 'Don't talk. Don't make trouble.' Calmly he began to untie the scarf he had worn over his face and which had now slipped into a noose around his neck.

I sat there, silent.

Paviot whistled thinly to himself as he drove. We went back as far as Argelès and then swung right-handed away from the coast. They made no attempt to hide their route from me. We were speeding now along the road to Le Boulou and for a while I wondered if they were heading for the Spanish border. Wherever they were going I told myself that it would be dangerous for them to remain on the road long in Didier's car.

We were some way out of Argeès when the car stopped. Watching the speedometer and checking the time on my wrist-watch, I made it about ten kilometres. That would be about half-way to Boulou. For the moment, I was glad to leave the big issues. I wanted time to come to that. I kept tabs on the small things like distance and place. So far I knew where we were.

The car stopped without any instructions from

George Sarrasin. Paviot got out of the driving seat and the other man slid across and took his place. Paviot opened my door and motioned me out. I obeyed and Sarrasin came behind me with the revolver.

I heard Sarrasin say to the driver: 'Take it as near Perthus as you can and then ditch it. Don't try to be brave.'

I knew what that meant. Le Perthus was beyond Le Boulou and on the border. If the ditched car were found there it would look as though we had gone across the Spanish frontier.

The car went off, its tail-light wreathed with a plume of exhaust gases. Sarrasin hustled me along into the side of the road and Paviot produced a long length of rope from around his waist. He tied it about himself and then, leaving a working length, looped it round my waist and passed the spare end to Sarrasin who fastened it about his own middle. We were roped like climbers. It would be difficult for me to make a break from them.

Sarrasin said, 'Keep going and don't give trouble. It will serve nothing but unpleasantness.'

I said nothing because I had nothing to say to them. I didn't understand what it was all about and for the moment I wasn't bothering. All I knew was that I meant to give them the slip as soon as I could. In the Army they had taught that if you are taken prisoner it is easier to escape in the first hour than the second. Every hour and day that passes makes escape harder. I knew this was true.

We began to climb by a small path through a plantation of young fir trees. The ground was slippery with loose needles. Very soon we were crossing a rocky plateau and the path dipped into a narrow valley. The wind was dead in our faces and I knew we were moving north. The young moon was up now, slipping in and out of a patchwork of small clouds. I saw that the far side of the valley was terraced with vines and away to the left I thought I could make out the shape of a house, probably the cabin of the *vigneron*. I put my hands in my raincoat pocket and plodded after Paviot. Behind me I could hear the even breathing of Sarrasin. The raincoat had slit pockets that allowed me to get at the pockets of my jacket. I got hold of my penknife and opened it. They should have searched me.

At the head of the valley slope the path got rougher, twisting through patches of tall white heather and a tangle of broken boulders. Leaning forward to the slope I brought my hands out of my pocket and holding lightly to the rope about my waist I cut into it. In a few moments I had sawn through the loop. With my left hand I held the two ends together. All I had to do now was to wait for the moon to go behind a cloud and then run for it. I was in good condition and I felt that if I got only a short start I stood a chance of losing them. I cocked an eye up to the sky. A largish cloud was scudding up towards the moon. I waited, plugging forward, and there was a growing edge of excitement in me. Fifteen seconds, I thought, and the moon would be covered.

'Paviot.' It was George Sarrasin.

Paviot stopped and looked back, and I half-turned too. Sarrasin came up close to me and I saw him look down towards my left hand which was holding, and hiding, the loose ends of the rope. He had his revolver out and he said evenly, 'I was a fool. We should search you.'

I took a chance. I kicked out at the revolver and threw myself sideways. I missed the revolver and fell and he was on me like a cat. He had that combination which is rare; a big man with the gift of speed. He came smashing on top of me and his weight drove the wind from my body. I didn't try to shake him off. He straddled over me, his knees gripping my sides and behind him was Paviot and I could see the knife in his hand. There was nothing I could do except curse myself for not having tried to escape in the first five minutes. I might have made it.

'You have caused trouble. *Eh bien*, you wish for unpleasantness.'

Sarrasin smacked my face with his open hand. It was a hard, fierce blow but less painful than insulting since he used his open hand, showing his contempt. From that moment I began to hate him, and it was a warm, comforting vigour inside me. I lay there and I think he contemplated hitting me again. But he changed his mind.

They went through my pockets as I lay on the ground and then, tossing my knife into the bushes, they roped me again. We went on, and I knew that so long as we were roped I was not going to have any chance with them.

And as I walked, roped between them like some slave, I could feel my face smarting from the blow. It was the same hand I thought that had struck at Sophie and bruised her. George Sarrasin, I thought; full of strength and vigour, who didn't care whether it was man or woman he struck, who breathed 'Beautiful' when a knife went home ... How I hated him, how I warmed myself with the hope that one day I should be free on my feet with a chance to get at him. I'm a Scot and we're good haters and I hadn't felt like this for years. I was almost happy as I looked forward to the moment when I could get at him. It was a wonderful, unchristian feeling and I nursed it tenderly.

CHAPTER EIGHT

There was that about these two men which slowly
began to impress me. Putting a word to it was difficult.
It was a combination of strength and resolution, not
fortitude because that had too much of a crusader
shine on it for them. The essence of their appearance
was seediness and shabbiness, their setting small, smoke-
filled rooms, unmade beds, bar-tops marked with Per-
nod and bock rings. Looking at them I should have said
I could place them; Paviot was straight from Marseilles,
from La Canebiére, and Sarrasin a boxing booth slugger
from some travelling fair. But I began to feel I was
wrong. They were both as hard and fit as apes. After
two hours of some of the roughest cross-country work
I have ever done they were almost unmarked. They
knew how to move in the dark and they knew how to
travel economically sparing all useless effort. They
spoke only once after the frustration of my attempt to
escape.

We crossed a high meadow, the wind taking the thin
grasses like smoke, a smell of wild thyme and basil
rising from the crushed turf under our feet. At the head
of the meadow, the narrow path we were following
led away to the left.

Paviot stopped and turned round to Sarrasin.

'The path, or over the top?'

Sarrasin said, 'Over the top. By the path we might
meet someone.'

Paviot said, '*Merde*' to no one in particular and was
off again.

Against the sky ahead of us I saw the sharp line of
a peak. It took us an hour to make the top and there
we rested in the lee of a boulder while Paviot smoked
a cigarette and I kept him company. No one spoke.
Sarrasin sat by himself. He was wearing a loose black
sweater and tight knee breeches and about his middle

he had a wide leather belt with what looked like a
large silver buckle worked in some intricate design. I
couldn't see clearly what it was. Far away and below
us—a good fifteen miles, I thought—was a great night
stretch of the coast laid out, a dark hem of land
embroidered here and there with faint whorls of light
from small towns and villages. I wondered what was
happening below there. An *agent de police* probably
dead. Didier snapping out instructions, and back at
the villa Colonel Drexel and Benson working out this
fresh complication.

As I went I was working it out myself. I understood
now what had been in Didier's mind when he had
shouted to me from the roadside. He had decided that
I was not being taken away by force, but that I was
being rescued. From his point of view it would seem
a reasonable interpretation. And now I saw that from
Sarrasin's point of view—if he were the brain behind
the abduction of Jabal—it was also a convenient
interpretation. It gave the impression that I was not
merely involved in this affair but had possibly organized
it and, when my innocent front had begun to fail, had
signalled for help. Sarrasin, Paviot . . . for a moment my
mind almost said Sophie, but I checked myself . . . were
unknown to the police. Now they had me they could
shelter behind me. But that was only a beginning. A
hundred following questions stirred in my brain. The
most important, since a man is a fool if he doesn't put
the highest value on his own skin, was what was going
to happen to me—and to Jabal. I hadn't thought of him
much, but now I started to. I liked the boy very much
and my anger against Sarrasin grew as I thought of
what would happen to Jabal if he were sold back to
Sheik Ahmed ben Fa'id.

Sometime after we had passed the peak and had made
three or four miles down the following slope through
groves of cork trees, we came out on to a rough cart-
track flanked on one side by a dry watercourse and on
the other side by a thick belt of trees, oak, beech and

birch with here and there the lacy white plumage of
an acacia showing against the shadows. Some way down
the road we swung right-handed into the trees and then
came out into a small clearing. To one side of it was
a small cabin with an outside verandah, the whole thing
reminding me of a country cricket pavilion. As we
went up to it Paviot gave a low whistle.

The door opened and a golden wedge of light struck
across the verandah. Someone stood beside the door and
we clumped up the wooden steps and into the hut, still
roped. For an instant I had a childish desire that all this
should be a dream, that really I was just coming back to
the Climber's Club hut at Helyg after a long day over
the Carnedds ... I suppose I must have been more
exhausted with our night trek than I had imagined.

I didn't take in the details of the hut. I just stood
there while Sarrasin cleared the ropes from us, and I saw
that the rough table held food and a large flask of wine.

Sarrasin nodded to the table and I sat down. Somewhere behind me the door closed, and then he was
saying.

'You go well. You are used to the hills.' Not a question but a statement and his tone a compliment for
which I had no need.

And then I saw Sophie. She came from the door to
the table and, lifting the flask, poured wine for us. She
wore a wind-breaker and a rough skirt and her thick,
black hair was caught up carelessly at the back with
a ribbon. She put a glass before me and I looked at her.
She made no sign. I might have been anyone sitting
there.

She half turned to Sarrasin, reaching past me to pour
wine for him, and she said, 'You have been quicker
than I thought.'

'Things went well.'

'Good.'

'Our friend here travels fast. He gave a little trouble
once. But after that ...'

He laughed and she smiled easily as she handed him

his glass. They talked over my head, as though I had no existence. Then she moved to attend to Paviot.

Paviot took his wine from her, raised the glass in a salute before drinking, and said, 'Coming over the hills. It is like the old days, eh? Night work puts an edge in a man. Makes the taste of a poor wine good.'

I tossed back my wine, feeling it rough and stimulating against my tiredness, and turning to Sarrasin, I said, 'Now we've time to breathe perhaps you'll tell me what all this is about? You've got Jabal, you've got me—and you've killed a policeman. You're doing fine.'

Sophie said, 'Have some more wine. There is also bread and ham.' She wasn't even looking at me. She bent over the table and began to slice a large ham. A hateful doubt crept into my mind. I loved her and I had faith in her, but this was the moment of trial and at such times a man is victim to his darkest thoughts. I tried to push them away. I believed in her. She would never betray me, and the force of my emotions came up in me with a great surge of anger directed against the others. It was more than I could hold.

'Come on, Sarrasin!' I shouted. 'What is all this about?'

He looked at me and smiled. 'You are angry. Don't be. In time you shall know all that is necessary.'

He spoke so placidly, was so damned sure of himself, that it made me lose control. I jumped to my feet. I didn't know what I was going to do or say. I didn't get a chance anyway. I saw the miracle of swift movement which was Sarrasin's pride. He was up and his revolver was out and levelled at me, and on the other side of the table Paviot, lounging back, had his knife ready. I don't know how he got it out so quickly. It seemed to have materialized in his hand. He sat there, tipping his chair back, a dog-like grin on his face. In jumping to my feet I had hit the table and Sarrasin's glass had gone over. The wine spread over the rough-grained wood in a dark pool.

'Sit down and be sensible,' said Sarrasin.

Sophie got a rag from somewhere and began to mop up the wine. And then it happened, the thing I had been waiting for. She was close to me and for a second, hidden from them, her hand touched mine. Just a touch and the swift movement of an eyelash as she straightened up. And it was all there, all the love and faith between us, and I knew that never again would I question them. There was a great shame in me that I had ever doubted them.

'Go to bed, Sophie,' said Sarrasin.

She moved to the only other door in the room. As she opened it she paused and turned towards Paviot. Outwardly she was dead to me again. Calmly she asked, 'Did you kill a policeman?' She might have been asking if he had watered the geraniums, put the cat out or remembered to pay a bill, her voice just touched with that hoarseness I knew so well. But underneath the acting, the indifference, I knew there must be anguish, anguish for an unknown policeman and anguish for me.

Paviot shook his head. 'I pricked him, no more. Our friend here exaggerates. Understandably, he is a little overwrought.'

She stood there and I loved her. She was with them, but she was for me. I didn't like the part she had to play, didn't understand all that lay behind her prudence, but I did understand the truth that was between us and it gave me hope and strength.

For a second her eyes were on me then she went through into the other room, closing the door on us.

Sarrasin said, 'If you do not wish to eat and you have had enough wine, you should sleep.' He nodded to a mattress that lay on the floor against the far wall. There was another mattress close to the door of Sophie's room.

I got up and went over to the mattress and he went to the main door and bolted it. I sat down on the mattress and was suddenly aware of my stiffness and fatigue. Maybe because of the long trip over the hills we had just made, I suddenly recalled my meeting with Drexel in Wales. For his sake, and gladly, I had given up the dream of Songa Manara. The choice had brought me trouble, but it had also brought me Sophie. The rough and the smooth ... the fascinating unpredictable future. Once I had seemed to have it all mapped out. Now I was groping in the dark.

His back to me, Sarrasin said, 'Tomorrow you shall have better quarters. Also, monsieur, take my advice— don't give any trouble. We are well able to deal with it.'

As he turned and faced me, I remembered the bruise on Sophie's shoulder. I said, 'If the chance comes I'll cause trouble. All I hope is that you're at the other end of it!'

Ignoring me completely, he went on, 'Paviot—you sleep first. I watch.'

He sat down by the table, hoisted his legs on to it and folded his arms across his chest; big, solid, all man, with a close-cropped head like a Roman gladiator, a Spartacus formidable with brutality and intelligence.

Paviot dropped on to his mattress and I lay down on mine, loosening my shoe-laces to ease my feet. I closed my eyes and I could hear them breathing. I hadn't behaved very well. I should have matched their sureness with reserve.

I woke once or twice during the short hours that were left before daylight. Each time either Sarrasin or Paviot was awake and watching, and the oil lamp on the table was turned low.

Sophie, humming to herself, made breakfast for us the next morning. We had coffee, fried eggs and then peach confiture on bread. I had one over-riding thought; to get away. Paviot did not eat much, but George ate enormously. I was reminded of Drexel's appetite. Thinking of Drexel was unpleasant. He was carrying so much.

Not only the collapse of his mission and the loss of Jabal ... but now he would have my disappearance as an extra load. No matter how much he had let me down before Didier, I knew he would feel responsible for anything that had happened to me.

After breakfast Paviot and George sat just outside the door on the verandah where they could see me and Sophie moved around the hut packing things away. I wondered where we were going from here and knew I would not find out by asking.

A couple of hours after breakfast, I heard the sound of a car engine. I went to the door. Sarrasin put his arm across it barring my way but not stopping me from looking. Paviot went down into the clearing and from behind me I heard Sophie say.

'Who is it?'

'Gerard and Fargette,' answered Sarrasin.

At this moment not one but two vehicles came into the clearing from the track beyond the trees. One was a small Fiat, shabby and dusty, and the other was one of those large wine tankers which they use in the Roussillon for transporting cheap grade wines. In England they use the same type of thing for petrol and milk. They stopped outside the hut. The man who got out of the cab of the wine tanker I knew. He had been in the row-boat with Sarrasin and he had driven the Citroën off last night. I had not realized before how small he was. Little more than four feet with rather sticking-out ears and a screwed-up, monkeyish face, an old-young face. He had some slight deformity of the left leg for he walked with a quick little lilt always to the left as though there was a large stone in his shoe.

The man from the Fiat was an individual whose chief characteristics were worry and dandruff. Although I wasn't going to like any of these people I felt vaguely sorry for him. He came across with quick, short steps to Paviot and in a low voice began to talk to him, shaking his head, rolling his eyes and now and again patting one hand against his forehead. I could almost see the dandruff falling from his stringy grey hair on to the dusty shoulders of his baggy blue suit. He must have been about sixty, thin-faced and white and everything suggesting that he had been shut away in a cellar too long. Worry, I decided, would probably kill him in the next five years.

He was ticking Paviot off about something and it was so much water over the mill-wheel as far as Paviot was concerned.

Then he came pitter-patter up the verandah steps and was greeted by Sarrasin.

'*Bonjour, Gerard. Tout va bien?*'

He rolled his head and, even if things had been going well, it was clear that as a matter of principle he would not admit it.

'It's this dirty Paviot. Why can't he watch his hands?'

Behind me I heard Sophie's voice.

'Is it the policeman?'

'Yes, it's the policeman. They think he'll die.'

I heard Sophie's breath drawn in sharply.

George said heavily, unconcerned, 'We all have to die. Paviot was handicapped by the dark.'

Then Gerard saw me. At once I was a fresh worry but he remembered his manners. He gave me a nod and said:

'Monsieur Fraser. You have, I hope, been treated well?'

I shrugged and he gave a suspicious glance round him at George and Paviot. I said, ' "Treated well" is a nice phrase. But I suppose you would call it that. What's the tanker for? We haven't run out of wine.'

He thought the joke was in poor taste and maybe it was. Not talking to anyone in particular he said, 'We must go ... I do not like this openness. One never knows ... some forester, a boy. Fargette, open that thing up!'

I saw Fargette climb to the top of the tanker and

begin to unscrew the wing nuts that held down the
large filler cap.

Sarrasin seeing me watch this operation said, 'That is
for you. It is a good way of travelling incognito. A
little stuffy perhaps.'

He touched my arm and I moved towards the tanker
with Paviot on one side and Sarrasin on the other. So
far they had not given me a chance and they were not
giving me one now. The revolver and the knife were
out in the open. Gerard fussed on ahead and I heard
him call to Fargette.

'You've got the little air thing fixed? He must
breathe.' It was nice of him, I thought, to want me to
go on breathing.

Fargette grunted and half raised a hand as though he
were brushing away a fly. Gerard must have been hell
to live with. I had met his kind before. Underneath the
fuss and anxiety—and maybe the cause of it—was a
clear-sighted, cold intellect, taking in so much more
than other minds did of any situation. If he had been
a fool he would have had no respect from these people.
They might brush him off but they did as he said
without question. As I climbed up to the top of the
tanker, I heard him direct Sophie and Paviot to travel
with him in the Fiat. I suppose I could have refused
to climb up and lower myself down into a space little
bigger than a barrel but, as that would have meant a
crack on the head and being tossed into the thing, I
preferred to go under my own steam.

When my feet touched the bottom my head was still
out of the small trap door. Fargette gave me a wink
and said, 'You will have to bend your legs, monsieur.
You will not travel well. However, it will not be un-
endurable.'

I said, 'The best wines never travel well.'

He roared with laughter, was reprimanded about
making a noise by Gerard, and then began to screw me
down, but I could hear him chuckling to himself. Somehow, it was comforting to find someone who would

laugh at a poor joke. Of them all I decided I disliked Fargette least.

From my watch, which I checked getting in and getting out, I know I was in that tin can for two hours, but how far we went or how fast I could not possibly judge. Cooped up there, jolted from side to side in the darkness, I lost all sense of speed or direction. For all I knew we might have been travelling round and round a bumpy circuit. In fact I imagined we were for I swear we kept on hitting the same bump, slewing round the same sharp corner time after time. I did not like it. Even though I knew it was going to end and I should see daylight again, I found it hard to hold down my claustrophobia. By the time it was over I was bruised and shaken and, I think, a little drunk from the wine fumes.

I think Fargette and Sarrasin must have expected this for when we stopped and they released me, they helped me down to the ground and stood by me, holding an arm each. I shut my eyes against the sunlight and the spinning world and then cautiously, as things began to steady, I opened my eyes. The first thing I saw was a magnificent tree covered with purple blossoms. It was like a great fountain, foaming with colour. Although I knew its name, at that moment I could not recall it.

I took a couple of steps forward and my guards released me. The giddiness went rapidly. Looking up above and beyond the tree I got my first sight of Chateau Minerve, thought it was not for a long time that I knew its name. That morning I only got a jumbled impression of it. It was a yellow-grey plug of towers and battlements, of steep walls cut by narrow windows ... It should have had banners flying from its highest tower, and knights and fine ladies strolling across the neat parterres. A gravelled causeway spanned the moat which ran around it; but the moat was dry and full of shrubs and flowering cherry trees. We went through a large gateway into a courtyard with a well in the

centre. Behind the well was a large marble statue of
Minerva, the goddess of wisdom, wearing a helmet and
carrying a shield. She was severe-faced and seemed to
frown at me and I told myself she had a right not to
like me. I wasn't doing very well in her subject. A
large vine covered one of the walls of the courtyard.
We entered a hallway that echoed to our footsteps like
a museum. I noticed suits of armour, old paintings and
weapons and a fine stretch of Persian rug. Monsieur
Gerard and Paviot were there. They watched us pass
as though we were another party looking over some
ancient monument, but at the last moment Gerard had
to impose his concern on us. He called :

'See that he has everything, for shaving, clean clothes.'
And then, as we were going up the stairs, 'And yes—
cigarettes, also. He must be comfortable.'

We went up three floors. He must be comfortable, I
thought. It was odd. That—and the fact that Sarrasin
had his revolver on me, and Paviot his knife to hand,
and both ready to use their weapons if I made any
trouble.

We stopped in front of a large oak door with an
enormous lock and two heavy bolts top and bottom.
Fargette opened it for me with a quick little hop-skip,
gave the suggestion of a bow, and waited for me to
enter. I stood there, looking across a great room to
a wide window which opened on to a rectangle of
pale blue sky. At that moment, from somewhere above
us, faint but unmistakable, I heard the sound of a
mouth-organ. The tune was a favourite one of Jabal's.
Something about *Frim Fram Sauce* ...

I don't want fish cakes and rye bread.
You heard what I said.
Waiter, please serve mine fried,
I want the frim fram sauce ...

Sarrasin gave me a little push and said, 'He is very
musical.'

I said, 'Monsieur Gerard probably insisted you should bring his mouth-organ to make him comfortable.'

The door was shut, locked and bolted on me and I heard Fargette laughing.

CHAPTER NINE

Chateau Minerve, except for the fact that I was locked in my room most of the time, might have been a hotel and myself a guest anxious for seclusion and rest, too shy or toffee-nosed to use the main dining-room, and having all meals sent up. I had a room which seemed as big as Piccadilly Circus and the likeness was increased by a black marble statuette in the middle of it. It was not Eros, but a grinning-faced faun in woolly pants. Part of the room had been partitioned off and converted to a bathroom and toilet. The water from the hot tap was boiling and whenever I turned it on I could hear the pipes singing and bumping in the walls. There was a four-poster bed with faded green silk hangings and a silver-thread counterpane. Over the open fireplace was an oil painting of some forbidding 18th-century bishop in mitre and full canonicals. He was holding up a disapproving hand at the faun statue who obviously didn't care a pagan damn. On one of the other walls was a painting of a sad-faced, anaemic-looking woman with a tower of white-powdered hair and unnaturally high, rounded breasts from which the paint was flaking badly. At the end of the first day I knew practically every detail of the room from the number of tiles on the floor to the places in the red and gold wall-paper where the pattern had not been properly matched when it had been put up.

There was one window and this I was free to open; but it offered no liberty. The chateau was perched on the top of a high crag that overlooked a deep river gorge. Below me the walls fell sheer for about sixty feet and below that there was a steep cliff face for another hundred feet and then a broken, boulder-and-tree-studded slope so sheer that the trees looked as though they had no time for anything but the business of hanging on. There was not a road or a house to be seen ... just the dark line of river below and then a sweep of wild mountain country. I could not place my whereabouts at all, except that the country was obviously Pyrennean. For all I knew, we might be over the Spanish border.

Fargette brought me my meals that first day, and there was always Paviot or Sarrasin waiting outside in case I tried to jump him. We had no conversation.

During the afternoon Monsieur Gerard came in to check that I had everything I wanted. They gave me clean linen, another jacket and a pair of trousers, shaving gear, some books to read and a carton of *Lucky Strike* cigarettes. But, most astonishing of all, before he went Monsieur Gerard produced a bottle of whisky, *Vat 69.*

'It is to be hoped, monsieur, you will give no trouble. We do everything we can for you ... Please behave, and in the end you will thank us.'

I was left wondering what the hell to make of that. His anxious, almost pathetic manner had a strange effect on me. It was hard not to believe that I was the one who was at fault and they were being patient with me. Being locked up in a room for hours can produce an exaggeration in the thoughts. I'm sure if I had told him that I wanted *Players* instead of *Lucky Strike*, or *White Horse* whisky instead of the other, he would instantly have done something about it.

My last meal was brought at five and after that I saw no one until morning. But around six—and I was to notice this in the following days—I heard the sound of a car leaving the chateau. From six until the morning the place seemed strangely quiet and empty, except for the passage-way outside my door. By listening I could hear the slight movement and sometimes the breathing of a watcher outside.

Monsieur Gerard came along early the second day and asked me if I had slept comfortably.

I said, 'I'd be more comfortable if I knew what all this was about.'

I saw at once that I had shocked him. This was a fairy story, and there was a spell over us. Remarks like that could break the enchantment.

'Monsieur ... in time, in time.' He wriggled his fingers through his patchy grey hair and I felt I wanted to go over and give him a brush down, pat his shoulder and tell him not to worry. That was one part of me. The other was cold, logical, still trying to work all this out, still wondering what their plans were for Jabal and myself, and not for one moment accepting anything he said as the truth. People who are prompt in their use of knives are ruthless, but people who use knives on policemen are more than ruthless; they either have to be very sure of themselves or desperate. None of these people struck me as being desperate.

'Who's getting Jabal?' I asked. 'The Regent or the oil company?'

'Monsieur ...!'

I really had broken the spell. It seemed to me that he turned and ran from the room, like Cinderella as the clock struck twelve, but all he left behind was a smell of tobacco, coarse *Gauloise Bleu*.

It was this second day that set the pattern for the others to follow. Not long after Gerard had gone Fargette opened the door and tipped his head to me to come out of the room. Paviot was waiting outside. The two of them stood a little way from me and although neither of them showed their weapons I knew they were there, warm with the touch of their palms, and ready for use.

I said, 'What now?'

Fargette, who seemed to have more natural cheerfulness than any of the others, answered, 'You are free to take some exercise. But, be wise, eh?'

I took him at his word. I was puzzled, but not ungrateful at being allowed to leave my room. I went down the main staircase and across the hall into the courtyard. They followed me, not too closely and not deceiving me by their casual manner.

The courtyard was full of sunshine. As I crossed towards the main gate into the gardens I looked up at the statue of Minerva. I don't know whether it was some trick of sunlight or whether seen from this side it was some vagary in the sculpturing but she seemed to have a softer, kinder aspect. When I had first seen her she had frowned, disapproving of me; now she was indulgent and understanding.

I was almost at the gate when a door banged away on the left. I turned and saw Sophie move quickly across the court towards the hall entrance. She looked at me and then quickly away.

I soon found that some parts of the grounds were closed to me. If I tried to move down a path that led towards the boundaries of the ground then either Paviot or Fargette would move up ahead of me or they would call a gentle reprimand. It was all done unhurriedly, almost off-handedly, and anyone watching us would never have guessed that they held hidden guns and knife ready for use if I proved intractable.

There was a little terrace to one side of the chateau, a stretch of gravel set with iron chairs and tables and overlooking the gorge. Behind was a wide camomile lawn with a large ornamental pool in its centre. We sat down at one of the tables after we had walked around a bit. Paviot rolled himself a cigarette and ignored me, but Fargette was quite ready to talk. I think that first morning we talked mostly about films. He was a great cinema-goer and loved romantic, musical films. Now and again when I got a chance I tried to pump him or slip in a question which might give me something more definite to go on, but he just screwed up his monkey face, pushed his tongue in his cheek and said, '*Vietato entrare, signore*'. It was the only thing he gave away about himself, that he spoke Italian as well as French. Paviot sat there listening to us, tipped back in his chair, eyes half closed against the sun, seeing how close he could let his ragged cigarette droop to his chin.

We had been there about fifteen minutes when there

were footsteps on the gravel behind us. I slewed round, smiling to myself as I saw how my movement brought Paviot's hand to his pocket. Sophie was coming towards us with a tray.

She looked fresh and very lovely, in a white blouse, a green skirt, and with a bloom on her bare arms and legs where the sun touched her skin. I felt my love rise inside me like a bird taking flight.

She set down the tray. Coffee and biscuits. She might have been a waitress and this a high-class country hotel. Even though I was sure of her, the whole set-up puzzled me and I would have given anything for the chance to be alone with her, to find out what it was all about, to learn what held her to these people and what their plans were.

Paviot said, 'What is for lunch?'

'A cheese soufflé and then cutlets,' she replied.

Fargette nodded approvingly, began to pour my coffee and said, 'Sophie makes a cheese soufflé like a summer cloud. I taught her how.' He touched her on the arm affectionately.

She smiled at him and then, as she turned away, her eyes met mine. It was all I needed. I watched her as she went back to the chateau. And even in the midst of this confusion and inimical politeness, I found myself glad that I was here, near her. I didn't know what was going to happen to me. There was a barrier between Sophie and myself, but one day—and the chance must come—I was going to break through.

At that moment there was the sound of a mouth-organ. It came from high up, thin and not very clear.

I looked up and back to the chateau and in a few seconds I had picked out Jabal. He was leaning over one of the crenellated battlements of a tower and gazing down at us. Just behind him I thought I could make out the head and shoulders of Sarrasin.

I raised my arm and waved to him, but though I could see that he was looking at us, he made no acknowledgement. Maybe, I told myself, at that distance he did not recognize me ... but I did not believe this.

I finished my coffee, trying to fit all this together; the way they were treating me, this chateau ... the whole confused business—and I got nowhere.

Just before lunch they took me in. I got the other side of Minerva's face as I crossed the courtyard. Cold and severe and obviously contemptuous of me for not being able to work the thing out for myself.

Sarrasin brought my lunch; a big, relaxed figure in a dirty singlet and canvas trousers. He said not a word to me, but his eyes were on me the whole time. We had no need of words. We knew exactly what was between us. One day, if we were lucky—and I am sure we would both regard it as luck—we should be loosed against each other. It was an unspoken, private understanding and we neither of us wanted to be disappointed.

If the morning had been strange so was the afternoon. I lay on my bed most of the time and for about two hours just after lunch the most puzzling noises echoed through the place. They seemed to come from the courtyard. I could hear people laughing, unrestrained, hearty laughter, and after a time I could even pick out the laughs. Sophie's husky but feminine and finishing in a little trickle of sound, Sarrasin's booming away and occasionally a short, gasping noise that might have been Gerard or Paviot. And with the laughter came the sound of dogs barking. Again and again the barking broke out, excited, frantic, then came silence, and then again the laughter and the barking. After a time there was no sound of dogs, but only voices and a persistent *thud, thud,* then silence, then *thud, thud,* then voices and silence again to be broken by more *thuds.*

At five Paviot brought me my evening meal.

Without any hope of an answer, I said, 'Why don't they let me down to join in the afternoon fun?'

To my surprise, he pulled his knife from his pocket and with a glance at Fargette who stood by the door, he said, 'I wish they would.' He laughed, flicked the knife open and ran his finger down the blade. Fargette flapped a hand at him, made an angry sound in his throat, and Paviot put the knife away. Then he picked up my empty tray and was gone.

An hour later I heard the sound of a car starting and then the chateau was silent, except for the quiet breathing of whoever was on guard outside my door.

It was a long time before I got to sleep that night. I didn't know what the hell it was all about. Quite clearly, I decided, they had probably rented this chateau for a hide-out while they held Jabal. None of them gave me the impression of belonging here. They would have rented it obviously under false names and with enough doubling back to prevent their ever being traced. But why were they holding me, giving me this quasi freedom? I knew too much about them to make it safe for them ever to release me. That meant they had to dispose of me. Why not do it right away? For the moment, since I sensed it was remote, I could not concern myself with my eventual fate—though Paviot's little act with the knife had for a second or two brought some reality into my situation. Why let me know Jabal was here, even see him, and ... a hundred questions floated in my mind keeping me awake. That they had incriminated me with the police I could see, but after that ... Why all this? I had served my purpose.

The next day did nothing to make it any plainer. I was let out and this time I had Sarrasin and Paviot for guards. I took my stroll, was served with coffee and chocolate biscuits on the terrace, given a short serenade by Jabal—it was *Red Sails in the Sunset*—and then back I went to get the cold side of Minerva's face. Sophie had brought the coffee tray and for a few moments, ignoring me, she had stood chatting to Sarrasin, something about the charcoal brazier in the kitchen and a blocked chimney pipe that sent the fumes back to her ... and I might have been a ghost. That afternoon there was the same hullabaloo from the courtyard and then at six the noise of the car starting, and then silence.

The following day I tried a few variations. Instead of going down to the courtyard I turned and began to make my way up towards Jabal's quarters. Gerard and Sarrasin were with me. In no time Sarrasin was on the stairs ahead of me, his face wooden, his great body blocking my passage.

I said, 'I just wanted to put in a request for a favourite number of mine. *Lazybones*.'

Gerard took my arm from behind, clicked his tongue like an old woman calling a hen, and down I went with them. Minerva gave me her going-out smile. Outside I tried to go round to the other side of the chateau, but again Sarrasin was in my way, and in the end I finished up on the terrace. When Sophie brought the coffee, I said to Gerard, 'I'd much rather have an *apéritif*.'

There was no surprise in me when he told her to bring out a bottle of Dubonnet and some ice.

I sat there sipping at my drink, and eventually Jabal came out, but I don't remember what he played for the thought had suddenly occurred to me that men who are condemned and wait for the day of execution are indulged. Any whim of mine was to be granted. The prisoner's last breakfast.

The afternoon was the same as always; laughter, barking dogs and that uneven *thud, thud*.

And so it went on. I often contemplated making a break while I was in the garden, but I knew I would not get five yards before I should have a bullet in my leg. There was a low wall round the chateau grounds and beyond this a rising slope of hillside thinly covered with cork oaks. A narrow, dusty roadway ran up to the iron gates in the wall, but I could see only about half a mile along it and then it twisted out of sight behind the hill.

But the truth was that it was Sophie who held me there. I could not go without talking to her, without having at least a few moments alone with her. Day after day I watched for my chance but I was too well guarded.

Then on the morning of the sixth day she came to me.

My door opened and she came in with the breakfast tray. I saw Fargette stand aside for her to pass. Then he gave me a wink and closed the door. Always before the door had been kept open.

Sophie came across to me and put the tray down on the table by the window. I stood to one side of it and, as she straightened up, she took from under her arm a bunch of newspapers and dropped them on to the window seat.

She said, 'Papers.'

Automatically, I said, 'Thank you.'

And there we were looking at one another. Her face was no longer a conventional mask. She was alive again, looking at me, knowing it was me. I saw the movement of her shoulders and breasts as she breathed and there was something laboured in the rise and fall as though she were conscious of unseen pressures bearing heavily on her.

I looked towards the closed door, thinking of Fargette. She saw my look and understood it. It was curious how we were both held back by an odd embarrassment. It was as though years of separation lay between us and we had to get to know each other again.

Then, in her funny hoarse voice, the words seeming not to come from her but to be diffused into the room from no fixed source, she said, 'Fargette is my friend . . .' Then urgently, the movement in her towards me already beginning, she went on, 'Oh, David . . . I had to come.'

But already I was reaching for her. The love that was inside me broke free. It was like an animal, a panther, swift and powerful, flashing out of the darkness into the sun, all light and strength and undying beauty.

'Sophie!' I cried. My arms were out wide and there was a sob in her throat. She came to me and was inside my arms and my hands were in her hair and her body

was shaking, and I was happy and mad, angry and
foolish, and nothing had any meaning for me except
that she was there. I heard her voice full of my name
and then moving into a torrent of words which slowly
took meaning.

'That first night in the hut ... How could I trust
myself to look or speak ... to give anything to you ...
And the stupid wine all over the table and you standing
there ...'

I said, 'I understood. I never doubted you.' And it
was true, for deep down there had never been any
doubt.

She laid her cheek against mine and her voice came
low. 'For them you have to be nothing to me ... Even
now I'm full of fear.'

I held her away from me gently and kissed her. I was
like a boy who had got more than he expected on his
birthday. I wanted to shout my happiness to the world.
And then I said slowly, forcing myself back to a practical world :

'You never knew they were going to take Jabal?'

'No. Not until it was too late to warn you. I thought
it was smuggling.'

'What are they going to do with him?'

'Ransom him to the oil company.'

At least that was something. It would only be money
involved and Jabal would be safe.

'You must get out of this, away from them.'

She freed herself from me and I knew what her
answer was going to be. She looked as she had done
the first time I met her, afraid, held down by her own
weakness and fears.

She said, 'I can't. Not yet. Believe me, David. You
must believe me. Everything will be all right and we
shall be together ... Nothing can happen so long as
they never know what we are to each other. If they
knew, they would never trust me. They would do
something.'

'To you?'

'Yes. They have so much at stake that they will take no risk.'

'But Fargette already knows you are here.'

'He is my one friend. I trust him.'

'And me—what happens to me? You must help me to escape.'

'No ... no ... that would do no good.'

I looked at her, not understanding.

'For God's sake, Sophie! I must get out. And you must go, too.'

'No, David.' She was adamant. 'Please believe me—'

'You've got to help me. Why shouldn't you?' I reached for her shoulders to shake courage, sense, I-don't-know-what into her. But at that moment the door opened and Fargette put his head in.

'You said five minutes, Sophie. You want George to knock my teeth in?'

He stood there, his hand on the door, the other holding a revolver. As she went towards him I followed. He held the revolver a little higher and said, 'Stay where you are, monsieur.'

I watched her go and, at the last moment, she turned briefly and her eyes were on me, warm and dark and bottomless.

The door slammed. I heard lock and bolts go home. And I stood there. I don't know how long I stood there but it seemed imperative not to move until life was fully with me again. And when I did move I knew that nothing was going to keep me here. I was going to tear this place apart and be free, and I was going to grab Sophie from the middle of whatever dark web held her and take her with me. I didn't care what she was or what she had been or what she had done. All I knew was that she was mine. All romantic poetry made sense and I was in danger of jumping out of the window to try my new wings on a flight to the nearest *gendarmerie.*

I ate breakfast, surprised at the appetite I had, and then began to read through the papers. Not even they took the edge off my new optimism, though they should have done. There were copies of the London *Daily Mail* and *Daily Express* and from Paris *Le Figaro* and *Le Temps*. The news had broken that Prince Jabal, staying in France on his way back to school, had been kidnapped and that his tutor, David Bladen Fraser, while being taken to Perpignan for police questioning, had been either abducted, too, or rescued by his accomplices if, as it seemed, he had had a hand in the organization of the kidnapping. This line did not surprise me. Some of the papers were more definite about it than others. The English papers were very cautious what they said about me for fear of libel cases. But the French boys just let themselves go. There was no doubt in their minds. I was a kidnapper whose well organized plan had come apart a little at the seams. One of them even said I had knifed a policeman. The *Daily Express* had an article about me written by an old army friend. It read like an obituary.

All over France the police were on the look-out for Jabal and myself, but it was thought that we had gone over the border into Spain or by this time were well away on the high seas. No destination was given. *Le Temps* had an article about Ramaut and the oil industry, but nowhere was the real political situation discussed and I could guess that government pressure was keeping the real truth hidden. There was no mention anywhere that the oil concession was due for renewal soon, and the reason for the kidnapping was felt to be mercenary. I could see how my abduction by Sarrasin had given strength to that point of view. It had also given Sarrasin and company a wonderful cover.

The most disturbing news item for me was a small stop-press paragraph in the *Daily Mail* which said that the policeman driver of the Citroën had died in a Perpignan hospital of his wound. Not only kidnapping, but murder, was at my door.

More than ever I wanted to get out of this place and
clear myself. That morning as I took my stroll in the
grounds I went over all the possibilities of escape. I
could see no way of making it. If I could talk to Sophie
again, she might help me. But I had a feeling that she
would risk nothing that might give away our relationship. If I escaped with her help she would have to go
with me ... I had a conviction that she didn't want me
to escape; that out of love for me, fear for herself and
loyalty to the men she worked with, she had seen some
easy compromise in the future and was content to wait
for it. Anyway, I fancied that the opportunities for me
to talk to her again would be too few and distant to be
of any help. I wanted to get away now.

After lunch I went all over my room, examining it.
I had done this before, but I did it again. In a chateau
like this part of the wall might easily have been boarded
up to cover some old doorway. There was nothing. The
walls were solid and the open fireplace, I knew, was
never used for the chimney had been bricked up. For
a time I wondered if I could get to work on the bricks
and pick them away. It would take days to do this with
a fork or a knife and I felt pretty certain I would be
discovered before I had finished the job.

I went to the window and looked out. It was not the
first time I had leaned over the ledge and looked at
the drop. Twelve feet below the window the face of the
chateau was broken by a weathered cornice nearly
six inches wide that ran along for about twenty yards
and then disappeared as the front of the chateau angled
back at a corner. What there was beyond this point
I did not know, but I guessed that there was more of
the chateau before the final turn was reached which
would bring me out above the moat with a small drop
to the rising ground of the gardens. I could get down
to the ledge easily. I could walk the ledge not so easily,
for it was weathered and crumbling and clearly unsafe
in places. But it could be done and without more risk
than an afternoon's climbing on Idwal Slabs. But I

could only walk the ledge so far. A few feet to the right of the window a great length of the cornice had fallen away completely, leaving a gap about six feet wide. It was a gap that could not be jumped for I should be spread-eagled against the wall without room for such a manoeuvre. I knew that if I could cross the gap I would take the risk of what lay beyond. I leaned out of the window, staring at the break. What I wanted was a plank to place across it to give me one foothold.

I turned back into the room. If I started breaking things up Fargette would hear and come to investigate. I had already considered one of the planks from the window seat, but they were only about four feet long and ran back into the wall mortar. The only other things were the wooden columns that supported the canopy of the four-poster bed. They might be long enough. I might be able to detach one of them, but they were round and would roll the moment I put my foot on one. The picture of myself slipping and the drop that waited was something I didn't care to think about.

I spent the afternoon roaming about the room, poking my head out the window and eyeing the cornice and then coming back and staring at the bed. The pole would roll. It was madness. If I wanted to commit suicide all I had to do was to jump out of the window. But I kept coming back and looking at the canopy supports. They were thin at the top and thick at the bottom. That would make the roll more certain.

Fargette brought me some food around five. I had no appetite for it. I was getting the feeling that it was today or not at all. This place had enchanted me. A heavy spell had been over it and me but now I had to break it or live forever under its charge. I was a new man, restless, full of desire to get out of this place.

I smoked and finished the last of the whisky in the bottle. It was not enough to give me courage or rashness. I felt depressed. It grew dark and I switched the light on. And in the end I went to the bed and began to examine one of the supports just to prove to myself that I couldn't, anyway, get it off without a lot of noise. The top I saw, was just socketed in to one of the canopy runners. The bottom ... I couldn't see how it went because of the mattress and bedcovers. I gave the mattress a heave over at the bottom—and there I had an immediate choice of six fine lengths of stout planking each about eight feet long.

I stood there knowing that luck is something you make for yourself. The bed-frame was a great shallow box, eight feet by four, and the base of the box on which the mattress fitted was made up of loose planks, just like the old army bedboards at the beginning of the war before things got soft. Good stout inch-thick oak planks. I decided to leave that night as soon as it was late enough.

CHAPTER TEN

It was past midnight before I left. For two hours I had had everything prepared and I sat in the window seat smoking and watching the night. The moon was up behind the chateau somewhere so that the whole wall-face was in dark shadow. There was a blaze of stars and a warmish light wind. Below me was the grey and purple depth of the gorge and, very thinly, I could hear the sound of the river over its bed. I had been thinking about Sophie, wondering what it was that kept her tied to these people, and wishing that I had had time to ask her far more questions than I had. Also, with the thought that I might with luck soon be free, I was thinking of the coming interview with Drexel and Didier. I had a lot to tell them. Enough easily to convince them that I was innocent, but there were still elements in this affair which had me puzzled. Today, for instance, I had not heard the car leave. Neither had I heard the usual noise of laughter and barking from the courtyard. I was sure, too, that there were people in the chateau for until late I had heard them moving about. This had never happened before and, although I found a reason for it, it still left me in the dark. I worked out that today was Sunday. Why should things be different on Sunday—except that they usually are?

I had said to myself that I would wait until one. But at half past twelve I could stand it no longer. I had to move.

I half closed the window and wedged a chair on the window seat so that it rested against the lower part of the frame. To this I tied a rope length which I had made from the bed sheets and covers. The plank I tied to my back with cord from the curtains. It was an uneasy, awkward fit but it was the best I could do. I had trouble backing out of the window because of the plank. It hit me on the head and got in the way of my feet.

With one hand on the sill I gradually took the strain of my body with the other hand on the rope. The chair creaked and groaned, but it held. Then I had both hands on the rope and went down gently. They were good stout linen sheets and I felt happy so long as I had my hands on them. A rope is a wonderful comfort when you have a long drop below you. My feet touched the ledge and I slowly let my weight on to it. It held but I knew I was not going to have any comfort from it. It was as crumbly and rotten as sandstone. It was dark in the shadow of the chateau, but the only eyes I needed were in my hands and feet. I reached out with my left hand and got a hold in a crack between the crudely cut blocks of stone. I waited for my breath to ease back to normal and then let go of the rope with my right hand. It was the most reluctant farewell of my life. The sheet swung away and then came back, brushing against my face. It didn't want to leave me. That went for both of us.

I found a hold with my right hand and there I was, spread-eagled hundreds of feet above the river, and the plank, unevenly balanced, came between my legs and tapped gently against the wall. Slowly I began to work my way along. I had a great temptation to go quickly. But I kept this down, moving one foot, one hand at a time and letting my weight gradually shift, testing each hold.

I made six feet and then, finding good hand-holds, I rested, letting the strain go in turn from each arm and leg. It was bliss. And then, from above me and to the right, I heard the clatter of something falling. I knew at once what it was. The chair had fallen back from the window seat. I knew exactly how much spare rope there was, and I knew that now, even if I went back, I would never be able to reach the end of it. I was out here and there was no return by my window.

I stood there with my face against the bare stone and

I was frightened. I felt sick and hopeless. At the back
of my mind had been the thought, hardly expressed but
a comfort to reach for if I needed it, that at any time
I could go back. But there was no going back now. And
then I was angry, angry with myself and everything
that had conspired to put me into this position. Anger
is the best antidote I know for fear. But it needs
watching.

I went on, too quickly, too violently, and suddenly
a great flake of stone broke away from under my foot.
For one moment I was clawing at the wall-face with
a leg swinging over space. The board on my back hit
the wall between my legs and then pivoted and crashed
against my head. I swung out sideways and then back
again. Somehow I got a hold and found my footing. I
pressed myself against the stones and my breath was
something between a sobbing and a whine. But it did
the trick. I was sober; free of anger and fear. From
that moment I became an automaton, allowing myself
nothing but movement and keeping my mind blank.

I came to the break in the cornice. I did not trust the
broken edge. I banged it with my foot, not wanting
it to break back when the plank was on it. It held. For
the other side I could make no test. I worked the plank
around so that it was between me and the wall, one
end resting on the cornice between my feet. I untied it
from my waist and then worked a loop of cord to the
end above my face. It was a manoeuvre I had done fifty
times in my mind as I had sat up above. To my surprise it worked without a hitch. Holding the bottom
of the plank in place with my left foot I let the top
slip away from me along the wall-face, controlling it
with the free cord from the loop in my right hand. It
went down gently, a slow-moving radial from my
left foot. It spanned the gap, edge upwards, and I
tipped it over with my foot.

By the time I had finished every muscle in my
strained body was trembling. I rested until the tension
eased down.

I reached out, took a new hand hold and then slid my left foot out on to the plank. It sagged a bit and I heard the board grating on the broken edges. I moved my other foot on to it and then inched along.

I was in the middle of the plank, taking all the strain I could on my arms. The board grated and sagged beneath me and I was talking to myself, growling between my clamped teeth, 'Don't hurry! Don't hurry!'

I forced myself to move more slowly, feeling my Adam's apple knocking in my throat like a faulty ballcock.

I got over and I was myself again. The plank moved as the last strain came off it. It slipped and fell away into the darkness, but I never heard it hit anything. It must have landed in bushes or a treetop. I didn't care. I was over. What happened behind me was of no importance, for there was no return. My future lay ahead, along this rotten strip of ledge. It was good to have a future I could measure in minutes not years. I felt more capable of handling it.

Although my movements were automatic, I was free to think now. I got to the point where the wall-face angled back on itself. A gargoyle decorated the turning point of the cornice. It was some kind of animal, its head covered with bird droppings. I turned the corner and was in moonlight. And I could see what lay before me. The wall ran back and then out again, forming a sharp V. The other side of the V was in darkness and I could not tell how far the ledge went. I was sweating now and it was odd how the warm night breeze seemed cold to my skin. My fingers were cut and scratched from the rough holds I took and I could feel my right-knee cap complaining about this work. That made me smile, for I remembered the army doctor who had fixed me up years ago when a bullet had cracked the cap for me. 'Climber, eh? Then don't ever trust it too long on a sticky traverse.' He should have been here now. The whole ledge was one long traverse. And the knee-cap brought Drexel into my mind ... that was the

time he had saved my life. Maybe now—if I got away
—I could repay a little of that debt. He'd get Jabal back
... save his pride and reputation. I knew just how
much he hated failure, just how much he needed the
stimulus of success ... it was food and drink to him,
to all heroes. A jerk of pain in my knee drove Drexel
from my head ... If my knee gave way now ... I tried
not to think of it.

Four yards beyond the corner there was a window
above the ledge. Just high enough for me to reach the
sill and pull myself up. I could see too that the window
was open, though the room beyond was in darkness.
I wanted to go in. I told myself that I could easily
find a way down through the chateau ... but I didn't
believe it. I rested under the window with my hands
reaching up to the stone sill. It was a good hold and
comfortable. All I had to do was to pull myself up. But
I wouldn't. I was outside the chateau and I meant to
stay outside. If I went back something would go wrong
... the strength of a fetish takes little from reason. I
rested and went on.

But I might have saved myself the trouble. When
I got into the apex of the V I saw that the cornice
finished. The out-running wall was bare and smooth.
I wasn't even glad that I had an easy trip back to the
window. I had made a decision not to use it and now
it was being forced on me. I don't know what it was
... Perhaps the strain of being hung out there over that
dark gorge with the black spikes of firs and pines
reaching up for me and the lisp of the distant river
shivering through the night ... Maybe I was a little
light-headed and open to any omen or token of luck ...
but I knew I didn't want to go through that window.

However, fetish, desire, want or not-want, I had
no choice. I went back and I hauled myself up. I swung
my legs into the room and I sat there, staring at it, with
my bottom hanging half over the drop outside. I didn't
take in the room for a while. It was enough to sit with
my muscles relaxed and take deep, sweet breaths of

air without fear that my expanding chest would push
me into space.

Nearly half the room was flooded by moonlight. And
now I began to take it in. It was large, a cross between
a study and a sitting-room. There was a big leather-
topped desk, very neat and no papers on it. One wall
was lined with books and against another was a wide,
deep cupboard, an Italianate looking affair with painted
door panels cut with open grill work at the top. Chairs,
a round table with a bowl of fruit, a tall glass case
full of china and a very fine spread of Savonnerie
carpet from which the moonlight took all the colour,
and then a tall Chinese screen that half-masked the
doorway ... a pleasant, reserved room, I thought.

I gave my knee a quick massage and then I started
for the door. So far as I could determine this room was
on the floor below mine. As I passed the round table,
I stuffed an orange and an apple in my pocket, like
a boy at a Sunday School treat. My throat was parched.

I was almost at the door when I heard the sound
of voices and footsteps outside. Then, as a switch was
thrown in the corridor, a thin edge of light came under
the door.

I thought: this is it; this is why you shouldn't have
come in through the window; and I started back. But as
I went I was looking for alternatives to the open
window. Now that I was in, I didn't want to go out
again. The Chinese screen was no good. It was too
near the door. I went to the cupboard and opened
the first full length door. The space inside was taken
up with shelves for linen. Hastily, as I heard the footsteps coming closer, I tried the door on the other side.
There was a full length cupboard except for a small
shelf at the top, a kind of cloak and hat place. I reached
up and found the shelf was loose. I slipped it down and
stepped inside, pulling the door as close as I could get
it.

I was there with about ten seconds' grace when the

room door was opened and the light switched on. I stood there and I found that I had a view of practically the whole room. On a level with my face the cupboard door panel had been cut into a fretted design of leaves, flowers and birds through which I could look.

Monsieur Gerard came in first. He went and stood by the round table and he was a pathetic sight. He was in a shabby old dressing-gown and bast slippers. The gown was made of grey feathers or towelling or something queer and he looked like a picture I had once seen of a young gannet, beaky nosed and big-eyed with worry. His whitish tufts of hair sprung upwards where he had run his fingers through them. But not in a hundred years would he ever feather up into any pleasing appearance.

He called out, half to himself, 'Why does he come at night? Why at night? Why at all, and why at this time? It's wrong and it's dangerous ...' He beat one hand against the other and he was a bad advertisement for would-be kidnappers to join his school.

It was Sarrasin he was talking to. He came forward into my view and quite obviously he had not been roused from his bed. He was wearing a neatish grey suit and polished brown shoes.

He said, 'Shut up!'

But he said it without any force, as though he knew it would produce no result.

Gerard began to pick at the end of his dressing-gown cord.

'What's he doing? Why doesn't he come?'

Sarrasin laughed. 'He's having a drink downstairs. And he's talking to Paviot. At this moment Paviot is feeling very uncomfortable.'

'And in a moment we shall.'

'What does it matter? These things happen. He told me to get you up.' Sarrasin went and sat on a corner of the desk and began to play with a paper knife. If Gerard was worrying his head off, it was clear that

George Sarrasin was completely unruffled.

He said, 'Karimba was much better today. But I don't get much time yet.'

'And you won't until this is over. Then you will have time and money. Santa Maria ... there are so many things we shall be able to do then with the money. Everything is falling to pieces and we have to take the cheapest ... that's no way to get anywhere. All my life I have wanted to do it big and—'

'Yes, I know. Do not tell me what you have wanted to do. We shall do it. Attention ... here he comes.'

Sarrasin looked at Gerard and he smiled. It was not the kind of smile that would have encouraged anyone.

'Try not to enrage him,' said Gerard.

'Idiot. It is already done,' answered Sarrasin unconcerned.

I stood there, cramped in my cupboard, watching the room through my fretwork and I had forgotten my own predicament. Most of what they had said was double-dutch to me. Who was Karimba? Sarrasin's girl friend? But most important, for I guessed from the reference to Paviot that it was something to do with Jabal's kidnapping, who was this person that Gerard feared so much?

There were quick, energetic footsteps coming down the corridor. Then the door, which I could not see, opened and was slammed shut again. And then into my field of view came a man; a shortish, alert figure in an old raincoat, the collar turned up, and carrying a soft hat in one hand.

He went up to Gerard and he stood in front of him, angry, spoiling with fury, and he said:

'Damn you! When I give an order for something to be done I want it done my way! My way! Do you hear? And only my way!'

Cramped in my cupboard, I watched through the fretwork and I saw the glint of light on Sarrasin's paper knife as he played with it. I saw Gerard, seeming to wither and shrink before the blast of words, his thin hands plucking at the fluffy material of his dressing-gown, saw the sheen on the fruit in the bowl and on the blood-red spread of leather on the desk top; and despair and hope, certainty and uncertainty warred in me.

It was Colonel Francis Drexel.

CHAPTER ELEVEN

I heard Gerard say, 'But Colonel, it was an accident.'

I thought Drexel was going to strike him.

'I told you there was to be no violence!' The words were shouted, venomous. 'Why the hell didn't you watch Paviot? You know what he's like with a knife. You—' he swung round towards Sarrasin and the skirt of his raincoat brushed against Gerard who started back as though he had been burnt. 'You were there. Why didn't you control him?'

Sarrasin dropped the paper knife, stood up and said calmly, more than calmly ... the touch of insolence in his voice, 'Paviot with a knife is his own man. What does it matter anyway? The policeman is dead and will recognize no one.'

'I don't care a damn about that! Dead or alive it doesn't matter. What matters is that I said it was not to happen! If we're going to pull this off—things go my way! My way! Do you hear?'

There was a note in his voice I had never heard before, the shrillness of almost hysterical anger.

That was the moment when hope died in me. Until then I hadn't been sure. Drexel was devious and unfathomable in his ways. Until then I had been feeding my hope with the thought that he was here on my side, that he was my Drexel ... the knight in shining armour, playing some dark role. But not now. I stood there and felt sick, knowing that the policeman's death meant nothing to Drexel, that he saw in it only trouble and the fact that his plans, whatever they were, had been mishandled. I remembered then the reluctance that had been in me to come through the window. I felt cold and empty, drained of all life. And in my mind was only a wild regret that I hadn't slipped from the cornice into the oblivion of the gorge for I knew now that there are some things which, at any price, are better not known.

'But even so, Colonel ...' Gerard drifted forward, one hand fluttering up to his loose hair, '... you should not come. Not here. It is dangerous ... Oh, so dangerous ...' His voice trailed off in a half-whisper.

'Stop whining to me about danger. I came to make you see that if you don't do as I say you'll put us all in danger.'

'But someone might have followed you ... seen you.'

'God! Why do I have to rely on such an old woman! No one followed me. I'm on my way to Paris for a few days. I left my car on the other road over the hill and walked here.'

'You go to Paris to see our friend about the arrangements with the oil company?' It was Sarrasin.

I shut my eyes. And I wished I could have shut my ears. I didn't want to believe what was happening. And if I had felt sick when they talked about the policeman, that was gone. I was filling with anger now. Anger, not against any person, but against the whole dirty sweep of things passing before me. It was all I could do to stay there. This was Drexel, my friend, the man who had once saved my life at the risk of his own. It was too awful. I was left with nothing but contemptuous rage. I could shut my eyes to put him out of my sight, but his bitter, almost hysterical voice rasped in my ears. He was nothing but a sordid, unscrupulous kidnapper. It didn't matter that I could, even then, find reasons for his degradation. I had in me only an anger that was like an unbearable pain. His voice rang in my ears and there was a quality in it of meanness and fine frenzy, the edge and strain and stress of a man dedicated to a purpose created out of his own baseness and weakness.

'Yes. I'm going to Paris. And if there's any more nonsense I'll cut down your share.'

'Not my share!'

I opened my eyes. There was the room again, jig-sawed into crazy sections by the fretwork. Gerard, drooping and worried, was by the table and Sarrasin was standing a few feet from Drexel, not intimidated by him.

'Not my share,' Sarrasin repeated.

'Be careful how you speak to me.' Drexel's body stiffened and his voice was strange to me. There was a new passion and strength in it, and I hated it as I hated him and the thing that had happened to him. 'You're in my hands—all of you.'

Sarrasin shook his head. I hated him, too—that went way back, but against my feeling for Drexel it was now colourless. I could even like him a little for not fearing this man. At least he was understandably animal, a strong body, and greedy appetites and no scruples as to how he fed them. He was simple.

'No, Colonel.' Sarrasin's face was unmoved; he was like a tower. 'You are in our hands as much as we are are in yours. So do not say things like that. We have followed your plan as well as we can. The policeman was an accident . . . but of no importance. The rest is as you said. Your friend is here safe. Jabal has seen him about the grounds, walking free, and he will think he is behind all this. But if there is any talk about cutting shares—then I do not promise to keep to the plan. There is another. It would be easy to slit your friend's throat and send Jabal back to the Regent where he will never talk. In fact, all along I have felt that the best plan.'

It was a long speech for Sarrasin and each word came deliberately, full of weight and a little awkward as though he were unused to marshalling his thoughts into open speech.

'You are not paid to think.' Drexel was pressing him hard. 'You're paid to do as I say. Do as I say and everything will be all right.'

'Yes, yes . . . if we do as the Colonel says it will be all right. That's so, isn't it, Colonel?' It was Gerard, poor fluttering Gerard.

And that was odd. I would have said that I had enough on my plate; that alive or dreaming there was only room in me for one emotion, the angry disgust centred on Drexel. But part of my mind could hold Gerard and pity him. I was sorry for him because he was so lost. He was eaten up with worry from his own rashness. More than anything he wanted reassurance. Sarrasin had no weakness. And the weakness in Drexel had been turned into a perverse strength fed by his own cupidity. But poor Gerard had nothing, only an echoing, fear-haunted spirit.

'Don't be a fool.' Drexel brushed Gerard away. 'Of course it will be all right. In a couple of weeks we shall have the money. Nothing will lead to us and Jabal will be free, and everything he says will incriminate Fraser more.'

'And Fraser?' Sarrasin was smiling. 'You really trust your plan for him?'

'Of course I do.'

'It sounds stupid to me. It leaves too much to him.'

Drexel swung round, quick, terrier-like, all the hardness and vitality of the man working in his face and movements, and he came past the cupboard, pacing the floor, and I knew he must be holding himself in now, goaded by the calm opposition in Sarrasin. And there he was, not three feet from me, with all my future in his hands.

'It's the only plan,' he snapped. 'Fraser is my responsibility. Keep your hands off him. I know him and I know how to deal with him. When he comes round, he'll be at sea, on his way to South America, and there'll be two thousand pounds in his case. He won't come back. I know him as I know my own hand. I'm giving him a fresh start, a new name, money—and too much against him in Europe for him ever to show his nose here again.'

Hidden there, silently watching this hideous scene, I began to understand so much ... how Drexel had at first made me look careless, how he, Brindle, and the others had muddled me up until I looked criminally involved, and then the final move of rescuing me from Didier. My comparative freedom at the chateau was explained. Jabal had seen me, marked me down as a kidnapper and when he was free who would doubt his word that I was criminally involved?

I stood there listening ... and the whole thing was a fantasy with cold truth and reason behind it. It was like

suddenly discovering a new room in a house you know
well. You can't believe it. But there it is. And inside the
room is a stranger who looks like yourself, And you
suddenly see that this is a you that you never suspected.
Drexel had a blazing belief in everything he had said.
And, in a moment of intense clarity, white-hot because
it was born in the heart of my anger, I could see how
right he was. He was telling something about myself
that was true. What would I do if I woke on some tramp
steamer with money, with a valid passport in another
name, and with a new future ahead of me to weigh
against all the weary complications and tortuous expla-
nations and accusations that waited in Europe? For two
days I would be mad to get back and clear myself. But
after four or five, I would have counted the money and
have known South America nearer and have been
saying, 'Oh, what the hell?' Going back was too much
bother—and what would it get me? Already the news-
paper publicity had pronounced me guilty. Profession-
ally I would have to fight prejudice, and I would have
Drexel and Jabal against me. I wouldn't have a chance
of clearing myself. God, Drexel knew me, and how well
he had worked it out, so that even his treachery was a
favour to me. I suppose that was how he could do it,
how he could stop himself from thinking about my feelings towards him. He was doing me a favour for which
I would thank him. Part of my anger turned against
myself for knowing that what he said was true.

But Sarrasin believed in one way only of making a
man silent.

'I would cut his throat. Cheaper and safer.'

Drexel said nothing for a few seconds. He stood there,
taut, strung up, a shabby figure in the grease-splotched
raincoat, his tanned face wooden, lips tight-stretched
across his teeth and his eyes were bright with a fierce-
ness I had never seen before. Then he pulled an automatic
from his pocket and levelled it at Sarrasin.

Sarrasin made no move. But his eyes were measuring
the distance between them, the animal body was tensing

and, without fear, he was feeling chance and time balance against the possible moment of attack. Only Gerard gave an anxious little cry that was wasted on them.

'Put one mark on Fraser,' said Drexel icily; 'put one foot out of line and I promise to fill your guts with lead. You and all the rest.'

I suppose I should have been glad that he could feel like that. But I wasn't. I didn't want his protection now that the friendship between us had been killed. I stood there, staring out at them.

'As long as I get my money—'

'But of course you will get it ...' Gerard moved to Sarrasin and made a flapping motion at the Colonel to put away his automatic. 'The Colonel is a clever man. His plan will work and we shall have the money ... Please, it is silly to show all this emotion. Bad feeling between us is unnecessary.' He patted Sarrasin on the arm. 'The Colonel says no violence. He is right!'

Gerard knew his Sarrasin. Maybe this was not the first time he had to handle him. For a moment I thought Sarrasin was going to persist. Then, abruptly, the tension went from his body and he shrugged his shoulders. The expression he used for a smile touched his face and he said slowly, 'All right. If the Colonel is sure. He wants to spend his money in peace. So do I. If he has no fear of Fraser—then why should I?'

They had settled it cosily at last. Would I or would I not let them down? The Colonel was right. I would not. I did not listen clearly to what they talked about now. It was a dry, leaf-skittering sound against the hammer of my thoughts. No fear of Fraser? How wrong they were. Two hours ago when I had been safely locked up the plan was perfect. Beautiful ... all the little things that had happened at the Villa Maruba; Drexel, or Brindle, I guessed, pinching my key; Sarrasin, Paviot and Sophie making my acquaintance ... everything ticking over nicely for Drexel. He was not going to hurt anyone. Jabal sold to the oil company. I wondered what price they had set. High, if they could afford to give me two thous-

and. Me—set up for life. (The successful kidnapper
Fraser, collects his money and disappears.) And Drexel
back in his London flat, to a retirement with honour and
luxury; and the others—what little dream world had
Gerard and the rest planned? But, whatever it was, no
one was to be hurt. No wonder Drexel was mad at the
death of the policeman. It had spoilt his plan, the essence
of which was to have been non-violence, and it had made
it awkward for him to see himself in the role of a beni-
ficient patron. It was all I could do not to take a chance
and walk out there and then and begin to kick the
heart out of him. If I nursed the hope that one day I
would come to grips with Sarrasin it was only an idle
pipe dream compared with the passion that filled me now
to come up with Drexel and be free to speak and act.
Sarrasin had made me feel unChristian. Nothing new.
Drexel made me feel lethal for the first time, and I was
anxious to be blooded.

When I came back to them, they were moving out of
the room. The Colonel was returning to his car. He'd left
it on some road over the hill. He didn't know it but I
was going with him.

I suppose because now I had the whole thing in my
hands practically, I should have been cautious. But there
was nothing of finesse in me. I'd come back through the
window knowing that I shouldn't. Come back to break
my heart over a dead faith. If it sounds hyperbolic it's
because it was. Strong emotion, the final dirtiness of the
human spirit can't be eased by under-statement. Not by
me, anyway: schoolmasters with English literature as
their subject are seldom laconic. There was no need for
caution. All the bad luck coming to me had arrived cash
on delivery.

They went out, leaving the light on and the door open.
I gave them one minute and then I left the cupboard.
Outside, the corridor was empty, but I could hear their
voices from the hallway at the bottom of the stairs.

The top of the stairs was in darkness. But below, the
hall was dimly lit. They stood there for a while, talking,

and I moved down the wide stone steps and found shelter
in the shadow of one of the suits of armour that lined
the steps at intervals. Hidden there, I waited. I knew
exactly what I was going to do. There was no choice. I
was going after the Colonel. I was going to be face to
face with him. He was going to know I knew and when
all that had been cleared from between us he was going
to know that I meant to throw him to the crowd. The
shout of the crowd in praise of a hero is one thing, but
against the noise that goes up as the dishonoured hero
falls it is no more than the sigh of stale air from a pricked
balloon. I didn't like myself for it, I never would like
myself for it, I knew. But in that moment, I knew I
was going to do it. And having settled that, I felt free
and my mind eased its pace and for relief began to take
little trips up side paths. I thought of Brindle. Didier
had said my crack over the head could have been part
of an act. He had the wrong man. Brindle had played
that part. And I saw how Brindle's love for Drexel was
stronger, stranger than mine. He had been able to follow
him anywhere without question. But love was the
wrong word for it. Must be. It was sorcery. In the past
I had felt the spell myself ... But not now. There was
not even the finest drawn hair-thread of sentiment re-
maining between myself and Drexel.

I heard the door shut and then the footsteps of Gerard
and Sarrasin coming up the stairs. Gerard was doing all
the talking, quick, fluttering words that set up echoes in
the lofty stairway which beat like bat's wings against the
dark vaultings.

'Oh, dear. Oh, dear ... how nearly you provoked him.
Why? Why do you do these things? You know his ways
are good, but always you set up against him.'

'He is English. I dislike him.'

'Stupid. Look at him and see him as money. We need it
so we do as he says. Oh, la, la ... tonight we are as poor
as crows. But soon.' Then, his tone changing, unexpectedly hard and brittle. 'That Paviot. Maybe it is his
throat should be cut. He causes this trouble.'

'No man takes a knife to Paviot.' Sarrasin laughed,
and they were passing me, hardly seen, a disturbance of
the dark air rather than form.

Their voices echoed away from me and then all was
silent. I went down into the hall. The outer door to the
courtyard was unlocked. I slipped through it and keeping
in the shadow of the walls made my way to the arch
that led to the causeway over the dry moat. Minerva
was white and softened by the moonlight. She gave me
the gentle side of her face. But I didn't want it. There
was no charity in me. Cold, hard justice was my want. I
was after Drexel and there was not a sliver of compassion
in me. War-like and stern—that was the Minerva I
wanted as a girl friend. I hurried on for I did not want to
lose Drexel. I need not have worried. As I edged into
the gateway, I saw him.

The gravelled space beyond the moat was bathed in
moonlight. At the foot of the causeway a ragged plume
of shadow was cast by the large tree with purple blossoms which had been almost the first thing I had seen
when I had been helped out of the wine tanker, a large,
splendid tree rich with flowers.

Drexel was standing just on the edge of the patch of
shadows. From the movements of his hands and arms I
could see that he was filling his pipe. I watched, waiting
for him to move on. He struck a match and one side of
his face came up in livid yellow colour. Faintly on the
night breeze I caught the fragrance of the tobacco smoke
coming to me. It was a smell I knew so well and instantly
it evoked a hundred pictures of him in my mind, and
none of them was wanted. Each one was a bitterness
now to me.

He tossed the match away and began to move across
the gravel and as he passed under the tree. I suddenly
remembered it's name, and that too was a bitterness for
me: *l'arbre de Judas*. The Judas Tree.

I went after him and I knew now that whatever risk
I had taken in the house, I could take no risk with him.
His eyes and ears would serve him well. One wrong

move and he would be prickly with suspicion. His whole life had conditioned him to walk watchfully.

He did not go down the drive to the gate. He went right-handed across the camomile lawn and through a small shrubbery. I kept well behind him, marking his passage by the slurred footsteps on the dew-heavy grass. He climbed the wall and disappeared. I gave him headway and then climbed it at another point in case he should already have sensed he was being followed. He was about a hundred yards ahead, moving up the sloping cork tree-studded hillside and I had to admire the way he followed his instincts. He went from one patch of tree shadow to another and there was never a sound from him. Thin on the air behind him was the trace of his tobacco smoke.

I followed him. From the top of the slope the ground dropped away down a rough hillside to the bottom of a small valley. The far side of the valley was steep and wooded with young birches and pines, and here and there I could see great shoulders of rock face thrusting out from the trees. I let him get into the wood before I started down the open slope. There was little cover for me and he might well turn in some break of the woods and look back to see me. But now I did not care. We were out of sight of the chateau and had the night and the woods to ourselves. A large white owl came drifting across the slope and from somewhere in the hills a nightjar screeched. It was good to be out and away from the chateau, to be moving somewhere and to know what I was going to do. I think I was calming down a bit, too.

There was a narrow, deep-cut of stream at the bottom of the valley. I jumped it and the soft thump of my feet on the far bank stopped the calling of the frogs. Where Drexel had disappeared into the trees there was the beginning of a small path. I followed this and, as I went, I took out my Sunday-school treat apple. My mouth was parched and I ate it greedily.

Someone had been working in the wood, cutting down the young birches and sawing them into small lengths

which were stacked in piles in some of the clearings.
They were posts to be used for staking the vines. After
a time the path swung out to the right and then went
steeply up over a shoulder of one of the big rock out-
crops. For a while I had to use my hands to climb and in
the bright moonlight I could see the marks of Drexel's
passage, the disturbed earth of the path, the long smears
on the dew-thick turf; and steady in my nostrils was the
tang of his tobacco.

When I came to the top of the great rock I stopped,
my head on a level with it and surveyed the flat plateau
carefully. I didn't want Drexel to surprise me. The surprise was to come from me.

It was a wide, flat space, dotted with myrtle bushes
and here and there the tall, straggly growths of wild
white lupins. Away to the right the rock broke away in
a ragged fall of about fifty feet towards the trees bank-
ing the lower slope of the valley. To the left there was a
dark palisade of pine trunks. Drexel's footsteps ran evenly
marked on the short wet grass right across the plateau
to the trees on the far side.

I pulled myself up and began to move across. I was
almost on the far side and about to enter the trees when
I heard a movement behind me. A voice said:

'Turn round and come back with your hands up.'

I knew the voice and I knew what had happened and
had to concede admiration for the man. In some uncanny
way he had sensed he was being followed. That can
happen. Just as in a crowd you can be aware of someone's eyes on you. He had gone right across the plateau,
his steps a marker for me, but once there he had doubled
back through the surrounding pines to the left and was
now behind me.

I raised my hands slowly and turned.

He was standing a few feet out from the pines, the
moonlight full on him. Against the tall trunks he looked
smaller than usual, a pygmy figure full of threat. He had
pushed his soft hat back from his forehead, the pipe was
still in his mouth and his right hand held his automatic.

I began to walk towards him. When I was four feet from him he said:

'That's near enough.'

I stopped. Cautiously, no expression on his face, strangers for the moment with nothing between us except the waiting tinder of violence needing only a spark to set it going, he circled round me and I felt him come up behind me and his hand ran skilfully over my clothes. I knew better than to try anything then.

I heard him step back and then he came round to my front and halted a wise four feet from me.

He took the pipe from his mouth, slipped it into his pocket and said:

'All right. You can lower your hands.'

I dropped my arms and reached to tuck in the loose material of my shirt that had pulled about my waist in raising my arms.

At once, he said, 'Keep your hands in the open.'

Then after a pause he said, his voice old and patient, 'Do as I say, David, and you won't regret it.'

It was odd how my name on his lips meant nothing. Always before he could touch me with my name. Not now. It was just a sound.

I said, 'You've finished arranging my future. This is where I take over.'

CHAPTER TWELVE

We stood there against the dark pine trunks and over-head there was a sky with stars and moon and needing only a trio of painted angels to be pure *quattro cento*. The air was sweet with night scents and the breeze was soft on my hot face. It was a good night, but not in my calendar. There was nothing good about it for me.

I picked up the wreck which had been our friendship, the broken splintered mess of it and I began to throw the pieces away. Turning out an old drawer or a junk room there is always something to make you linger, to rouse nostalgia, to bring the hot sting of remembered goodness and happiness into the eyes. Maybe that's why that kind of job is never finished. But there was nothing like that here. I cleared the broken, useless junk from my heart without a qualm, without feeling except the anger which was cold and controlled in me.

I said, 'You saved my life once. I wish you'd left me there in the desert.'

He jerked a little, as though I had flicked at his face contemptuously. I didn't have to tell him anything, or explain anything. It was all in my face.

He said, 'Turn round and start back for the chateau.'

'No.'

'Start.'

The automatic came up a little and I saw it tremble in his hand.

'No. You can't tell me what to do. You played at God, but that's forbidden, and it's over. You took me and you arranged my life. South America and a new start. You took your reputation and the love people have for their heroes and you would have used them to pay your wine bills, your tailor and to give you a rich old age. But the game's over.'

'Shut up!'

He came a step forward. I kept my eyes on his face

and it was the face of a stranger to me. A hard, lean, tormented face and the eyes almost colourless in the moonlight, the pale blue washed away; cold, white eyes. I saw his mouth move as though he talked to himself, as though inside he was answering me; and I knew what was happening to him because it had happened to me an hour before. He was beginning to hate me. He was beginning to throw me away ... but it was harder for him because for his own sake he would have liked to save it all, to have kept the comfort of his god-like interference with my life to off-set the future he had planned.

'Give me the gun,' I said. 'You're finished.'

He laughed and it was like the coughing sound a sheep makes at night. 'You're a fool,' he said. 'A bigger fool than I thought. I'm not finished. I'm just beginning. But, by God, if you get in my way I'll finish you. I don't know how you found all this out, but what have you got to grumble about? No harm's been done. Only good. You were never really happy as a schoolmaster. In your heart you've always wanted a fresh start. But you're too louse-gutted ever to have done anything about it. I went out of my way to put you right.'

'Thanks for worrying about me. And what about the policeman? You gave him a nice future. You gave his wife and kids a nice future!'

'I never planned that. Things went wrong!' But he wasn't thinking of the *gendarme* even now. He was thinking of himself, of his precious plan.

I said, 'If you play God, you mustn't let things go wrong. Give me the gun.'

'This is my plan and it's not going to fail! I've waited years for this chance!'

He wasn't talking now. He was shouting. It was horrible. Out there on the moonswept plateau with its bare turf and clumps of myrtle, perched high up over the valley with the wind rattling gently at the black seed-pods of the lupins, there were the two of us, both full of hate but mine now pale and tired against his. It was pure nightmare and if there had been a price within my power to pay to stop it, to put the clock back, I would have paid it. But there was no going back. I stood there listening to him, and my eyes went from his face because it was agony to watch the spirit that moved there. He was not talking to me any more. He was talking to himself, to his *alter ego*, to the spirit which had possessed him and, while it would have been easy to say he was mad, tormented and warped by his past life into this new creature, I knew he was not mad. He was naked and I didn't want to look at him. He was being himself; his full self, showing the dark and savage side of his nature; the evil principle, which in all of us must be held down and disciplined, now clear in the light and vibrant with a fierce vigour.

'It's not going to fail! What do you know about me? What do you know about what goes on inside here—' he smacked at his chest, and if it had not been tragic it would have been funny. 'For years I've been a hero. I've walked the tightrope and risked my life. I've put my hand in the fire and held it there. I've seen everything I had when I started slowly destroyed. I had ideals and I let them roll in the gutter to serve a handful of officials. I had pity but I killed men who didn't even know my name or that death was settled for them. I had health and I saw it go ... malaria, typhus. The man who stands here now isn't the man who started out.' He paused, panting; his breathing an anguished sound across the still night.

'I hate your guts,' I said. 'Do you hear? It's me. The man who was your best friend saying it. I hate your guts.'

'Don't throw your hate and your disgust at me,' he shouted. 'I did that to myself years ago. And what have I got from it all? A few pence, the niggardly thanks of the Foreign Office. What *have* I got? A good name on one side and on the other a mass of debts. A rich past and a miserable future ... To hell with that! To hell with you! I'm going to have a future. I'm going to have money. I'm going to have my name and a rich retirement. I've earned it in a thousand shabby ways. I'm going to have it.

Do you hear? And, by God, I'll finish anyone who gets in my way!'

His left hand came up to steady the one with the automatic and I saw the soiled linen of the bandage he still wore round it. I could have cried for there was that happening inside me which I could neither welcome nor hold down. I didn't want it, but it came. It was as though I saw all of his life laid out before me ... and the misery of it tore at my heart. He had taken too much from life. It had battered and warped him. He'd given so much of the good in him that now only the bad remained. And because of that, because I could see how it had brought him to this moment, what he had done to me was unimportant for the real evil lay in what he had done to himself. In that moment I had nothing but compassion for him but I would not give it full life. I could not.

He said, suddenly calm, 'You've got no choice, David. You're going back to the chateau. Even now we can arrange something. One day, maybe, in South America you'll thank me.'

'I won't go to the chateau.'

'I shall count five. After that I shall shoot you in the leg. You'll lie here until I get help to carry you back.'

'You can do what you like,' I said. 'But it won't save you.'

He began to count and from the tone of his voice he might have been checking off stores in a quartermaster's office.

'One.

'Two.

'Three.'

I listened to him and I knew what I was going to do. When he said, 'Five,' I was going to jump and he was going to shoot. He might get my leg or my heart in the movement. I was not fool enough to have no care which it was, but there was that in me which left no choice. Sometimes we can only go one way. We have no choice.

He said, 'Five.'

And I jumped for him. I saw the spurt of flame, felt

and smelt the quick reek and sting of powder like a
handful of dust thrown suddenly into my face. I did not
know it until later but the bullet passed between my left
arm and my side tearing away and scorching the stuff of
my jacket. I got my hands on him and we both went
down under the momentum of my body. As I hit the
ground he slipped sideways from me and clubbed me
across the forehead with the snout of the automatic.
But even as it hit me, my hand went up to his wrist and
I held on as we twisted and rolled across the plateau.

For all his age he was strong and wiry, and his smallness made him difficult to hold. We struck and battered at
one another, our heels tearing up the short turf, our
bodies crashing through myrtle and lupin, and all the
time his face was close to mine and his breath was hot
against my neck and cheek. There was no word, no cry
from us except the short, desperate sigh of throat and
lungs for air. I bent his wrist back, putting all my
strength into it, and sometime or other the automatic
went because suddenly I realized that he had both hands
free and tight about my throat. He hung on to me like a
terrier gripping a large dog. I shook him and pummelled
him and tried to rise but he held me down and we
thrashed around, sometimes myself on top and sometimes
Drexel. And the curious thing was that somewhere some
part of me stayed aloof, wanting no share in this. It was
an indecency which sickened me. It was like a son fighting with his father. That I should lay hands on Drexel
was unthinkable. If anyone had ever told me I would I
should have said that it was not in the nature of my hand
to strike him. But the other me was there on the ground
now, hitting out, savage, feeling his flesh beneath the
shock of my fists and taking his violence, too, on my
body. His hands tightened against my throat and I knew
that, whatever plan had been formed in his quick mind
when he had ordered me to return to the chateau, he had
only one thought now. If he could kill me he would. I
got an arm locked across his throat and forced his head
back. I saw the stubby line of his jaw, the thin grimace

of his mouth and a wet splash of earth against his cheek.
He jerked his knee up and drove the little of breath that
was with me from my lungs and, at the same moment,
he rolled, his body arching and straining. I went with
him and the next instant we were falling together. It
was no clean fall.

We went down through space and then our bodies
crashed into loose stones and we slid, still grappling one
another, for a few feet and then fell again. A great circle
of hillside seemed to whirl round me. I saw rocks, a
swift cascade of stones and then a blur of bushes, and
then I knew we had gone over the edge of the plateau.
We struck the steep slope again and he was torn from
me with the shock. I saw him whipped away as though
he were a puppet roughly jerked by some hidden wire.
And at the same time I fell into a great cool well of
shadow. A monstrous rocky fist drove up from the darkness below me and punched into me with a force that
was robbed of pain by the immediate blackness that
engulfed my mind and body.

When I came to, the sky was grey and purple with
dawn. Somewhere a bird was singing incessantly and I lay
there and let myself get irritated by the noise. My head
ached and I was thirsty. Thirst was like a beast in me
and I knew I had to do something about it. I shut my
eyes against the ache in my head and at once it got worse.
I opened them. A small spider with a white cross on its
back was spinning an untidy web between two twigs
of the heather bush under which I lay. I watched him.
At a guess I should have said his heart wasn't in the job.
He kept resting and taking time off to polish his white
cross with a pair of back legs. I got irritated with him,
then. And I think I must have gone off again. But I
couldn't say for how long. It might have been a minute
or an hour.

When I came back again I was still thirsty, but I was
sensible enough to do something about it. I sat up and

found a squashed orange in my pocket. I sucked at the pulpy mess and felt better.

I stood up, feeling my body creak with strain and ache as though it were a badly contrived machine, a contraption of loose cords and stiff leather straps.

I was standing at the foot of a drop of sheer rock twice as tall as myself. Above the rock was a loose drift of stone, held in places by thin grass tufts and bushes. I could see the long score our falling bodies had made across it. Above the loose stone the side of the rock out-thrust went up, strewn with boulders and more bushes. Looking at the rock face I remembered Drexel.

I turned, searching for him, and saw him at once. He was lying about five yards from me, right up against the base of a tree. He was sprawled on his back, his rain-coat torn and open, one arm flung out and the other folded under his head. He had a deep cut down one cheek and his mouth was open in the stupid laxness of one who sleeps and snores. From his throat came a curious low sound as though he were complaining at some horror seen in a dream. I bent down and shook him gently but his eyes were shut and he gave no sign.

I stood there, not knowing what to do, fighting off the haziness which still kept sweeping over me. Then I saw his soft hat which had fallen from the plateau with us and lay now some distance from him. And I remembered the stream at the bottom of the valley. I picked up his hat and went away, down through the pines.

When I reached the stream I knelt down by it. There was a pad of moss under my knees and I felt the dampness work up from it into the cloth of my trousers. I leaned over the water and saw myself. There was a gash on my forehead where the automatic had hit me. My face was filthy with earth and stone dust. I frowned at the face, not liking it, not liking the hollowness of the eyes or the dirt and fatigue written all over it. The frown made me wince with pain as the dried blood of my forehead gash pulled with the movement of skin. I drank, filling myself with water and then I shoved my head under. I began to feel better. I found my handkerchief, wiped myself, and then tied it around my forehead where the blood had started to flow from my wound again.

I filled the soft hat with water, plugged the ventilation holes with my fingers and hurried back to Drexel. I got some water down his throat and the rest I used to bathe his face. His breathing evened off a bit but he still made no movement. I went over him anxiously—there was no past for me then; only this moment and his motionless body. So far as I could tell he had nothing broken, but I saw now that there was an ugly bruise under his left ear.

I went down for more water and poured it over his head but he still lay like a log.

For a moment I did not know what to do. I lit a cigarette and sat on a stone beside him, smoking and looking at him. I wanted five minutes, a clear, unhazed five minutes to think, in the hope that I should know what to do. I didn't know, there and then, what to do because I was myself so much involved. This really was a job for Minerva, and I guessed she would have had trouble deciding which face to show, which line to take ... the wisdom of the law, hard justice, or the wisdom of the heart. Christian forgiveness ... ?

I don't know how decisions are made. Sometimes the mind in its wisdom puts two and two together and it makes four. Sometimes the heart, with no faith in mathematics, just takes over and impels one to inexplicable charity. Sometimes they both work together. But whatever it is, there is the one thing, the thing which is yourself, the needle point of the ego on which every desire has to balance perfectly or be discarded. Half the time we may not know the balancing and rejecting is going on. All we know for certain is that we suddenly stand up acknowledging what we must do in order to live with ourselves. Disregard that moment and no peace remains.

Sitting there, I suddenly knew that I didn't even want five minutes and a clear brain. I knew it now and may be I'd known it when I brought the water to him. What

he had done to me was nothing. It had been purged up
there on the plateau. What he had done to himself was
paramount and he would have to live with it. But I knew
that I wanted him to live with it alone. I wanted no other
man to know it but myself and if it could have been
wiped from my knowledge I could have wanted that. I
wanted to save him from everyone but himself.

The person I had been last night was a stranger to me.
My real self sat there on a rock, smoking and watching
him. And I knew I could not throw him to the wolves.
Once the decision was made, I saw other advantages, but
even though one of them concerned Sophie none of them
had any true part in my decision.

How to do it was a problem and I knew I was asking
for trouble. But this time it would be my own trouble.

There was a clatter of stones from above. I looked up.
A man had come over the edge of the plateau and was
working his way downwards over the loose stones. He
lowered himself over the edge of the rock-fall and climbed
down it awkwardly. Then he came across to me. I knew
him but it took me a little while to place him.

CHAPTER THIRTEEN

It was Mr Leslie Dunwoody, the Englishman with the motor-cycle who had been camping near the Villa Maruba. He came across to me, rolling a little on his short legs, a half-length leather jacket belted tightly round his ample waist and a black, fur-edged motoring helmet cocked a little to one side on his head, the chin straps flapping loose. Anything he put on his head seemed to slide sideways, and as he came over I wondered whether he wore his toupee under the helmet.

He stood in front of me and he smiled, the red, soft baby face beaming with pleasure and his eyes twinkling. Life seemed a great joke to him ... Well, that was one way of looking at it.

He said, 'You all right?'

I nodded.

He looked back up the slope of rock and went on, 'Nasty fall—even when you've got company for it.' Then looking back at Drexel, he said, 'He's not so good?'

'No. I think he's got concussion.'

'Wonder you didn't both break your necks. Funny way, if I may say so, for friends to carry on.' Then with a shrewd but still humorous glance at me, and I could fancy him hugging himself with the pleasure of being in on all this, he said, 'You're Fraser, aren't you? The great kidnapper.'

'I'm Fraser.' I was thinking hard, wondering how much he knew, and how much I could depend on him. He had walked straight into my problem and unless I got his co-operation I was going to be in a mess. He did not give me the impression of a man who would be difficult to handle. I said, feeling the ground, 'How do you come to be here?'

With a casual frankness, he answered, 'Followed him when he left Banyuls last night. Waited around by his car and then I heard a revolver shot. Took me a long time to find you both. Tell you the truth, took me a long time to make up my mind to look. Didn't want to get mixed up in anything. But curiosity finally killed the cat, if you know what I mean.'

He took off his helmet and I saw that he was wearing his Edwardian toupee. He mopped his face with a handkerchief.

'Why were you following Drexel?'

He shook his head. 'Not important at the moment. Thing is—we ought to do something about him.'

I stood up and moved closer to him. I think for a moment he was suspicious of me for I saw the half-stir of his body to draw back. But he stood his ground and I liked him for that. He had courage and not for one moment did the twinkle go from his eyes. I don't suppose he knew how to make it go. He would go on twinkling all his life, life's joke never palling on him.

I said, 'Look—I'm in a jam.'

'You are. The police want you. Fact is, if the telephone had been working they would know where you are now.' He paused and scratched at his chin. 'It's funny that. If it had worked, I'd have done it. My duty and all that. But now I'm here, talking to you ... seems different.'

'What telephone?'

He seemed surprised by this.

'The one in the chateau, of course. Blimey, what do you think I did when I found you both? Went for help of course.'

'Where?' But I knew.

'Big chateau over there. But there ain't a soul there. Not a soul. And the phone doesn't work. So I came back here.'

I knew what that meant. They had discovered my disappearance and thinking I was on my way to the police they had cleared out of the Chateau Minerve. I didn't stop to go into all the implications of that, but I did see that if they had left the chateau the last thing they would do would be to come back. They had probably rented it furnished for this operation. All I had to do to give me some grace to work out my plans was to go back there. My only problem right now was Dunwoody.

I said, 'I'm in a jam, but I assure you that I've done nothing wrong. I want your help. Later, I'll explain everything.'

He did not answer for a while. He stood there looking at me and then his eyes went to Drexel. I could hear the flies buzzing about the flowers and bushes as the morning sun strengthened and I had a curious hope ... no, certainty. With a French peasant I would have had real trouble. But this was an Englishman, as English as Walthamstow, and he was obviously a man with a lively curiosity.

He nodded suddenly and then said, 'That's it. Talk later. Got to do something about him first.' He moved towards Drexel and I could have taken him in my arms and hugged him.

'We'll carry him to the chateau,' I said.

'Lucky he don't come in the same weight class as me,' he said. 'Come on then.' But as he bent down to take Drexel's legs he suddenly twisted his head round to me and his face was comically serious as he said, 'Let's have this straight, though. Don't try any fancy tricks with me. I can look after myself. Also,' he played it as a trump card and with a smile that flooded his face, 'I got his automatic. Picked it up when I was looking for you.'

I didn't reply, because the answer was in my face. I took Drexel's shoulders and we lifted him.

It was a bad thing to have to carry him the way we did. I realized that. But there was no alternative. Although I was pretty sure that he had broken no bones, I couldn't know whether he had internal injuries and the rough passage we gave him would do that kind of thing no good.

I didn't think much on the way back to the chateau. All my mind was concentrated on carrying Drexel, on easing the jolting and swinging as much as I could.

Dunwoody surprised me by his strength. For all his

roundness and plumpness he kept going, a dumpy Shet-
land pony of a man.

He was right about the chateau. When we got there it
was empty. In the hallway the lights were still burning.
I wondered when they had missed me. I tried to remember if I had left the cupboard door open when I had
quitted Gerard's room. If he had gone back there, full of
worry after Drexel's visit, he might have noticed it and
felt impelled to check on my safety. For all I knew he
might have noticed the apple and orange missing from
his table bowl. Anyway, miss me they had, and now we
had the chateau to ourselves.

We undressed Drexel and put him to bed in a room on
the ground floor. Dunwoody, who said he had had some
first aid training, went over him.

'Concussion,' he said. 'He'll come out of it, but I
wouldn't say when.'

We left him, still mumbling a little to himself, and I
locked the room door. Dunwoody cocked an eye at me,
but I offered no explanation then.

I said, 'What about his car and your motor-cycle?'

'They're on the other road. I can bring them round.
Means two trips. Or we could go together.'

'I don't want to take the risk of being seen on any
road yet. I don't want his car to stay there, either.'

'All right, I'll fetch 'em.' And then as he turned to
go, cheerful and willing, he paused and said, 'I ought to
go down to the police, you know. It's me duty.'

He may have been teasing or he may have wanted
to test me, to be sure that I was set in whatever plan I
had.

I said, 'I don't want you to do that. Not yet, anyway.'

'All right—but you got to promise to keep me out of
trouble.'

'I will.'

He put his hand into his pocket at that and he pulled
out Drexel's automatic.

'Here, you take this.'

I did, but I could not help saying, 'You trust me that far?'

He said brightly, 'It ain't just that. You come into this house and it don't take a telescope to see you've been here before. It's empty now, but maybe your friends ... or whatever you call them ... might come back. You'll feel better with that. Besides'—he grinned and patted his toupee straight—'it ain't a question of trust. Got a gun of me own. Never travel abroad without it.'

He was three hours making the two trips. He came back first with the motor-cycle and when I said, 'Can you manage the Bentley?' he replied, 'Drive anything on wheels,' and was off again, his short legs twinkling, a Tweedledum quite happy without a Tweedledee. Watching him go, I realized how grateful I was for his company and help. I'd been alone a long time. It was good to talk to someone other than myself.

I searched all over the chateau, but there was no one in the place. I went into every room, every tower and cellar. It was easy to see which had been Jabal's room. It was a little round, monkish kind of a cell in one of the towers, and he had amused himself by writing in pencil the pedigrees of his kidnappers all over the walls. He didn't know their names, but his characterization was clear enough. It was done in Arabic, colourful, fluent abuse, and I was sorry that it hadn't been done in French so they could have read it.

I found the kitchen, a long, white-tiled room on the right just inside the courtyard portal, and I opened a tin of chicken soup and warmed it up. I took it into Drexel and tried to get some of it down him. I think he took some but most of it dribbled over his chin. However, he seemed to have a better colour and was breathing easier and I think that for a moment his eyelids flickered as though he were trying to come back. I did not worry overmuch about him. He was hard and he would pull out of it.

I went back to the kitchen and found some food for

myself. While I was eating Dunwoody came and
joined me. We made some coffee and carried it outside
into the sunlit courtyard and sat on the seat by the wall.
We didn't talk right away. We just sat there busy with
our own thoughts and waiting for the right moment to
begin.

I stared across at the statue of Minerva and it was
hard to get my thoughts sorted out. Odd irrelevancies
came popping into my head. Minerva was wisdom and
she looked pretty serious about it. But if I went round to
the other side of her, she'd be different: a kind, understanding creature. No help at all. I didn't want any
double-faced woman. I wanted to know which was the
true Minerva. True wisdom was what I wanted at this
moment and it was hard to come by. One thing about
her, I thought, was that she wore her helmet with a
more natural carriage than Dunwoody wore his *Invita
Minerva* ... that was an echo from some drowsy afternoon in form and not one of the boys a damn bit interested. *Invita Minerva ... against the grain.* I remembered
now how it had come up; the use of Latin tags in English
composition. To do something against the grain, or something for which nature has not fitted you. Horace, *Ars
Poetica* 1.385. That was my card index memory.

But the thing I wanted to do now was in my nature, the
trouble was to find the right way the grain went and to
go with it. What I wanted to do was to pull Drexel's
chestnuts out of the fire. He was in my hands and he
would have no choice but to do as I told him. But if I
knew what I wanted to do, I was far from certain how to
do it. The ways and means were beyond me at the
moment. A great deal depended on how much co-
operation I could get from Dunwoody. I sat there trying
to sort it out. Drexel wasn't the only person I was concerned with. I was thinking, too, of Sophie. If this thing
could be hushed up she would be untouched. As far as
the police were concerned if the full truth came out
she was as guilty as Drexel or any of the others. I sat
there becoming more than ever convinced that the truth

must not be known. I wanted it hidden for Drexel's
sake, for Sophie's sake, and so for my own. With Drexel's
help there must be some way of tracing where Gerard
and the rest had taken Jabal. If I could get Jabal back
I would talk to him like a Dutch uncle and I felt I knew
him well enough to bet on his playing the game my way.
Drexel and I between us could cook up some story of
his having rescued me and Jabal from the chateau but
the kidnappers had got away and we had no means of
identifying them. It would work, I knew. Drexel's word,
and my word and Jabal backing us up . . . No one would
doubt us. And even if they did there would not be a
damn thing they could do about it. But how was I to
find Jabal? Drexel might know where they would have
taken him. They obviously had had to act on their own
initiative when they had discovered my escape. Gerard
was probably sick with worry at this moment. Parti-
cularly as he thought Drexel was on his way to Paris for
a few days.

My more immediate worry was Dunwoody. What was
I going to tell him? I'm a fair judge of men and so far
he had impressed me as a reasonable sort, no fool, and
certainly not hide-bound or stiff with rectitude. In the
end I decided to tell him the truth. At least as much as I
thought he ought to know. I would say nothing to him
about the relationship between Sophie and myself (that
belonged to me and I didn't want him to have cause to
think it might be my real reason for covering up for
Drexel).

If my plan did not work—if for any reason we could
not get Jabal back, I didn't know what was going to
happen. We could still cook up a story to keep Drexel
cleared. Gerard would get his ransom money and Jabal
would return. Jabal had no idea, I was sure, that Drexel
had organized the kidnapping, and if he pointed an accus-
ing finger at me I could clear myself by proving I was
framed and Drexel would say he had rescued me. But I
did not let myself think much about the plan failing.
It had to work.

It was at this point that Dunwoody said to me:

'Who is that old girl?'

I said, 'She's Minerva. The goddess of wisdom. She's supposed to have been born, fully clothed and full grown, through the left ear of Jupiter.'

He said, 'Obstetrics have altered since those days.' And then with a grin, he went on, 'She ought to wear her nightdress inside that coat of armour. Warmer that way.'

I said, 'Why were you following Colonel Drexel?'

For answer he fished inside his open leather jacket and produced a rather dirty card. It read—

The Dunwoody Detective Agency
Discreet
Confidential
Divorce Work a Speciality
Ex-Metropolitan Police.

In one corner was a North London address.

I could not help it. I laughed. Anyone less like a detective than Dunwoody I could not imagine. But that's how it should be.

I said, 'You were never in the Metropolitan Police. You're not tall enough.'

'True. That's me brother, Albert. He really runs the business. I'm the second hangman.'

'How does this tie up with the Colonel?'

'His wife. The second one. She wants a divorce and he won't give it to her. Too busy to bother is his line. But he was sure he wasn't behaving for all that. So here I am. Must say I haven't got anything to put in the old notebook so far.'

I knew the Colonel had this kind of trouble. In fact I'd heard long before I left England that he separated from his wife.

'How did you know he was going to be at the Villa Marubu?' I asked.

His eyes twinkled. 'You should be in this business. From you, of course. Or rather, your landlady.'

I remembered now that I had given my address to my landlady in case anything had gone wrong.

'And how did you know about me?'

'Take nothing for granted, do you?' But it was said kindly.

'Not at the moment. I've got too much on my hands. But I'll be equally frank with you in a moment.'

'Fair enough. We been watching the Grosvenor Square house for some time. Saw you go there twice and then the Colonel hops it and we can't find him. So we did a routine check on you. If I may say so you've got what I would call a gabby landlady. Told me your address and all about you.'

'And so you came to France? Just on the strength of my address?' I did not know this man and I had to be careful. I had to be sure. There was irony in it for if anyone should have been suspicious it was he.

'Not as easy as that. Albert was all against it. Wild goose chase, he said. But then he's not a romantic man, and he didn't need a holiday. I am and I did. So I talked him into it. I was right, too. Except that there were'nt no lady. But, correct me if I'm wrong, I've an idea I've tumbled into something much more interesting?'

I said, 'You have. I'm going to put myself in your hands.'

He looked down at his pudgy hands as though he was not sure whether he wanted them full of me.

'I've said my piece. Let's hear yours.'

I hesitated for a moment. It was hard to begin, and now the time had come I was suddenly full of doubt, not doubt of him, but of the whole plan. Putting it into words was going to make it sound quixotically stupid. Some trick of sun and shadow on Minerva's face seemed to make her frown and I knew she wasn't on my side. I knew that she would say and probably in Horatian metres, 'Don't be a clot. Go straight to the police and let Drexel take whatever is coming to him.' That was wisdom. Something told me that we don't live by wisdom. It doesn't warm any heart.

I plunged. I told him the whole story, except the pieces about myself and Sophie. He was a good listener. Never asked a question and, as I talked, I could see he was with me. I began to realize that it is a heart of gold that puts that kind of twinkle into a man's eyes. He heard me right through and when I had finished he was silent for a while. He sat there with his fat lips pursed, making a little nodding motion of his head that caused helmet and toupee to slide. He stood up and thrust his hands in his trouser pockets and took a few paces up and down. Then he stopped in front of me.

He said very soberly, 'You ain't going to like me for this. But I got to say it. In fact I got to say two things. And you ain't going to like me for either.'

'I like you already,' I said. And I meant it. Not just because I wanted his help. 'You can say anything you like.'

'All right. One. You're a bloody fool. You'll never pull this off. You should go right to the police.'

'I can't do that.'

'Sure?'

'Yes.'

'All right. Good enough for me. Now—two. I'll string along with you on one condition. If it comes off I want a hundred pounds for my trouble and a fair share of any reward money going.'

I stood up, and my heart was lighter than it had been for many a long time, I was with him and I understood him. In fact, I told myself, if I hadn't asked for money, if he hadn't kept one eye on the main chance, I should have been uncertain of him.

I said, 'It's a deal.'

He grinned and said, 'And a bloody silly one. But then, I was always one for a crazy deal. Well, all you got to do now is to avoid fifty thousand police looking for you —and pretty soon for the Colonel, too—and find Jabal. That shouldn't be difficult for a superman. Ask me and I'd say you'd better invite Mrs Minerva over to make up the quorum.'

With that he walked back to the kitchen and very soon I heard him rattling the dishes as he washed up from our meal. And, although I had no idea what to do at that moment, it was somehow comforting to hear him in there. I was not alone.

I sat there and wondered how long it would be before the Colonel came out from his coma. So far as I could see there wasn't a thing I could do until then.

That afternoon while Dunwoody sat with the Colonel in case he came round, I poked about the chateau again. It would have been hard to say exactly what I was looking for, but at the back of my mind I began to have a conviction that somewhere there might be one solid piece of information that would help me enormously. The thing I had to know, of course, was where Jabal had been taken. To answer that it was obvious that I had to know all I could about Gerard, Sarrasin and the others. And the curious thing was that I felt that between them all there was some exceptional bond. They were not so much individuals but a group and wherever one was would be found also the others. Even Sophie came into this enclave.

Ignoring the main facts of the kidnapping and my own framing ... all of which were clear enough now to me ... I went back over the small details which still puzzled me for in them—perhaps undeservedly—I felt there lurked the other truth I now had to have. I think I was doing this because I was half afraid that the Colonel might be too long coming round, or that when he did he would refuse to co-operate or might not be able to offer much. In that case I would be on my own. That being so it was wise to act now as though I were on my own.

I had already gone through his clothes. But he carried nothing which seemed to help me; money, keys and in his wallet only the usual dog-eared junk of letters and club membership cards that men hang on to. There was even a very old letter from me asking for a character reference just after I had left the army. On the back he

had scribbled in pencil the draft of his testimonial. I
had never seen it before and I smiled at one sentence in
it and wondered how the school governors had taken it.
'A man of high intellectual integrity and one whose
personal qualities are outstanding. In my opinion he
will be wasting himself in the teaching profession, but's
that's what he wants to do—and he takes a lot of stopping.' Loose in an inside pocket was a small piece of
paper that did seem to have something to say but I could
not fathom it. It was just a short list of figures and
numbers.

PE	2 — 7
PV	9 — 11
LB	12 — 14
BM	16 — 21

It meant nothing to me unless it was the key to some
code, or the letters might be initials, but the only one
that seemed to fit anyone I knew was the PV which
might have stood for Paviot. The first and last set of
numbers had an interval of five between them, and the
middle two an interval of two. It was a neat pattern
which inclined me to think it was some code key. Even
so, it gave me no help. In addition it was so crumpled and
dirty it might have been in his pockets for months.

I went down the gravelled drive as far as the lodge
gate, following the telephone line to see where it had been
cut, and as I walked in the sun I tried to marshal everything neatly in my head ... the things which I did not
understand.

Why hadn't the dogs barked when Sarrasin and Fargette had come that evening to carry off Jabal? They
always barked at me when I came in, but that evening
the old bitch hound by my side had done no more than
growl softly as the boat came inshore. The only answer
I could give to that one was that Drexel had got the dogs
from Sarrasin and Fargette originally and the dogs, knowing them, had kept quiet. Which led to the next point.

Here in the chateau there had been the afternoon noise, dogs barking, people laughing, and that distant, hollow *thud, thud*. In my walks around the grounds I had never seen a dog, but I knew now that there had been dogs here for behind the kitchen there was a run of kennels and all the signs pointed to the recent presence of animals. Something told me that the dogs were important. What were they, hunting dogs, watchdogs?

Something, I was sure, held all these people together. I recalled Gerard talking to Sarrasin. 'Everything is falling to pieces and we have to take the cheapest ... that's no way to get anywhere. All my life I have wanted to do it big ...' That didn't sound like a man who just wanted money for itself ... money was a means to feed some ambition. But what?

I didn't achieve anything except to pile up a stack of questions which just confused me.

Just this side of the gates I found where the line had been cut. However, I made no attempt to put the wire right. I had no need of the telephone yet.

I returned to the chateau and went over it again. This time I made more discoveries, probing and poking and getting into a state of mind which reminded me of the days when I used to do *The Times* crossword puzzle, priding myself always to do it in less than sixty minutes flat, and finding myself looking at the last empty space, the clue hammering in my head and knowing I had the answer there ... just over the border of memory, so near and so far, but knowing that in a moment it would come flashing into sight.

Only this was no crossword puzzle. This was Drexel and Sophie, and my own arrogant determination to put things right. Or as right as they could be. A shabby knight-errant, I thought, in a ripped and scorched tweed jacket and dirty flannels. But I was not sure even whether I was acting out of chivalry or self-interest. I didn't care much. If self-interest was the reason I'd settle for that. I just knew what I had to do.

In Gerard's room the only thing I found was in the

wastepaper basket. It was a small page, torn from a
loose-leaf pocket book, stuck right through with a pencil,
crumpled and smelling of the cigarette dog-ends that
littered the basket. On it in a tight, hard hand which
might have been Gerard's since anxious, fretting people
often write concisely, taking a pleasure in dragooning
their words even if they can't control their fears, were
a few notes in French:

>   Sunday. Karimba. Cut nails.
>   I. Myna   3000 frs.
>   Golden-eye   2150 frs.
>   Remember money due on Arab.

Here was Karimba again, from whom the others took
their cue. Was Karimba an Arab? Man or woman? I.
Myna and Golden-eye meant nothing unless Gerard was
a betting man and they were race-horse names with the
amounts he had lost or won. Cut nails left me floundering. And what money was due on what Arab? Did this
refer to Jabal?

Going over the chateau it was clear to me that they
had taken the place unfurnished. Except for their unmade
beds they had left little sign of their occupancy. In a
closet opening off the hall there was a large and dirty
celluloid collar hanging over a corner of the mirror.
Sophie's room I knew at once because it was full of her
perfume. I stood there looking at the bed in which she
had slept and suddenly she seemed to be in the room
with me. I wanted her more than I wanted anything at
that moment. I didn't care a damn what she had been or
what she had done. I didn't care about the past, about
morality, right or wrong, about anything except the
future and the force in me to pluck her from whatever
tangle held her and to carry her away with me.

There was a small white button on the floor which had
been pulled from a dress or a jumper. I picked it up and
put it in my pocket. It was good to have something
which had been hers on me. It was silly, I knew, but if

that was the way love took one then I believed in it and didn't care who knew my silliness.

I went down into the courtyard, had a word with Dunwoody on my way and strolled around trying to sort things out. The Colonel was easing into a quiet sleep but he was still as communicative as a log.

I walked around so many times that I shouldn't have been surprised if Minerva had told me to shut up, that I was making her giddy. And then, a little way up from the kitchen door, I saw something. I had my eyes on the ground. Maybe when I'd passed the spot before I had been staring moodily ahead. On the gravel, quite close to the wall which at this spot was made up of a smooth run of planks forming part of a lean-to coal store for the kitchen, was a scattering of cigarettes. But they were very odd cigarettes. None of them was complete. Most seemed to have been cut in half or to have had the last third cut off them. The pieces lay about the ground quite haphazardly and were clearly not cigarette-ends dropped from some waste-paper basket for none of them had been smoked. I picked a few up and saw that they were a very cheap brand. The thing beat me. I glanced over at Minerva. But she was no help.

CHAPTER FOURTEEN

I was getting nowhere fast. The Colonel just lay as good as a corpse on his bed and did nothing to help us get soup or brandy into him. Maybe it was the wrong treatment for concussion.

Dunwoody and I knocked up a meal of sorts in the kitchen that evening. I was not very good company because there was too much on my mind, mostly a feeling that time was going by and that time was valuable. From a map he had Dunwoody showed me the situation of the chateau. We were dead in the middle of a hilly triangle of country which had for its corners Le Perthus, Le Boulou and Amelie Les Bains. It was well over forty kilometres back to Banyuls-sur-Mer.

As we ate I gave Dunwoody an account of all the things I had discovered. He was a professional detective. If anyone could make anything of them, then he should. But he shook his head.

'Your only hope is the Colonel,' he said. 'By tomorrow morning maybe he'll be round.'

'I don't like sitting here doing nothing.'

'Neither do I. What is more, Albert's going to have a few words to say when he hears about this.'

'You aren't going to tell Albert a thing about this. This is between us.'

He didn't say anything for a while. He just looked at me, chewing away at a piece of brown bread he had spread thick with Brie. Then reaching for a glass of wine, he said, 'All right. I understand how you feel. If Albert was to cross me up the way the Colonel did you ... I know how it would be. I'd kick his guts out first and then do all I could for him.'

We found a bottle of whisky—I should think it was part of the store got in for me—and helped ourselves liberally to it before we went to bed. Under the influence of the whisky I began to let things slip from my mind a bit. Dunwoody was good company and his professional stories were very funny.

That night I slept on a mattress in the Colonel's room. I spread it on the floor close to his bed so that if he came round I could get to him easily. I went off to sleep easily. Dunwoody had found himself a bunk in one of the other bedrooms.

It must have been well after midnight when I was awakened. I got up and switched on the light. The Colonel was sitting up in bed with his hands against his forehead and he was moving his head slowly to and fro. The movement and the fact that his eyes were screwed up tight gave me the impression that he was suffering from a frightful headache. He probably was.

I sat by him, and reaching for a glass of water from the bed-table, said quietly, 'Here, drink this.'

He opened his eyes and quite normally put out his hand and took the glass. He drank it all in one long movement and I saw the rise and fall of his Adam's apple against the leathery skin of his throat.

I took the glass back. He sat there staring straight in front of him and his eyes had that bright, out-of-this-world look which I remembered from the time long ago when he had come a cropper from his horse and lost his memory.

Very gently, I said, 'How do you feel?'

And very quietly he replied with a scurrilous Arab phrase which answered my question but was quite untranslatable.

I said, 'You're at Chateau Minerve. You're all right. I'm looking after you.'

He said, dully, 'Who the hell are you?'

I said, 'I'm David. David Fraser.'

He frowned at this and it was clear that I meant nothing to him.

I went on, 'You know who you are, don't you?'

He said nothing. Then he shook his head. It was uncanny and disturbing. I'd known this kind of thing before and in a way I understood it. But, even so, something

turned over inside me unpleasantly as I sat there with a
Drexel who was out of touch, not only with the world,
but with his own personality.

I said, 'You're Colonel Francis Drexel and I'm David
Fraser, your friend.'

I could say that last and still mean it. I was his friend.
I was for him whether I wanted to be or not. I was
beginning to understand that friendship isn't something
you come to the end of easily.

He said, 'I wish this room would keep still.' And his
voice was suddenly guttural as though the words wanted
to slip back down his throat all the time. He dropped
stiffly to his pillows, lay there for a while with his eyes
open and then was asleep.

I let him be. I kept the light on and stayed awake for
maybe two hours, but he showed no further signs of
coming round. In the end I got back on to my mattress
and dropped off.

Dunwoody woke me about six with a great mug of
steaming coffee. He was a good soul. Just having him
around did things for me.

I told him about the Colonel's waking up in the night.

He said, 'That's a good sign. Today, maybe, we'll get
some sense out of him.' He went over and stooped above
the Colonel. He was still sleeping. He shook him gently
by the shoulder but there was no response. He rolled back
his lids and looked into his eyes.

I said, 'The last time he took a bang like that he had
amnesia for two days.'

He shook his head at this. 'Let's hope he cuts something
off his record this go. Funny box of eggs the brain. Albert
had a chum who started to drive himself mad about
fire. Couldn't smoke, couldn't strike a match, a flame or
a light drove him to a jelly. He was headin' straight for
the nut house. Then they took a bit of bone out of his
skull, relieved some pressure ... You should see him now.
Don't care a damn. Smokes in bed, burns holes in his
sheets and suits, and he's been black-listed as a bad risk
by every fire insurance company in the City. But he's

happy. Took a job on the London Fire Brigade.'

I laughed, not believing a word of it, but knowing it was meant to cheer me up.

He took over and I went off to have a wash and a breather. There was a radio in the kitchen and I switched this on while I was having a second mug of coffee. I got the news from Paris. It mentioned the Jabal disappearance, but there was nothing of importance. The French police were working away at it. Apparently Drexel had not been missed yet, or if he had the police were not letting it be known. I wondered how Didier was making out.

I went back to the Colonel's room. As I approached it I heard the sound of someone talking and a swift hope leapt up in me.

But when I went in the Colonel was stretched out flat and Dunwoody was sitting in a chair by the bed.

'I thought I heard someone talking,' I said.

He grinned. 'So you did. Trying a new treatment. I sit here and I keep saying aloud, 'Come on. Wake up, you old bastard! Wake up!' Thought maybe it would reach down into his subconscious. You never know.'

I said, 'If he doesn't make sense by lunch-time I've got to do something. I can't sit here for ever.'

'If he don't come round there's only one thing you can do.'

I knew what he meant.

'That's the last thing I want to do.'

'You're going to be bloody unpopular with the police if you do have to go to 'em in the end. They won't like the wasted time.'

'I couldn't help them much, even now. They've got a description of all the men, except Gerard. And as long as Drexel's unconscious he's no good to them.'

'You're the boss.'

I began to feel that even though Dunwoody was going to get a hundred pounds, win-or-lose, he was forming the opinion that I was playing a poor hand. I hadn't even got one card that looked like a winner.

The Colonel did not come round by lunch time and I started to ask myself seriously if I should give it all up and go to the police. By all the rules it was what I should have done; but every instinct in me was against it. I told myself that by hanging on for a while I was not doing anyone harm, and the chance might come to clear up the whole mess tidily. Jabal was safe enough for a while. The worst that was intended for him was ransom and a return to safety. It would only be when Gerard failed to get any word from Drexel—and that was a few days off yet—that he would start to panic. What he would do then, I didn't know. He might turn Jabal loose ... I tried to believe this, but at the back of my mind I was worrying that he might do far worse. However, I had some days' grace yet.

But no matter what I told myself, I began to worry. I was in the unhappy position of wanting to do the wrong thing for the right-to-me motives. My common sense fought against my instinct.

I mooched around, coming back now and again to look at the Colonel. He lay there, sleeping or in a light coma, and he was useless to me. I began to feel angry towards him. He was the man I wanted to help and I could do nothing without him. I wanted to shake him into life. More than once I was on the point of sending the whole thing to hell and going for the police. I only had to get into the Colonel's car and the thing would be done in an hour. I even went and sat in his car; testing myself, knowing I only had to reach out a hand for the switch. But I couldn't do it. Not even if I painted for myself a picture of Jabal with his throat cut in a few days' time when Gerard found himself alone without guidance or instructions. But I still could not touch the switch.

Dunwoody went off on his motor-cycle during the afternoon to get some provisions for the kitchen. He did not bring much back and I could guess why. He didn't think we were going to be here long, but he said nothing.

That evening we had no whisky, but we finished a flask of wine he had bought. When it was time for bed, he insisted on taking his turn sleeping with the Colonel. I found myself a bed in a small room overlooking the courtyard. Before leaving Dunwoody for the night, I made up my mind suddenly. It was no good drifting.

Standing at the door of the Colonel's room, I said, 'If he doesn't come round tomorrow, I'm going to the police. I'll give him until the evening. After that I've finished playing around.'

Dunwoody pursed his fat lips and then said, 'If it had been me, I'd have gone today.'

I went up to my bed and for a while I stared out into the courtyard. There was a moon and Minerva looked cold and distant. I had no affection for her. Tomorrow, maybe, I was going to be wise and without pity—like her. I got into bed and had a hard time persuading sleep to come.

It must have been well on towards morning when I woke. I was suddenly alert and I knew that I had not come out of sleep naturally. I sat up and listened and away in the distance there was the faint drone of an airplane. I wondered if it had come over the chateau and disturbed me. During the day quite a few aircraft came over and I guessed we must be on some airline route. But at the back of my mind I did not believe that I had been awakened by the machine. I got up and went to the window. The moon was gone and there was a greyness outside like the belly of a tabby-cat. A little scud of mist was floating over the surface of the courtyard and Minerva rose above it. She would. She rose above everything. I disliked her more than ever. I thought I saw something moving in the mist, but the mist itself curled and lifted gently and might have been an enormous blanket held on the backs of a slow-pulsing crowd. Mist can play hell with a suspicious mind. Sentries have wasted thousands of rounds of ammunition mowing down the attack of advancing mist.

But I was uneasy and I went down. I walked around the courtyard and out to the gravel space under the judas tree.

There was no one about and far away the first cock was jabbing away at the morning to waken it. I came back and, switching on the light looked in on Dunwoody and the Colonel. They were both asleep. I had to smile at Dunwoody; false teeth in a little glass and his toupee balanced on the knob of a chair. The Colonel was snoring unattractively and he looked grey and old and really not worth bothering about. That I thought was the trouble with life, half the things we bothered about weren't worth it. I took this banal thought back to bed and slept soundly until the sun was up and striking hot through the window.

When Dunwoody came into the kitchen where I was making coffee, he said cheerfully, 'Well, this is the day.'

He made it sound like the morning of a school treat or an important cricket match.

'You're glad?'

'I think you're doing the right thing. He's showing no signs. Tell you what I'll do, too—I'll cut that hundred to fifty. I don't feel I've earned more. After lunch, too, I'm going down the village to send Albert a telegram. He'll be worried not hearing from me. All right by you?'

'Yes. If we've got no sense out of him by then.'

I sat with the Colonel that morning, but there was little hope in my mood. Not even when he woke up. He just lay there with his eyes open, staring in front of him. I talked to him, tried to bring him back, but when he did answer it was in a stupid, confused way and he was obviously lost in some other world. I began to wonder whether he was not more badly injured than I thought. I tried not to tell myself that the kindest thing I could do would be to get a doctor to him. After about half an hour I could see the fatigue cloud his eyes and then he was sleeping again.

I was not going to get anything from him. That was clear. Not that day. And today was my limit.

After lunch Dunwoody got on his motor-cycle to go down to the village—it was about six miles away—to send his telegram. As near as damn-it I got on the back

with him, but even then something held me back. I had
said I would wait until the evening and I felt tied to my
limit. Dunwoody looked at me and I knew what he was
waiting for, but I waved him off and he went down the
roadway, bouncing like a fat elf on the powerful
machine.

Ten minutes later I was glad I had not gone with him
for I came across something which made me feel that my
luck was turning. I went back into the kitchen to clear
away the lunch things. I washed up our few plates and
knives and forks. We'd had mortadella sausage and a
salad Dunwoody had made. There was a kitchen garden
full of stuff. The bin for scraps stood near the sink and
I was just going to toss into it some bits of skin from the
sausage when a splash of coloured paper in the bin caught
my eye. It was well down at the bottom and the paper
was damp. All I saw at first was the head and shoulders
of a tiger snarling, arresting in orange, black and red.
I bent down and retrieved it. If I had any reason for
doing it than it was an idle one. My mind was in a dull
state, the colour attracted me. I spread it out on the sink
board. It was a largish handbill, splotched with damp
and grease as though it had been used for wrapping food.

I stood there, staring down at it. Across the top was a
large banner: *GRAND CIRQUE PYRÉNÉEN*. Underneath was a picture of four performing tigers in a cage.
Three of them were seated on high stools and the fourth
was flying through the air towards a paper hoop held by
a herculean character in a leopard skin, waxed moustaches and glossy black hair. Underneath the picture
were a few lines of the usual exaggerated circus adver-
tising stuff, and then in a small box the legend—*Visitez-
le à Banyuls-sur-Mer le 16–21 Avril.*

But the thing which held my eye and in some way
began to stir up my dulled mind was the lion- or tiger-
tamer person. He was magnificent. And around his waist,
to hold his leopard skin he wore a belt. It was the belt
which said something to me. It was a black belt with a
curious-shaped buckle. The reproduction was bad and

garish, but it was clear enough to wake my memories
and I knew where I had seen a belt like this. Sarrasin
had worn one on the night I had been abducted. And
this man might easily be an idealized picture of Sarrasin,
plus waxed moustaches and a black wig.

Why not, I asked myself? Long ago I remembered
thinking that Sarrasin was a boxing-booth type from a
country fair. But an animal trainer in a third-rate circus
was just as good. All these people I had told myself
recently belonged to a group. Why not a circus? And if
they did, that would account for the strange silence about
the chateau at night when I had been kept here. They
had to go off to their performances. Only on Sundays—
when the changed pitches or rested—would they be free
of that. And there *had* been one day when the chateau
had not been silent during the evening. And what more
likely if they were coming up here each day and bringing food with them that they would wrap it in a circus
handbill?

I did not stop to think about it any more. It was a
chance, and a good one, I felt. At once I knew I was not
going to the police until I had tried it. There was a calendar in the kitchen. The Banyuls-sur-Mer dates were the
16th to the 21st April. Today was the 18th, a Wednesday.

I started to get ready at once. Dunwoody could stay
here and look after the Colonel while I went to Banyuls
for the performance that evening. Banyuls was just over
forty kilometres—twenty-five miles—away. There was
an old bicycle in the shed by the gates and I could make
the distance on that easily. In the staff quarters behind
the kitchen I found a beret and an old pair of blue workman's overalls. It was no good thinking of using the
Colonel's car. The police knew that too well. And if I
were dressed as a working man, then Dunwoody's
motor-cycle with its GB plates was out of the question
... anyway, I was not pressed for time. The main thing
was to keep clear of the police. The last thing they would
expect would be to find me riding a bicycle. They saw

me as the clever, well-organized kidnapper tucked safely away in some retreat until my plans had worked out.

I looked fairly natural in the overalls, but I decided against the beret. One thing an Englishman cannot wear convincingly is a beret. I found instead an old motoring cap of the Colonel's in his car, mucked it up with grease and dirt, and pulled that on. I don't know what I looked like, but certainly not myself.

I was all ready to go when Dunwoody returned. I told him of my discovery and the chance I was going to take. I could see at once he did not like it.

'I don't say you're not on to something. But the police'll pick you up. Let me go.'

'But you don't know these people. I'll be all right. And if I'm not back by tomorrow morning—you go to the police.'

He argued for a bit, but in the end I persuaded him.

'All right. But take your revolver with you—and watch yourself.'

He came down to the lodge gates with me fussing cheerfully. He wanted me to take his motor-cycle but I was against this. For all I knew the police might have a line on him and be watching for his machine. To take it as far afield as Banyuls would be madness. Besides, I had plenty of time and I was looking forward to the ride. I put Dunwoody's map in my pocket and off I went.

The simple fact of moving, of going forward, did things to my spirits. I was not thinking too much of what I should do if I established that Gerard and company were at the circus. That could wait. All I knew was that once I found them I would have a chance of tracing Jabal, and when I knew that then Dunwoody and I—and Drexel if he was able—would make a plan of action.

It was bad cycling country, up and down hill the whole time, but I was in no hurry. I had worked out a route on the map which would eventually bring me by the back road down into Banyuls. I had no wish to show myself on the coast road.

As I cycled along I remembered the scrap of paper

I had found in the Colonel's wallet. I pulled it out and examined it and I knew the circus was not going to disappoint me. I realized now that it was a list of the places, with dates, at which the circus was playing that month. BM was Banyuls-sur-Mer; PE—Perpignan; PV—Port-Vendres, and LB was Le Boulou. Drexel had the list so that he would know where to find them at any time during the month. I wondered how Drexel had got to know them and why he had brought them into his plan. *Cirque Pyréréen* meant that they probably played a circuit that covered the central and southern part of France. From Perpignan down the coast and then right across to Biarritz and maybe up as far as Bordeaux ... And then I remembered that at one time Drexel had been dropped in France for work with the resistance movement and that he had come out over the border into Spain. Maybe he had met up with Sarrasin or Gerard then.

Some ten miles short of Banyuls I was thirsty and went into a small *estaminet* called *Le Point du Jour* for a drink. It was in a hamlet of about six houses perched just below the bare, rocky shoulder of a hill. An old woman in man's boots and with her hair drawn back in a tight bun from her ancient face served me with a *blonde bière*. On one of the walls was a poster for the circus. It was the same as my handbill only larger. I asked her about the circus. I was the only one in the place and she had kept me company to see I didn't steal anything, though there was nothing in the place that would have fetched five hundred francs. She told me, grudgingly, that the circus came through these parts once every two years. She hadn't seen it herself, but her grandson went. He also went to the cinema in Banyuls once a month. She seemed to think he was too fond of entertainments and was still grumbling about him when I left. I felt I was on his side. He probably broke his back fourteen hours a day hoeing and tending the vines on some mountain slope and then had to help run the *Point du Jour* at night.

CHAPTER FIFTEEN

I tucked my bicycle away in the lee of a stone wall a couple of miles outside Banyuls and started to walk towards the town. I came to it by a footpath that led down the long flank of a hill behind it. I stopped half-way down the hill and made myself comfortable on a patch of turf, my back against a tree. I was hot and tired from the ride and it was good just to sit. It was seven o'clock and I knew the circus did not begin until eight when it would just be getting dark.

The town was spread out in a long line below me, red roofs and pink, ochre and white walls. Over the roofs I could just see the edge of the thin strip of sand, and away to the right the block of buildings which was the Arago Laboratory and Aquarium.

It seemed a long time ago that I had gone in there and met Sophie. And a whole lifetime since I had met Drexel in Wales and sacrificed gladly the Songa Manara project. There was bitterness in that thought. Still the sacrifice had brought me to Sophie. Drexel I had lost. But there was Sophie now ... I loved Sophie. It was the easiest statement in the world, and the most difficult to understand. I didn't try to understand it. I sat there hugging it and, for a little while, not worrying about the circus or what I would do—except that somehow I was going to haul Sophie out of it.

A couple of men came down the path. They passed me with hardly a glance. In these parts there was nothing strange in the sight of a workman stretched out on the grass having a rest. Now and again a car hooted in the town below and far out on the dusky horizon I saw the lights of one of the Port-Vendres streamers.

I waited until a quarter to eight and then I went down. It was just twilight and dark enough for me to feel that I did not have to walk with my head down to hide my face. The circus was camped on an open space at the back of the town, not far from the Banyuls stream which was now a succession of dirty pools fringed with tall reed and bamboo growths. I joined a trickle of people moving towards the open space.

Against the paling sky I could see the silhouette of the big top and the hunched backs of the parked caravans and mobile cages. It was a small circus and the first few caravans I passed wanted repainting badly. There were one or two sideshows and a small roundabout for children worked by a man turning a wooden wheel. There was nothing impressive about it, not even the crowd which was sparse. If Gerard had anything to do with this affair, I thought, then he would have plenty of worry over the receipts. I could hear his voice fretting away back in that room in the chateau ... *Everything is falling to pieces and we have to take the cheapest* ... And what was it he had said on the stairs as he passed me? *Tonight we are as poor as crows. But soon* ... He didn't know it, and I certainly hoped it, but disappointment was probably walking up to his paybox at this moment.

Some children came dashing through the sprinkling of crowd, chasing a dog and, as I stepped aside to avoid them, I bumped gently into someone.

A familiar voice, but now a little slurred with drink, said, '*Monsieur, vous voulez les espadrilles?*'

I half-turned and there was Jean Cagou. He was not quite so brisk and glossy as usual. He swayed a little as he opened his case and his hair was ruffled and the smile on his face was slipping all over the place.

I shook my head and was going to turn away when he caught my arm, protesting—

'But, monsieur has not seen—'

Then he broke off, peered forward and up, as though I were an umbrella and he wanted to come under it, and nearly fell into my arms. He went on, tripping over his tongue, 'But surely I know ...'

I grunted angrily and at the same moment gave his case a nudge which tipped some of his espadrilles to the ground. He gave a wail and sat down, gathering them up quickly to avoid their being trampled by the feet of the passers-by. I left him hurriedly and hoped that his tipsy mind would soon forget the encounter.

There was a queue formed at the paydesk before the large marquee and I joined the end of it. I had gone up about three places when I saw Dunwoody. He was standing a little apart near the paybox and looking down the queue. He saw me at the same time as I saw him, and with a nod of his head for me to join him, walked away.

I left the queue and went after him. He stopped in the lee of a flat-topped trailer and gave me a cheerful grin as I came up. I wasn't pleased to see him and I was at no pains to hide my feeling.

'What the hell are you doing here?'

'It's all right, Don't fly off the handle.'

'But why are you here? What about the Colonel?'

'He's all right. I've locked him in and I've got his clothes in my saddle-bags. He can't move. Anyway he's dead to the wide.'

'I still don't see—'

'You won't if you don't give me a chance to tell you. I got to thinking when you left. If anything went wrong down here ... somebody recognized you or something ... Well, then, you ain't mobile enough. Now, with me standin' by—you got speed. The old bike's just outside the grounds. It's sensible, you know. Anyway, two heads are better than one.'

I did not say anything for a moment, but I guessed I was not getting the full truth. He knew what I was thinking.

'What else?' I asked.

Dunwoody looked around at the parked caravans and trailers and said reflectively, 'If your hunch is right, Jabal might be here. Plenty of places to hide him.' He patted his leather jerkin. 'We've both got guns. We might be able to lift him this evening. You couldn't do it alone.'

I laughed. He might be pudgy and look like nothing, but he was game.

'You just didn't want to miss any fun!'

He nodded. 'That's true. Albert's always saying I'm too impetuous. But if you're going to do a thing—do it quick, I say.'

I gave in. 'All right. Let's go in.' I started for the pay-box.

He held out his hand. 'I got the tickets. Two. I've an idea the old boy in the paybox is your friend Gerard. He might have recognized you.'

He was right. The man in the paybox was Gerard. I went back and had a look from a safe distance. Even in the half-light and with the little of him that was visible there was no mistaking that scruffy, tufty hair and the thin tight-drawn face, cross-hatched with its anxiety lines.

Seeing him there, his head bobbing about and his hands scraping in the crumpled and dirty franc notes, did something for me, something that had been lacking for a long time. I came awake, came out of a dusty dream and everything became hard and clear. I was right. This was the place and these were the people. But more than anything else I knew that somewhere close at hand was Sophie and that no matter what happened I was going to see her. I was going to get her away and after that we were going to have Jabal. Everything was falling into place, everything was working for me and I knew my own luck well enough not to question it or to let any doubt in. This morning I had been in the doldrums. Now I was sailing.

Dunwoody and I went in. The real entrance to the big-top was masked by a small marquee which held a menagerie. It was lit by electric light that came from a generator that thumped away somewhere in the near distance. The crowd going into the circus passed first through the menagerie. Dunwoody and I circled slowly round with them and it was not long before I recognized two old friends. I Myna and Golden-eye. The first was an Indian myna bird—it didn't look like 3,000 francs worth, not for size or colour anyway—and the second was a golden-eyed pheasant, a beautiful cock bird, We walked around the cages. It was a poor show; a few monkeys with worn coats, a jackal that went round and round its pen practising for the mile walk, a honey bear, curled in a ball, and smelling like a damp rug. I know there are people who make a good case for caging animals, but they don't count with me. When I meet an animal that puts up a good case for being caged, I'll listen.

Dunwoody led the way in and we took seats in the front row below a small band which was raised on a wooden tier some way behind us. The ring was larger than I had expected. I kept my cap pulled well forward, but there was little danger of being recognized for the lighting, except in the ring centre, was poor. We sat there amidst the chatter and hum of voices and the band played selections from Offenbach and Verdi with more enthusiasm than style.

And within an hour I had seen them all, Fargette, Paviot, Sarrasin and Sophie. But if I had not known them and been there looking for them I should not have recognized them. Any policeman watching the show and with my descriptions of them in mind would have passed them over. In fact there was a policeman, the local gendarme from Banyuls, sitting about four places away from me. He must have had their descriptions from Didier, but he was enjoying himself, unworried by professional cares.

There were the usual acts; the band blaring away while a couple of trampolinists bounced up and down on their good-tempered bed; the long roll of the drum for the high-wire and the trapeze artists ... and then Fargette. He came in dressed in baggy clown's clothes and with a troupe of performing dogs. The dogs were all shapes and sizes, but there was a wolf-hound amongst them. His face was painted but there was no mistaking him and I saw that round his neck he wore an enormous celluloid collar like the one I had seen hanging in the toilet at the chateau. He put the dogs through a series of antics which they carried out with a quiet brisk indifference as though they disapproved of the whole thing. It was funny and the audience loved it. But I was remembering how the dogs

at the Villa Maruba had not barked, and also the noise
of barking and laughter in the afternoons at the Chateau
Minerve. Fargette must have been rehearsing, or training, a new act up there.

When the turn was finished the dogs went off but Fargette stayed behind, wiped his brow as though exhausted
and reached for a cigarette. He stood against a property
door and the spot-light isolated him from the surrounding darkness. As he reached to light his cigarette a knife
flew out of the darkness and cut the cigarette in half. The
knife thudded into the door. Fargette, clownlike, puzzled,
reached for another cigarette, but again a knife came
from the darkness and chopped it in half for him and
then the spotlight swung away from him to reveal a
man dressed in Mexican gaucho clothes, wide-brimmed
hat, and a belt festooned with knives.

I leaned over to Dunwoody and said, 'That's Paviot.'

'Handy with a knife,' said Dunwoody and I heard him
chuckle.

Paviot *was* handy with a knife, as handy as anyone I
had ever seen. As I watched him fling knives at Fargette,
outlining him against the door, I thought of the chopped
cigarettes I had picked up in the courtyard. Now ...
here, in the circus, seeing it all ... it was hard to realize
that I had been puzzled then.

Everything was clear now. Sarrasin came on with his
tigers. The clowns tumbled in horse-play about the ring
as the great cage was set up. Sarrasin was the man on
the circus poster and he was also my Sarrasin, a big,
splendid brute carrying his leopard skin more naturally
than any clothes. He put his tigers through their paces
and I could feel the power and the pride in the man and
there was no doubt that he was enjoying himself. But
that didn't make me like him any better. For Fargette I
had some sympathy, for Paviot disgust, but Sarrasin drew
hatred from me and I knew why. He had used his strength
contemptuously against Sophie and against me. I thought
of the day Sophie and I had lain together on the cliff
and of the dark bruise on her shoulder. I lit a cigarette

and for a while the great bowl of the ring was lost to me,
no more than a maze of shifting colours. Sophie whom I
loved, and Sarrasin whom I hated. Whatever else seemed
fantasy, those two things were hard and real. Against
them even my feeling for Drexel was wan and spiritless.
Drexel had gone out of my life in a sense when he had
mutilated our friendship. All I had for him now was a
charity which I could not avoid, but which I knew set
people apart.

It's not easy to get one's motives and reasons sorted
out, perhaps it was impossible for me to come to real
truth in this affair. I could only hang on to the easy things
that emerged from my thoughts ... my love for Sophie,
my hatred for Sarrasin and my compassion for Drexel
which I suspected drew its life from the other two. I
wished I had a clear, cold mind that could cut through
cant and deediness to truth. All I had was a hodge-podge
of half-baked thoughts and the conviction that that was
how most people were unless they were saints and could
command a spiritual ruthlessness and logic.

Dunwoody touched me on the shoulder and said, 'This
the girl?'

I came alive and said, 'Yes.'

'Thought she had dark hair?'

'It's a wig.'

Sophie's hair was silver. She was going round the ring
a foot on each of the backs of two white Arab horses.
They were lovely things, lovely with movement and
form that makes a horse not an animal but a divinity
and on their backs was a goddess. For me, anyway. She
wore a short, white, Greek-looking tunic with a green
belt and her dark hair was hidden by a tight-fitting silver
wig. She was straight from some grey and gold island
held by a wine-coloured sea. The vulgar crowd fell away,
the patched and stained canvas canopy rolled back and
the velvet night was full of heavy stars. She seemed to
float from one horse to another, part of a slow-moving,
graceful arabesque; she was neither maiden nor youth
but some wonderful equivocal being that an incautious

sound, a rude movement would startle into invisibility. I sat there holding my breath, stupid with love and un-critical adoration ... It sounds adolescent but for me it was a poetry in the blood and I didn't care who knew it. Time stood still without any awkwardness and the world stopped rolling without jolting a pebble out of place. Round and round she went and my eyes never left her.

When she had finished and gone out, I couldn't sit there. I had to go to her. I stood up. There were only a couple of people between me and the aisle.

Dunwoody held my arm for a moment and said, 'Where you going?'

'I'll be back in a moment,' I said and I pushed my way towards the aisle. I don't know how I got outside, through some slit in the canvas at the back of the seats I think. It was dark and the air was cool after the tent atmosphere. I could hear the generator pounding away and over its noise the crash and thunder of the band inside. Little lights showed in some of the caravans and a big arc light cast a great cone of pale yellow down by the main entrance to the marquee. Gerard, I thought, could count his money by it. Stepping over the stout guy ropes I went round to the back of the marquee towards the performers' entrance. Through the wide doorway of a small marquee I saw a circus hand holding the white Arabs ... *Remember money due on Arab.* It came to me now from Gerard's memorandum. Poor old Gerard, even the horses weren't fully paid for. How he must have jumped at Drexel's plan for some easy money.

And then, some way from the marquee, I saw the flash of a white tunic and a figure go up the short steps to a small trailer caravan.

I stood at the foot of the steps. The door was half-open for coolness and Sophie was sitting at a narrow dressing-table littered with make-up pots and odds and ends. She'd taken her wig off and thrown a dressing-gown over her shoulders, and she had her elbows on the table and was looking at herself in the mirror. Her legs were pushed out to one side of her chair and the pose was the same almost as the one she had had that first time I saw her. The princess who had lost her golden ball. Not unhappy but empty of hope.

I went up the steps and when I was inside I closed the door behind me. She turned and looked at me and at first I thought she hadn't recognized me because of my cap and the overalls. I pulled the cap off and smiled, but there was no need for that. She had recognized me but she was not believing it. She stood up and the dressing-gown fell back loosely from her shoulders and slid to the floor. It curled and twisted round her feet, and it was green and yellow and looked like a grass mound decked with flowers. Her skin was very brown against the white of her tunic and her face was very still with a fine-chiselled grace and firmness. The dark eyes which had been clouded with that familiar apprehension suddenly cleared and were bright and sparkling as though there was distant candlelight behind them ... That's how she was for me.

I said, 'Sophie.' But it wasn't a name or word. It was the movement of love in me.

She came into my arms and she rested there, not trembling, not excited, a bird coming down from the air, settling its wings and feathers, coming home; and the breath from her mouth as she raised it to me was a sigh which expressed all happiness and yet, too, the gentle ease of a long fatigue passing.

She was back at her dressing-table and I sat at the foot of her narrow bunk. I could see her face in the small mirror as she leaned forward and absently repaired her make-up. For the moment there were no more words between us; just that tranquil silence in which she turned and smiled at me and reached back her hand to take mine. There was no world for me but this caravan, four hundred and fifty cubic feet of happiness, the chintz curtains tied with ribbons, an ivory crucifix above the mirror, a row of books, a blue and white stove and a curtain in a corner half-drawn back to show dresses, costumes and an untidy jumble of shoes.

Then she said, 'At first they were all sure you would go to the police. But there was nothing on the radio, nothing in the newspapers. Gerard was worried and they quarrelled among themselves ... all wanting to do different things, until last night when he came. Where were you?'

I sat there, not really listening to her words but to her voice with its faint huskiness and the odd, affectionate thought in my mind that when she had a cold it would sound like a croak....

I said, 'I didn't go to the police for a lot of reasons. You ... I wanted to find you first.'

Her hand tightened on mine and she went on, 'I was sure something terrible had happened to you. Otherwise, why should they have been so confident after he came? They wouldn't tell me anything today. I wanted to know but I daren't ask, daren't show what I was feeling. That's why when you walked in I couldn't believe it at first. Not after last night.'

I came back from the mists and said sharply, 'What are you talking about? What about last night?'

'I was in Gerard's caravan. I do the accounts with him and it must have been two o'clock when he walked in. They sent me away. But today everything was different. Gerard and the others like new men ... So confident. We've got a poor crowd tonight, and normally Gerard would be frantic. But he doesn't care.'

I said, 'Listen, Sophie, I'm at sea. Who is this "he" you're talking about? And why shouldn't he walk in and why anyway should it make you think anything had happened to me?'

'Who?' I saw the surprise on her face. 'Haven't you been listening to me?'

'Of course I have. But you've just said he. What he?'

She stood up and I honestly believe she thought I was teasing her.

'Colonel Drexel, of course, David.'

'What?'

I was on my feet in a flash.

I took her by the shoulders and I almost shouted, 'Has he been here? Colonel Drexel? No—he can't have been!'

She said, 'What's the matter, David? Why shouldn't he? He'd only gone to Paris they told me. Why shouldn't he come back?'

But her words now were only a wash of sound in my ears. Drexel had been here last night! I didn't get it. If someone had struck me hard between the eyes I couldn't have been more dazed. I stood there looking at her stupidly, but the stupidity didn't last. It exploded in a blast of anger that was almost physical. Drexel. The damned, black-hearted, devious snake! Here I'd been sweating my guts out and walking the edge for him and all the time ...

My face must have been an ugly sight for she suddenly shook me and said, 'David, don't look like that. Tell me what is it? You make me feel afraid again.'

'It's all right,' I said.

It was the understatement of the century. But I couldn't go into it all with her now.

I stood there with my hands on her shoulders and she waited for me, afraid for me. And at that moment I am not sure that there was no fear in me. Drexel had been here the previous night. And then I saw it, saw how I had underrated him, underestimated the devilry and the courage of the man. He had started to play for high stakes and when the game had gone against him he had staked higher. He had come out of his coma. He had recognized me all right, but he had gone on playing the invalid ... He must have enjoyed that. Me, sitting there, itching for him to come to his senses and he laughing, knowing that he was immobilizing me and waiting for his chance. And he had taken it last night. He must have slipped out, leaving Dunwoody sleeping, wheeled the motor-cycle down the drive and been away to Gerard. It was a hell of a risk ... but just the kind of risk that delighted him. I knew now that I had not been mistaken when I thought I heard someone in the courtyard. It was Drexel, and he must have got back into bed only a few seconds before I looked in on him.... I swore to myself and couldn't help admiring the audacity of the man. This was the kind of thing which had made him a public hero ... And I saw it all. Last night he had made his arrangements with Gerard ... and tonight, after the show, the whole gang was to come down on Dunwoody and myself and restore the *status quo*. But the plan would be a little different now. Neither Dunwoody nor myself would survive the ransoming of Jabal.

Sophie said, 'You haven't told me a thing about what you've been doing or what you're going to do. Why are you here?'

I saw myself in the glass beyond her, tall, untidy in overalls, the cut on my forehead still raw-looking and my face was angry. I seemed to be staring at a stranger, a tight-lipped, angry-eyed being, tense now with an ugly but necessary resolution.

'Don't worry. It's all going to be fixed.' And it was. I was throwing Drexel overboard. I was going to the police. It was the only thing to do. Minerva with the cold, stern face was the girl for my money. Doing the right thing would hurt Drexel all right—it would hurt me, too. But there was no other damned way out.

'I've never seen you look like this.'

'I've never felt like this before.'

'What do you mean? David ...'

'It's all right. What have they done with Jabal?'

'He's in one of the box cars. They keep him drugged, I think.'

I said, 'How much money have you got? Enough to take you to Paris?'

She nodded.

'Give me a pencil.'

I found a scrap of paper and I wrote a name and address on it.

'You're going to Paris tonight. Take one of their cars

and drive to Perpignan. You can get a train there. Go to this address. It's a friend of mine. Tell him I sent you and stay with him until I come. You're staying out of this mess if I can fix it.'

'But I can't go.'

'Yes, you can, and right away.'

'But I've got another turn after the interval.'

I thought that one over. I meant to go to the police and throw the whole thing in. But if Sophie cleared off before the end of the circus it might make them suspicious.

'Do your show and then go. I won't go to the police until you're well on your way to Perpignan. Do as I say, Sophie, and everything will be all right.'

She was worried, I could see that. Too often in her life she had been worried and that dark look had lived in her eyes. Too long she had lived on the fringe of darkness and sunlight. Now she was coming out into the sunlight and I was going to be with her.

I bent down and kissed her gently. 'Go to Paris after the show and wait for me. I can't explain more.'

She stood up. It was hard for hope to take hold of her.

'You'll go to the police,' she said, 'but they'll bring me back. The others won't let me go free.'

'Nobody's going to bring you back. You're staying with me for good.' I could do it, too, I knew. Behind Jabal there was power and discretion. Behind Drexel's coming disgrace lay my strength. The Foreign Office, the *Bureau des Affaires Etrangères* and the oil interests ... they owed me something and I knew the price I was going to ask. Sophie's name stayed out of this. After all she had played a part she had never understood, forced into by fear. It was a small price and I knew they would pay it.

She said, 'But they will bring me back. You don't understand.' She was stubborn with the conviction in her.

'What can they do to you? What hold have they got on you?'

She looked up at me. 'I'm not French. I've no papers—only forged ones. They got them for me when the circus came out of Spain, years ago, when I was a child. A word from them and the authorities would send me back.'

'They wouldn't do that.'

'They would ...'

I got it from her but it took some getting. Even to me she didn't like talking about it though when it came it didn't seem all that dreadful to me. But if a threat and a fear may have been held over you since you were a child and you've grown up with it, it becomes so much part of you that you can't shake it off or see its proper proportions. And every year that passes makes it more hopeless to contemplate ever being free of it. All her family, except her brother, were dead. They were from Barcelona and had got on the wrong side of the Falangists. Her brother still lived in Spain, an outlaw, a price on his head ... working against Franco. If she was sent back she would be a wonderful hostage. They wouldn't care a damn what they did with her so long as it brought her brother in—and he would come; she knew that. He would give himself up to save her. And she was sure that the French would send her back because she had helped Gerard and Sarrasin to smuggle stuff between the two countries. She'd been useful to them on the French end, and they had a nice hold on her ... They were a prize lot, all right. They had brought her out of Spain and looked after her, given her a job when she had been a destitute child and then had used her. Gratitude and fear, it's an ugly mixture, but it works.

When she had finished I put my arm around her.

'You're going to have a nationality,' I said. 'You're going to have mine as soon as I get to Paris.' I kissed her and she was inside my arms.

'David ... it can't be.'

'Don't be a fool.' I held her, driving out fear and warming hope in her. 'You're not going back to Spain. You're coming with me to England as my wife. As for the rest of the stuff about smuggling and the French authorities

—don't worry. No matter what Gerard may say about you, I can fix that. You'll have helped to get Jabal back ... God, they owe me something, too!'

But even while she was in my arms I began to think about Gerard and Sarrasin. They'd played on the fears of a child and built them up ... It was dirty, mean dirty, and I was sorry that I was going to finish them off cleanly by going to the police. They rated something less formal ...

'I'll give you an hour after the show is over,' I said. 'Then I go to the police. If you aren't in Perpignan on your way to Paris by then ...' I raised my hand, threatening her with love and for the first time she laughed, really laughed, a low, gentle sound that was music to me.

I went down the steps and she closed the door behind me. And I went back through the darkness and hoped I would not meet Gerard or Sarrasin because I knew I would not wait for the niceties of police procedure ...

When I got back the interval was nearly over. Dunwoody was twisting about in his seat with a strained expression on his face which I supposed was worry, but his habitual cheerfulness and twinkle wouldn't let it appear authentic. He said, 'Where the hell have you been? I began to think they'd nabbed you.'

'I've been talking to the girl.'

'The girl?'

'Sophie. I've never told you ... but she and I are going to be married.'

He stared at me with his mouth open and for once there was no twinkle in his eyes. Then slowly his mouth closed and he shook his head and blew out his cheeks.

'Either you like things to be difficult—or you're crazy.'

'No, I'm not, I'm sane and I know exactly what I'm going to do. When this show's finished I'm going to the police. We're finishing with this game altogether.' I put out a hand and held his arm. 'You've been a great help to me. But the best turn you ever did me was to sleep heavily.'

'Sleep heavily? Look, save the riddles for some party. What is happening?'

I told him how Drexel had visited the circus the previous night. Sitting there in the front row with a gendarme a few places away and the ring hands smoothing out the sawdust and tan bark for the last half of the show, I felt confident and my mind was clearly made up. When I had finished talking, Dunwoody said:

'If you're going to the police after the show, I know where I'm going now. I'm going back to the chateau. If Drexel really is all right, he may not stay put. I've got his clothes and he's locked in, but that cove's a Houdini. You know that. He may get out and he'll find something to wear if it's only a couple of chair covers ... I'll be back there in an hour and I'll take up the gendarme from the village and we'll sit tight until we hear from you. You don't want the big fish to slip from you now ... Blimey, fancy him sneaking out on me like that! And he must have used my bike, too!'

I think this last must have been the biggest insult. I had to smile.

I said, 'Yes, I think you should go back.'

'No doubt about it. If he got out he might see that circus handbill in the kitchen. He'd guess what we were doing and he might warn these people. If Gerard and company knew we were in here they'd stop at nothing. Paviot would have a knife in us ... or something.'

'You'd better get going,' I said. I felt that he was a bit cut-up that the Colonel should have slipped out while he was supposed to be watching him. That touched his professional pride. It was the kind of thing, I guessed, that his brother Albert would never let him forget.

He stood up to go and said quietly, 'Keep out of trouble.'

'Don't worry.' I nodded towards the gendarme. 'When I get out of here I'm sticking to him. He's sure to go and have a drink somewhere. As soon as Sophie is clear I'm going to join him.'

I could see the moment coming, a big moment for the

gendarme and one he would talk about for years.

Dunwoody went and I was left alone. I slouched back in my seat, pulled my cap forward a shade more and lit a cigarette. There was only a little time left now. Jabal was going to be safe. There was going to be a hell of an awakening for a lot of people. I couldn't even guess what would happen to Drexel. But at the back of my mind I had a feeling that international and oil interests might decide to keep the real truth from the public ... it would be better that way. Whatever happened, though, it would be the end of Drexel. I could think of that without pity. The end of Drexel ... Prison for a while, maybe ... then he would drift into a shabby obscurity, become a lonely, eccentric anonymity ... And for once I could find no compassion in me for him or any of the others. I was thinking of the child Sophie, her innocent simplicity warped by fears and threats ... and, then, of the woman Sophie, waiting now to step out into the sunshine.

CHAPTER SIXTEEN

I think it was the spotlight which first made me uneasy.
But I couldn't be sure of this. Maybe just waiting there,
knowing that the end was approaching worked on my
nerves and filled me with a growing impatience for the
show to be done.

While the acts were going on the bowl of the ring was
flooded with lights and the surrounding tiers of seats
were in a half gloom, but every now and again a small
spotlight from a box on the far side of the ring would
detach itself from the other lights and the beam would
drift gently round the sea of faces as though the electri-
cian, tired of his real duties, was searching out some
friend. This happened again and again. The light would
come gently towards me. For a moment it would be full
in my face and then gone. Maybe I was hypersensitive
now but I got the impression that each time it reached
me it paused for a moment and that somewhere a voice
was saying, 'Ah, there you are. Still there. Good.'

I told myself not to be a fool, but my uneasiness per-
sisted. I wondered if Gerard and company had found out
I was in the circus. Maybe Drexel had got out and got in
touch with them. But I could not believe this. And, anyway, I told myself, even if they did know there was nothing they could do. There were dozens of people around
me, and a gendarme only a few places away. There was
no way they could touch me. I don't remember much
about the acts for I watched the gendarme most of the
time. I didn't want to lose him. He was a big, capable-
looking man, stolid and probably not very intelligent
but comforting to look at.

But each time that spot came wandering across the
seats and flicked over me, I stirred uncomfortably.

Sophie came on about half-way through the second
half. There were two men with her and four easy-step-
ping, broad-backed grey horses. I wondered which were

her favourites, the greys or the Arabs, and which got the bigger sugar ration. It was a curious sensation watching her turn somersaults, fly from one man to another and then, perched high on the pyramid of their shoulders, swing lazily round the ring. Out there she had a vitality new to me, her body quicksilver, every moment sure and fluid. I thought: I'm going to marry her. She's going to be my wife; a bare-back rider, a circus queen. When I went back to teaching it was going to be amusing. Mrs Davis Bladen Fraser, late of the *Grand Cirque Pyrénéen*. The Board of Governors, the head's wife and the other women might look old-fashioned, but the boys would love it ... But was I going back? Could I go back after all this? And then, quite definitely, I knew I was going back. I liked teaching. Nothing had been changed for me. It was my profession and I didn't care a damn that there were no big money rewards ... there were other rewards. Sophie wouldn't let me down. I knew that. Yes, I was going back. Drexel had always had me wrong. I wasn't pelagic; just a simple barn-yard creature ... I smiled to myself and the spotlight hit me full in the face and then was gone.

There was great burst of hand-clapping and shouting as Sophie and her team went off. The band burst into a noisy fanfare and into the ring came tumbling half a dozen clowns and a crazy-looking motor-car which spouted flour from its horn and sent a jet of water shooting up from its radiator when the cap was lifted. It was all traditional, well-loved stuff. I watched them and I could pick out Fargette, and, I thought, Paviot and there was an enormous fellow in a battered top-hat and tight morning-clothes whom I guessed was Sarrasin. But this was no surprise. In a poor circus everyone plays many parts. I watched them trip one another over, produce strings of sausages from inside their coats, pour water and flour about and, in their efforts to start the car, gradually shake the thing to pieces. Sarrasin did a strong man act and failed to lift a great dumb-bell and then Fargette came along and lifted Sarrasin and the bar. The audience roared with delight. There may not be a touch of the poet in us all but there's a fair-sized slice of the clown. I laughed with the rest, but part of my mind was with Sophie in her caravan. She was changing now. She would pack a bag and soon be away. It was a long trip to Paris. I wondered what she would be thinking about all the way, saw her sitting in her carriage, staring out of the window while league after league of France flew by her ... Sophie moving ahead to a future whose strangeness I would have to temper for her.

The clowns had now given up the motor-car in disgust. In angry voices they were blaming one another and shouting that they must have a mechanic. With one accord they turned to the audience appealing.

'A mechanic! A mechanic! Is there a mechanic here?'

Voices called back to them and from behind me someone offered them fifty francs for the car as scrap.

But Fargette began to bounce up and down, his baggy check trousers ballooning, his great collar rising and falling about his ears and he shouted—

'Francois! There's Francois—he'll fix it.' He pretended to recognize someone. Then, followed by the others, he began to run across the ring. They came straight towards me.

'Francois! Oh, the good Francois!'

'Francois!'

They came tumbling and running towards me. I had a suspicion of what might happen and I think I even began to rise. But the spot swung round suddenly and isolated me. There I was half-risen in my seat and I heard my own voice shout angrily, 'No! No!'

Then my cry was swallowed in a burst of laughter from the audience as Fargette, Paviot, Sarrasin and another were on me. They grabbed me and hauled me roughly over the protecting bank into the ring.

'Francois! Francois!'

Laughing and pushing around me, they fought over my body. I was tripped and fell on my back. Someone squirted water in my face and I was half-blinded. I struggled up and swung out at them, but I went down again and my ears were full of the laughter and delighted shouts of the audience who saw in it all part of a carefully rehearsed act. I got to my feet and began to run back ... back towards the gendarme. I must have looked a fool, not desperate, but funny. I shouted something but the next instant I was sprawling as Paviot tripped me and my mouth was full of sawdust. They jumped for me, picked me up by my arms and legs and carried me into the centre of the ring, swinging me stretcher fashion and chanting my name—

'Francois! Francois!'

They dumped me down and as I tried to rise, swearing at them, and striking with my fists, Fargette jumped on my shoulders and clamped his legs round my neck. I swayed upwards, nearly made it and collapsed. And now they just took me and sported with me. I could feel their blows no pantomime, no mockery. Sarrasin kicked me skilfully in the side and the breath went from me. I had no power to shout or resist. I was conscious only of the roaring crowd and this frenzied, dancing circle clothes ringing about me.

They rolled me over on to a large tarpaulin, grabbed the corners and the next instant I was flying up into the air, arms and legs spread-eagled and the whole place reeling in front of my eyes. They caught me as I came down and up I went again, and I think I must have been weak, not physically, but with frustration. Right here, under the eyes of hundreds of people, they were carrying me off and only a few yards away was the security I had thought so certain ... my gendarme friend, his red face convulsed with laughter.

It was a nightmare, the shouting, the blaring of the band, the flying up into space and then the slow dip back to earth, and the spotlights, coloured now, whirling and intertwining, the whole thing a mad, desperate medley. Once, as I came down and rested for a moment on the sheet, I saw Sarrasin's face leaning over me. It was painted with great streaks of red and yellow and his top-hat was cocked to one side, and I could see the quick heave of his throat above the tight hard collar, and he was smiling grotesquely through the grease-paint. No, not smiling, but laughing, roaring with laughter.

I think, in my confusion, the one thing I feared, if I had time for fear, was a quick knife-thrust from Paviot as I came down. But they had other plans.

I came down for the last time and lay for a second or two, so winded that I could not move. Fargette snatched up an enormous pepper-pot and sprinkled me with sand while another clown from an equally large container flicked white chalk for salt over me. Then with a great shout of triumph they suddenly rolled me over in the sheet. They screwed me up in it as a sausage is wrapped in a pastry roll. I was in darkness and half-stifled and then almost sick with giddiness as they began to swing me round and round.

I felt myself dumped roughly in the car, and then heard the spluttering roar of its motor. I was jolted and bumped about as it drove off. Someone sat on me heavily. I don't know what happened then. I was in darkness with only sensation for company. I heard the blare of the band die away and the roaring of the crowd thin to a faint murmur and there was only the clear, beating sound of the car. Then silence. Then voices. Something banged, a door clattered. I was lifted. I was thrown, flying upwards, and then, wrapped like a cocoon, crashed on to hardness. My head hit something and there was a galaxy of light before my eyes. A slow, irresistible tiredness swept over me. I didn't pass out, but I had no will or strength. I just lay there and groaned gently to myself against the nausea in me and idly wondered how long I would be able to go on breathing in this cocoon.

It was the regular jolting and the sound of the engine which brought me out of my stupor. I could breathe evenly and somewhere above my head and beyond me was a meagre light set in a glass bowl protected by an iron grillwork. I struggled to a sitting position and saw that the tarpaulin had been cleared from my head and shoulders but was still wrapped around my feet. I was on a wooden floor covered with a loose litter of straw.

A woman's hand came towards me, took my wrist gently and I heard Sophie say, 'Are you all right?'

I said, 'Yes,' absently, and wondered what she was doing there. The floor jolted violently and I was tipped sideways. An arm held me and I turned my head to find that she was sitting beside me. Her arm held me firmly by the shoulder.

I said, 'So you didn't get off to Paris?'

She smiled and put up a hand and brushed my hair from my forehead.

'No.'

'Where are we?'

'In one of the lorried box-cages.'

I pulled myself up a bit more and shook my head to get the bleariness from my eyes, and suddenly my mind cleared.

Sophie was sitting close to me with a raincoat over a blouse and skirt. I saw the plank-ribbed walls of the swaying box-cage and a little grilled window high up on my right. It came back then. Not only had I been taken, but she had been caught as well. That meant they knew about us. I said urgently, 'How did they know about you? Sophie, what's happened?'

She gave no answer in words, but her eyes left mine and she looked towards the far end of the lorry. I followed her gaze and in the shadows I saw two men sitting on a long packing-case. They sat close together, their backs touching, both of them moving a little with the swing of the lorry. One was Fargette, still in his clown's clothes, and in his hand, glinting under the feeble light, I saw that he held an automatic. The sight of it reminded me of my own gun and instinctively my hand went to my overalls for it. It was gone.

But its loss hardly impinged on me. At the moment the second man swayed forward a little and the thin rays of the overhead light illuminated his face.

I couldn't believe it. I stared at him like an idiot and somewhere in my mind a voice was hammering away saying, 'No! No!' and there was a vast emptiness inside me. It couldn't be! It damned well couldn't be! I almost shouted the words and at the same time some instinctive, rageful reaction sent me forward, trying to untangle the layers of tarpaulin from my legs.

Fargette raised his revolver and he said throatily, 'Stay where you are, monsieur. If not—' The weapon swung towards Sophie, and, at that moment, her hand pulled me back.

'It's no use, David.' Her voice was heavy with hopelessness.

I dropped back against the wall of the lorry, the jolt and bang of the boards beating against my shoulders. The man sitting by Fargette began to chuckle. The chuckle grew to a laugh. I could see the tears squeeze from the corners of his small eyes, and the rich shake of his plump cheeks. He raised the hand which was free of a gun and thumped himself on the chest to relieve the choking humour in him. The motion set his familiar toupee askew and his drooping Edwardian quiff trembled like the curled tail feathers of a drake.

'Oh,' he choked. 'Lord, it was funny! Funny ... If you could have seen yourself! Up and down, up and down and shouting your head off ... I'll never forget it. Not if I live to be a hundred!'

I said evenly, feeling small and with no advantage, hating to see him with all the honours, and hating the feebleness of my own words, 'Don't laugh your head off, Dunwoody. One day I'm going to knock it off.'

'Not you, chum ...' The bubble of dying humour was still in his voice and his tear-moist eyes twinkled as though they were set with brilliants. 'Not you, chum. I don't like to say it, but you're the one who's going to be knocked off. You and the girl.'

It didn't come through at once. Only slowly. Like ink dropped on to a blotting-pad, a small ugly spot and then spreading into an uneven, dirty patch.

'You and the girl.' He said it again and the odd thing
was that though there was no menace or force in his
voice, just a plump old bastard with a shining face talking in a matter-of-fact tone, the words chilled me. Because Dunwoody meant it. The man was incapable of
rhetoric. He meant what he said.

My hand found Sophie's and I held it tight.

'You're a bastard, Dunwoody,' I said. 'A dirty bastard ...'

'Naughty ...' He shook his head and I knew that I
hadn't touched him. There was nothing there that I
could touch.

And that filled me with a spleen that I wished I could
have taken out on him. The words were there now, all
the rich and pungent vocabulary that years in a Scots
regiment had given me, but I let them lie. Not words,
but action was what I wanted, and that was denied me.

'Don't try anything, Mr Fraser,' he said. 'Keep in
your little Jack Horner. If you don't we'll let the girl have
it first.'

I got myself in hand then. A lot of things were suddenly clear to me and I began to wonder that I could
have been such an innocent. But then that is how one is
betrayed; by one's own innocence, by the trust one puts
in faces and words, by the blindness that keeps men's
hearts shrouded. First Drexel, and now Dunwoody. I
was getting my share this trip.

I said, 'Mr Greatheart Dunwoody. The heavy sleeper.
The Dunwoody Detective Agency ... No wonder your
card was dirty and crumpled. Did you only have one
printed?'

He chuckled and shrugged himself more comfortably
into his leather jacket.

'You take too narrow a view ... uncharitable, I call
it. I'm just doin' a job. My job. It ain't the kind you
can do with love and kisses. But believe me I'm real
sorry about what's coming to you and the lady. Real
sorry.'

I didn't believe it. Real sorry, where other people were concerned, was only a literary term for him.

'What have you done with the Colonel?' I asked.

His eyes opened a little wider. 'Nothing—except a deal. You'll see him later, maybe.'

'A deal?'

He nodded, and then flicked a fat finger towards the far side of the lorry. Lying in the shadows I saw something which had so far escaped me. A slight, curled-up form, a head cushioned peacefully on an arm. It was Jabal, apparently sleeping peacefully.

'Drugged,' said Dunwoody a little severely, even disapprovingly, 'and I hope they haven't overdone it because he's got a trip ahead of him early this morning . . .' He chuckled and I hated to see him enjoying himself so much. 'A nice little trip . . . back to Ramaut, by way of Spain, Mr Fraser. And I'm real grateful to you. I am really. If it hadn't been for you I'd have never pulled it off. Lummy, it's odd, ain't it, the way things work out?'

He was like a man who'd won a prize in a sweepstake. Talkative and wanting to go back over it all, from the moment he'd thought of buying a ticket, what his wife had said and how it was Wednesday the something his lucky day and lucky number . . . I knew how he felt. Right into his lap. Right into his broad, capable hands . . . the twinkling-eyed, chubby-faced bastard. But suddenly, beyond and above all this, came the lightning sear of panic. Jabal back to Ramaut. My head must still have been a bit muzzy for I heard myself in class saying ' "Jabal back to Ramaut". Translate'. And then the hesitant words, '*Jabal va vers sa mort*'. Oh, yes, and no mistake. Jabal back to Ramaut meant Jabal to his death.

'You're a Regent's man. You're a murderer.'

'I'm doing a job. Didn't you ever send a platoon out knowing that some wouldn't come back? Death ain't so hard, not even your own if you get to thinkin' right about it. Anyway, you fixed it for him. I offered the Colonel a deal from Ahmed ben Fa'id ages ago, but he turned it down. Then you mucked him up. You did it, chum. If you'd sat tight in the chateau he'd have gone to the oil company and Jabal wouldn't be putting up his shutters. You—' He jabbed his forefinger towards me. 'You, chum, fixed Jabal up. You gave me my chance to talk the Colonel round. And it was easy when he learned you meant to play guardian angel to him. Blimey, you should have heard his language. Come to think of it you did hear some. Remember the time you come in and said you thought you'd heard voices. Well, chum, you did. His and mine. Life's tricky, ain't it? The little ins and outs, I mean.'

Life was tricky, all right. But it wasn't the little ins-and-outs as he called them. It was the people in life. People like Dunwoody and Drexel.

Dunwoody sat there, beaming, and I think he expected me to say something, to protest, curse him or even make some move. He was disappointed. But I didn't enjoy just lying there, jolted by the rapid progress of the lorry, feeling Sophie close against my shoulder and seeing Jabal curled up in a drugged sleep. It was no good telling myself that I could not be blamed if the things I had done from the best motives had inevitably brought them very close to death ... I couldn't believe it. Every breath we take involves us in some unexpected responsibility. I *was* to blame.

Drexel had the whole thing nicely planned. Originally Jabal was to be taken off and then ransomed to the oil company. No harm would have come to him. I would have been the scapegoat, safey out of it on my way to South America with plenty of money. Even if I had dared to come back, I could have proved nothing. The Chateau Minerve would have been empty and no trace of the people who had hired it. They would make sure of that. Gerard and company would be nicely hidden away in their circus, and Jabal's word would destroy mine.

But I had spoilt that by escaping and then holding Drexel. Dunwoody must have been watching his chance for a long time, and I had given it to him. My quixotic plan to save Drexel could not have been more convenient for him. Drexel must have come to his senses that first morning and he and Dunwoody had fixed the whole thing up. Drexel, now hating me, determined not to lose his chance of money, had gone right over. He had been forced into ruthlessness. He was selling Jabal right back to Sheikh Ahmed ben Fa'id and to cover himself he was prepared to see me and Sophie go under. It was the final passage in his deterioration. You made the first step, an easy one, but after that time and chance took over and there was no going back, no giving up, not if you had the stiff pride and hungry determination which marked Drexel.

At the chateau he and Dunwoody had fixed it all up beautifully between them. When the Colonel had gone to see Gerard he had, no doubt, given orders for Sarrasin and his boys to come up and take me. My coming to the circus must have put Dunwoody in a desperate mood. But not a hint of it had he shown me and, when I had told him about Sophie and my intention to go to the police, he had left me, slipped round and seen Gerard and they had worked out the clown act there and then. I could imagine Gerard's moment of panic and then the swift, capable decision to take me right under the noses of hundreds of people. If you play for big stakes you must take big risks—and they had not hesitated.

We were in the lorry a good two hours. We said nothing. Just the five of us. I had Sophie's hand in mine and I had the comforting feeling that she had found a new strength. She was no longer afraid ... but I was, for her and Jabal and, frankly, for myself. Yet while we were in this shadowed straw-littered world the real potency was slowly withdrawn from fear. Nothing could happen here so long as no movement was made. This was an interregnum. Real life, and the prospect of life's end, would come when we stepped out.

Fargette yawned occasionally and Dunwoody whistled very gently to himself. They were like a couple of nightwatchmen, bored, waiting for the end of the spell. Looking at Dunwoody I could be coldly curious as to the kind of man that really lurked under that plump, cheerful exterior. He was a superb actor, and a man with a ready, unfaltering courage ... it was odd that the qualities which made a hero went for a villain, too. Only that thin line of dedication separated them, the choice of a banner to fight under.

The lorry stopped and I was jerked forward. Somewhere outside I heard men's voices and then the bang of doors and the squeal of hinges. The lorry moved again and then stopped.

The doors at the back of the lorry were pulled back and as Fargette and Dunwoody rose, covering us still, I saw Gerard, Sarrasin and Paviot standing in a welcoming committee outside. Sarrasin was wearing a long, loose coat which I guessed covered his clown's clothes. Paviot had changed and both of them had wiped the make-up roughly from their faces. Gerard was in his wrinkled blue suit, his scraggy neck thrust forward as he peered into the lorry.

'All right? Is everything all right?' he fussed.

Fargette nodded and jumped down and Dunwoody followed, lowering himself bulkily.

I stood up and Sophie rose with me. We walked to the end of the lorry and halted. The five of them stood in a tight semicircle waiting for us.

So far as I could see we were in a large, barn-like structure, the lorry driven well in. A couple of hurricane lamps were burning on two cases near the wide open double doors and outside was a moonlit stretch of rough ground. Across the open space the corner of some farmbuilding, white, bone-like in the pale light, showed and beyond it I glimpsed a pewter-stretch of water and the dark plumes of poplars. There was a pungent smell and suddenly, from the darkness at the side of the barn, I heard the disturbed grunt of some animal.

'Come down and behave yourselves,' said Gerard, and he might have been a fussy parent who had caught two

children in some naughtiness. 'Come down! Come down
at once!'

We did not move for a moment. And in that pause,
that moment of waiting, my eyes came back to their
faces and there was that in them which was unpleasant
to see. They weren't angry, they weren't resentful, they
weren't anything but faces suddenly stripped of all feeling. They were looking at us and not seeing us as human
beings. We were things, just things with which they had
to deal ... objects that were soon to be put away and
forgotten, and maybe in their minds they had already
disposed of us. Gerard like an untidy sparrow, pursing
his lips and impatient with our slowness; Dunwoody
bland, patient, knowing his cards were good; Paviot,
dark and shabby, full of a frayed energy and violence;
Fargette, dwarf-like and with a simple good natured
disregard of pain in others—and then Sarrasin. My eyes
met his, and we spoke to one another without words,
spoke our hatred of each other, and I could see that his
had grown in pace with mine, and instinctively I knew
that it was because of Sophie. Somewhere in him was
a capacity for affection that was linked to Sophie. The
nearer she came to me and disaster, the more he hated
me as he acknowledged that he would do nothing for
her.

I jumped down and then turned, reaching up a hand
for Sophie. She joined me and they closed in around
us. We were shepherded across the barn. The whole of
one side was taken up by animal cages raised about three
feet off the ground. Gerard opened the cage on the ex-
treme left by the door. There was no point in protesting
or fighting. There were too many of them. Sophie climbed up and I followed her. Gerard slammed the bolt over,
padlocked it and they all stood back, looking at us. We
might have been new animal stock, just arrived, and
they watched us with an intense curiosity to see how
we would take to our new quarters.

Then, as we did not move or speak, did nothing to
feed their curiosity, they turned and left us. I saw Gerard

hang his keys on a nail by the large doors. One of them closed and locked the back of the lorry with Jabal in it and they went out, swinging over the double doors behind them.

CHAPTER SEVENTEEN

Sophie told me where we were. It was the farm which was used as the winter quarters and training establishment for the circus. It was looked after by Gerard's married sister and her husband. The barn we were in, a large corrugated iron affair, housed sick animals and those which were under training and not yet ready to go into the circus. The farm itself was about forty miles from Banyuls and well up in the mountains. The Franco-Spanish border was within five miles by a route, over very rough country, which Gerard and Sarrasin had used in the past for smuggling. The farm stood on the edge of a lake ringed about by the hills.

We sat on the bare boards of the cage floor and talked in low voices that echoed strangely about the cavernous interior. The cage next to ours on the right was full of of birds. I could see them moving restlessly on their long bamboo perches. Our presence disturbed them. A large hornbill sidled up to the bars and stared at us magisterially. Somewhere in the far shadows there was a shrill cry and the beat of large wings, and then a thin, piping complaint. Somehow I was reminded of the dusk and lonely coastal flats and the weird sounds of unseen night birds ... of the emphasis and menace that solitude can carry.

Further along the barn I could see the dark movement of animals, the occasional green glitter of eyes caught in the dim light of the hurricane lamps and hear the slither and rustle of straw as bodies turned restlessly. Once a monkey chattered and screeched indignantly and then was answered by the raucous, short growl of a lion.

'That's Karimba,' said Sophie. 'Sarrasin has four new lions and is training them. The far end of the barn can be turned into a large training cage. You're cold?'

She took off her raincoat and sitting close to me draped it over our shoulders. Then she looked across at the lorry which had brought us here. 'Why have they left Jabal there?'

'He won't be there long.' I tried not to think of what lay ahead for Jabal ... and of us. But my mind refused to free itself of the thoughts. Somewhere the night wind rattled a loose sheet of corrugated iron—a shivering, apprehensive sound.

I said, 'It's clear how they mean to take Jabal out. Over the Spanish border ... God knows what will happen to him after that.' I slipped my arm round her and she put her head against my neck and she was warm, strong and untrembling, but I knew what was in her mind. It was something neither of us had to speak about.

She said, 'This farm was one of the first places I came to in France. I used to bathe in the lake, but even in summer the water is very cold ... Even now, you feel the night air is cold. Animals like cold, not draughts, but cold. It improves their coats. There is another barn near the farm-house where we keep the horses ...'

It was hard to say whether she was talking to me or herself ... But I knew how she felt. It was hard to sit waiting in this gloom. I held her closer. My Sophie ... If it had been possible then I could have gladly had it that we might go back over the past days, never to have met, and me, never to have loved, that she might be free and in no danger. I remembered my moment of first seeing her ... remembered the lumps of wrapped sugar spilling from her bag in the aquarium. We sat there and she told me about the early years she had spent on this farm, how under Gerard—who was wonderful with horses—she had been trained. But all the time she was talking part of me was away from her. Now and again I could hear Jabal turn over and mutter to himself in the locked lorry. A toucan, looking like a Jewish rabbi, sidled along its perch in the next cage and looked down its great nose at us. Karimba grumbled hoarsely in its throat from the far darkness. The place was restless, full of life, but none of it carrying any pity or understanding for us. I watched a rat come out and forage along the bottom of some stacked bales of straw by the door. But time and again my eyes came back to the bunch of large double doors. I had already tried the padlock and the bars of the cage but they were not to be forced. I looked at my watch. It was three o'clock. Soon now —if Dunwoody were right—Jabal would be taken off. An early morning trip. A trip from which he would not return and, after he had left, what would happen to us ... or rather, how would it happen to us?

I held Sophie more closely and she was saying, 'There's a little stream runs down behind the farm. This time of the year it's lined with arum lilies ... a white pathway of them and the farm ducks lay their eggs amongst them so that you have to walk carefully ...'

I said, 'We had ducks when I was a boy. But we never let them out of the duck-house until eight o'clock in the morning. That made sure they always laid in the house.'

She said, 'These have no house.' Then she was silent for a while and it was clear to me that her thoughts were back with those first days when she had been a child here. When time runs short one looks back on the good things and finds courage in them.

She went on, 'Fargette came with me from Barcelona ... You know, he's not nearly as old as you would imagine.'

I said, 'I hate their guts. The whole lot of them.'

Her hand tightened on mine and very quietly, she said, 'In their way they were good to me. When you're poor you can be good to people—and then cruel. I don't hate them. I just want to forget them.'

I knew what she meant. People are good to you from their virtues, offer friendship and protection; and then, from their evil, from their own desperate needs, they are cruel. Why expect only the gifts of their virtues? If you take friendship, you must take the person who offers it, too. Very few jewels get a perfect setting.

She was saying, 'Fargette is a good clown ... It is in his family. He fishes, too. There's a little boat we would take on the lake and he would fish and talk ... With grown-ups he is usually silent, but with children he talks. He used to tell me stories ... the tales from Perrault, and the Fables of La Fontaine ... with a different voice for each animal. And he would tell my fortune ... Oh, David, you've no idea of the silly, lovely things he used to say. I'd be bruised and scratched from falling off the horses, convinced I would never be any good, and he would tell me what lay ahead. All the great cities of Europe and the wide tan-bark rings with thousands of faces watching like a spread of rice on the darkness and me going round and round and the whole world falling in love with me. I used to worry him for details. I was so young. Who would I marry and how many children would I have? And it would be an emperor with a row of stables so long that, as you looked down the stall-doors with the horses' heads hanging over them, the head of the last horse would be no bigger than a pea. And, standing by each horse, a child, a long line of sons and daughters ... We used to laugh until the boat rocked ... inventing names for the children and the horses.'

I said, 'When you marry me, we'll be poor. It'll be one horse from a hackney stable at ten bob an hour.' I wished I had not spoken. Though I wanted to keep it from my voice, there was the note of angry despair in it which was my only answer to the dimming brightness of the future.

'Oh, David ... I don't mind. I don't mind. The other's only a fairy story, and you, you're real and ...' I heard her voice falter and, turning, saw her face. Her eyes were moist with sudden tears and her mouth trembled. I knew that her thoughts had caught up with her, and I cursed myself for the bitterness which had been in my voice when I spoke last, cursed myself for dragging her out of the comfort that lay in the past. She came to me, throwing her arms around my neck, and she said, '*Chéri* ... *Chéri* ...' I held her, caressing her, trying to still the trembling which was in her.

Momentarily she was all weakness and I would have given anything to be all strength. I tried to be, tried to

force courage and hope from myself into her, and maybe
I succeeded a little. She lay still after a while, my arms
around her, and the shadowed enmity which seemed to
wreathe about the barn receded a little.

The rat by the straw bales sat up and polished his
whiskers like an old colonel in a club window and took
no interest in us. We weren't human, no menace lay in
us, we were just two more caged animals. And I suppose the rat was right. What did we have more than the
animals around us? A little more intelligence which, un-
fortunately, gave us a sense of the future. It would have
been better if we had not known what the word future
meant—for we had so little of it to come, and our intelligence was turned to a frustrated restlessness and vain
desire to escape.

Now and again, at the far end of the barn I could hear
the *pad*, *pad* of some animal circling its cage. Maybe a
wolf or a hyena. The darkness beyond the pale ring of
light from the hurricane lamps was pregnant with unseen life, the stir and the cough, the sudden sharp snarl
and the quick, shaking settle of wings like small twigs
falling ... And the warmth and smell of the creatures was
like a fog, harsh with ammonia, a dusty rankness in the
throat. After a time the atmosphere, the unquiet gloom
and the sense of futility and shortening time ahead, began to work on the spirits until a brute dejection took
one. This was it. We were back where we belonged ...
with the animals. What did we rank more than they,
except a different label on a strip of perspex outside the
cage? *Homo sapiens, European—male and female—
presented by Colonel Francis Drexel. Hyena crocuta—
Abyssinian—presented by Monsieur George Sarrasin.
Felis leo—'Karimba'—African—female. (Purchased out
of the proceeds of smuggling penicillin over the Franco-
Spanish border.)*

But no matter how dejected I got, I didn't like it. Man's
spirit doesn't take to cages. I was an outrage to the body
and the mind ... and I had a feeling that Sarrasin would
appreciate this only too well. This was an insulting jest

... Somewhere down the row something began to shake at the bars of the cage frantically, chattering with a garbled fluency.

Sophie stirred and said, 'That's a baboon we have. He cut his leg on a cigarette tin someone gave him. He has a very bad temper.'

The rat sat and stared at us, undisturbed by our voices or the chattering of the baboon, a chattering that echoed strangely under the lofty iron roof. Then, in a flash the rat was gone. The baboon stopped cursing his fate and in the silence I heard footsteps outside the big doors. A small slip-door cut into the big right-hand door opened and a man stepped into the barn. He turned momentarily and called back through the moonlit rectangle:

'Get that mule over as soon as you can.'

It was the voice of Colonel Francis Drexel, curt and full of authority. I watched him come towards our cage. My friend, Drexel; the man who had once saved my life and now, I supposed, felt he had the right to take it away. Logically it was a fair deal. He has given me more years of living than I had expected, a bonus paid from his own courage. It might have been comforting if I could have seen it that way.

He wore his tight-belted, shabby raincoat and there was a fullness of silk scarf about his throat. No hat, the iron-grey hair dark in the poor light, the trim, small body full of cut and thrust, he came right up to the cage and stood there looking in at us. His face was as grey as pumice stone and as rough, worn and old. But the eyes were alive and they had now a brightness I had never seen before, and he kept blinking as though there was sand in them. This was a new habit ... and although it was a small thing, it changed him for me, made him febrile, uncertain and unpleasant. I had the swift impression that for the first time I was looking at the real Drexel, that for the first time in his life he had caught up with himself ... that until now he had been playing a part which others had dictated to him. And because he was a stranger to me I had no words for him that came easily, either out of contempt or compassion. My Drexel had died years ago.

I don't know how long he stood there before he spoke. Sophie and I, close together, watched him, and it would have been hard to say what was in his mind until he spoke and then I knew that this stranger was an unhappy man, knowing himself to be the creature of his own evil, and obstinately determined to live with it.

He said, 'You did wrong, Fraser. You did wrong.' His voice was rough, overwrought. 'You forced me and you know I'm not a man to be forced.'

He waited for me to reply. But I had nothing to say to him. He had called me Fraser. I was a stranger to him, too. What was there for me to say? Argue with him? Plead with him? Beg him at least to let Sophie go and rely on her honour to be silent? He had nothing in him which would respond. I only had to look at him to see that.

Drawn by my silence, he said quickly, 'I wish I'd never seen you. And when you're gone from here, I'm going to forget you.'

He waited again and I could see that he hated talking to silence.

'Do you hear me? Say something.'

I spoke then, but I wasted few words on him.

'That's right Drexel. You forget us. Forget Jabal, forget Sophie here, and forget me. You'll find it the easiest thing in the world.'

And moving gently from Sophie I drew cigarettes and matches from my overalls and lit a cigarette and ignored him. There was nothing between us. Exactly nothing.

I saw his shoulders move inside his coat and then with an abrupt movement he turned away towards the lorry. He went over and unlocked the rear doors and climbed up inside. As he did so I heard the sound of hooves clopping up to the big barn doors. The sound stopped and then there was the rasp of a wooden bar being pulled over. The doors opened.

Dunwoody and Paviot came in leading a mule between them.

They took no notice of us. Dunwoody climbed up into the lorry and he and Drexel brought Jabal out. They lowered him over the edge to Paviot. Jabal stood there swaying on his feet, hardly able to keep upright and quite clearly unaware of what was happening to him.

Paviot held him until the other two were down and they they half-walked, half-lifted him across to the mule. He was hoisted up and sagged forward, his hands clasping the saddle-horn. Paviot squatted down and tied Jabal's ankles together under the mule's belly. The animal moved restlessly as this was done but Drexel hit it across the muzzle and quieted it.

Sophie and I stood there, watching them, listening to Drexel's quiet word of command. I don't know how she felt, but I guessed it was much the same as I did. I had forgotten myself, my own danger, for it seemed all to have been transferred to Jabal. He was more helpless, more innocent than we. He had done nothing active to ensure himself the role of a victim, done nothing except be himself and so excite the venality of others. A tallish slim figure, dark-haired and young ... little more than a boy, normally full of life ... and he was going to be killed. I used the word bluntly to myself, for it was death that waited for him; maybe just over the Spanish border, maybe on some boat back to Remaut or in one of the rooms of the palace of Sheikh Ahmed ben Fa'id. He was going to die to feed the greed of others for the oil which was the blood of his homeland. The whole thing made me feel sick and angry.

Instinctively, I found my hands gripping the bars of the cage and the muscles of my body tensing.

Drexel said, 'We shall have to watch him at first to see he doesn't slip. But once he's got some fresh air in him he'll come round enough to hang on.'

He began to wheel the mule about and Paviot and Dunwoody moved at its flanks, a hand each on Jabal.

Paviot said, looking over at Dunwoody, 'Your men better be waiting. It's not safe to hang about up there in daylight too long.'

Dunwoody, in much better French than I had ever thought him capable of producing, said, 'Don't worry. They'll be there—and with the money, too.'

When they got to the door Drexel halted the mule. I saw him pause, saw the back of his hand rub slowly across his mouth in the manner of a man who has forgotten something and wonders if he should return for it. Then he turned his head slightly and looked across to us. Dunwoody and Paviot followed his glance. I expected something to be said. But nothing was. There were no words in them for this moment. Just Drexel's eyes on me, his small, neat head showing above the bowed neck of the mule; Drexel going out and away from me, for I knew he was saying good-bye, and that in some odd way he wanted something from me if only an angry acknowledgment of the dead faith between us. But I had nothing for him.

He turned away. Dunwoody raised a hand gently, valedictory, and the beam and twinkle were in his eyes still and there was in him the ease and affability of singleminded roguery. He had put his conscience in store years ago. And I could respect him for it.

Paviot? Nothing, except the coldness of the moonlit morning to match his inner coldness. He and the mule accepting the early hours and the work ahead, following their natures, and as indifferent to suffering in others as they were to the brute drive in themselves.

They went out and the big doors were closed and the bar dropped into place. And a moment after they were gone I found I was standing there, shaking at the bars, and swearing to myself. I wanted to be outside . . . to be after them . . . to be free to loose the animal ferocity which every moment in this cage drew from the black core of my anger.

Sophie took my hands away from the bars and looking at my watch, pretending not to notice my mood, said,

'Four o'clock. They will be over the border by eight.
I know the path so well ... In the spring, at this time
of year, it is a lovely walk ...'

I sat down with her. We talked quietly to one another
for a while. But I could not sit still nor would my mind
stay with our talk. I was restless ... driven frankly by fear
fear of what lay ahead of Jabal and waited for us. When
Drexel and Paviot returned, their money safe, our turn
would come. I knew Drexel. Nothing would be done to
us until the money was safe in his hands. One step at a
time ... the whole thing a neat military operation ...
0400 hours move off with Jabal on mule ... and so on
until, possibly, 1200 hours ... disposal of prisoners. Cold,
inflexible planning.

I got up and walked around the cage. Karimba roared
once and somewhere outside a cock began to crow. Time
and again I stopped at the front of the cage and my eyes
went to the length of wall by the big doors. The bunch
of keys on its wire loop hung there; fifteen feet away
which might have been fifty miles. I went over the cage
again, tried the floor-boards and even climbed to the iron-
barred roof, but there was no weak point, nothing that
could be moved.

One of the hurricane lamps guttered and went out and
the oil smeach of the smoking wick came across on the
draught to us. The rat came back and started its foraging.
I kept looking at my watch, greedy of time as a miser of
gold, and the impatience from frustration began to kick
in me as though it were a living thing.

'Sit down, David. There's nothing you can do.' Sophie
said it with all her love in her voice, but it was of no
help to me. Women, after their first fears are curbed, are
more resigned, full of a deeper, calmer courage than men.

'You'll wear yourself out, chéri ... Nothing can be
done.'

But I could not accept this. I kept seeing that mule,
with Jabal on its back, picking its way up the mountain

track, and the three men plodding with it. Somewhere
up amongst the grey, pine flanked peaks was the border,
and that to me became a symbol, a thick black band of
mourning. Once across it I knew there was no power
could save Jabal. And when I didn't think of that, my
mind went on punishing me. I looked at my watch and
saw the slip of the seconds, and each one as it peeled
off into limbo brought nearer the morning and the daylight and those last few moments when we, too, should
take the beastly shock of not-life and slip away ... And
how desperate my thoughts were I knew because the
spirit refused to acknowledge the real word, the real act
and called it 'not-life', trying to coat the pill for the
panic-poised child within me. At any other time I might
have been braver, had been braver; but there had been
no Sophie then, no love, no eagerness for the future
which went beyond my mere self ...

The baboon, sensing perhaps this uneasiness in a cage
not far from him, had begun to chatter and now and
again gave a queer half-strangled cry as though its body
were charged with some strange agony. Its cries disturbed the other animals, for one by one they woke and pro-
tested and a bedlam of noise filled the barn. It would
break out, rise to a mad pitch, and then suddenly stop
and the darkness beyond the thistle head of pale light
from the one hurricane would be thick with a low, ur-
gent, breathing sound, and this was almost worse than
the noise. It was a sequence which worked on the imagination, and set nerve and muscle on edge. When I
held Sophie, I could feel it in her, and once when I
kissed her cheek it was salt with the secret tears she had
wept and wiped away.

Five times that awful noise coughed and barked and
screeched and rasped its way to a crescendo, and each
time we were held in the following trough of low, desperate panting and stirring, and then, as it started again
for the sixth time, I could stand it no longer.

I swung away from Sophie to the side of the cage and

grabbing the bars I shook them and yelled at the top of
my voice:

'Stop it you bastards! Stop it!'

It was odd. I don't know whether it was the ferocity
of my voice, or because it was human and the human
voice confuses all wild animals into silence; but they
stopped.

Behind me Sophie laughed, an edgy, unreal sound. But
I scarcely heard her, was not really aware of the effect
my voice had had, for I was staring straight ahead of
me into the next cage, and my mind was suddenly cold
and clear with hard shock. I was drunk one moment and
then, a bucket of water in my face, standing sober, wondering where the idiot I had known myself to be two
seconds before had gone.

The birds in the next cage were restless, disturbed,
shuffling about their perches. It was these perches that
held my attention. They ran from side to side of the
cage at different levels; long, thick lengths of bamboo.
My hands on the bars were now only a few inches from
the end of one of them. I looked at it and saw that it was.
held to one of the horizontal cage bars by a thin looping
of soft wire.

I turned to Sophie and called her over. She stood by
me and I pointed to the perches which were about eight
feet long.

'Look, Sophie—if we can get three of those bamboos,
we can lash them together and then reach those keys on
the loop by the door.'

Before I had finished speaking my fingers were at work
on the wire fixing nearest to me. It untwisted easily and
by pushing the bamboo up I got my fingers between the
bars and had a grip on it. The birds on the bamboo squaw-
ked and flew off. The large toucan flopped to the ground
and stalked away indignantly. The end of the bamboo
was attached on the far side of the cage in a wire loop
also. I pulled the perch back towards me to free it. It
would not come at first and I swore as I tried to get a

better grip with my fingers in the limited space between the bars. Then suddenly it came away. The far end dropped to the floor of the cage and I almost lost my grasp on the end I held. But I just saved it and then I was pulling it through into our cage. Eight feet of beautiful, smooth bamboo, marked here and there by bird droppings. I could have shouted with joy.

Sophie called to me. She had climbed up the cage side a little and was working at another perch. I went over and held her and she made a better, quicker job than I had done because her hand was smaller. The birds now were alarmed. Some of them flew around the cage, their wings beating against the bars, a dark, soft movement that sent up quick gusts of stale, dusty air in our faces.

Very soon we had the three lengths we needed. And now I was taking back all I had said about men and animals. The cage had made us animals and stopped us thinking, filling us with a desire for freedom and dwarfing our ability to conceive a design for it. I was suddenly cocky, self-sure and elated ... hope was blossoming in me like a great red flower opening to a new sun. I took the thin belt off my overalls and lashed two of the bamboos together, giving them a good overlap to ensure rigidity. I poked one end out of the cage in the direction of the keys and set to work to lash the third bamboo on. For thongs I tore my large handkerchief into four strips. Then I pushed the long rod through the bars, keeping a butt of about two feet under my arm for steadiness. The rod reached the keys easily.

Sophie said, 'You'll never do it. The end droops too much.'

And she was right. The weight of the bamboos made the far end dip. I could get the end into the loop and lift it off the nail but the moment it was free it would slide down and off the drooping tip. And whichever way I turned the bamboo I could not get rid of the dip at the end.

'I'll do it.' I was determined to do it. I pulled the rod back until the end was inside our cage. Then I lay down

on the floor and pushed the rod out again at floor level
and then up towards the loop of keys. The whole rod
now sloped upwards at an angle of about thirty degrees
until it was within two feet of the loop and then the dip,
corrected by the long upward slant, evened out almost
parallel with the ground. Once I got the wire loop on the
far end of the rod all I had to do was to raise it higher
and the keys would slide down towards me.

And they did. I got the end through the loop and then
raised the tip. The loop came up free of the nail and half
an inch back from the end of the rod. I shook the rod
gently, raising it, and the next moment the loop was
sliding down towards us, the keys swinging and touching
off soft lights where the hurricane glow hit them.

We pulled the rod in and took the keys from it. I stood
there, keys in my hand, and saw Sophie's face close to
mine. All the anxiety which had been in my love went.
It was a fighting, hopeful love now. I flung my arms
around her, gave her a hug and a kiss and then swung
round to the padlock. But I had to give the keys to her.
Her hand was smaller and could go through the bars.

Quickly she found the right key and we swung the bolt
back and then pushed the barred door open. We jumped
to the floor. She would have moved at once to the small
door in the big barn doors but I held her. We had to
know what we were to do once we were outside.

I looked at my watch. Drexel and his party had been
gone nearly three-quarters of an hour.

I said, 'How far is this place from a village or the
police?'

'Ten or twelve miles.'

'We'd never get any help in time. We've got to go
after them ourselves. But they've got a big start on us.'

Sophie was silent for a moment, frowning as she
thought.

'You know the path,' I said. 'What chance have we
got?'

She said, 'They have to go right round the other side
of the lake before they begin to climb. There's a rough

road and they won't be travelling fast if they have to keep
Jabal on that mule. If we could get a car we could drive
round the lake. That would save time. Once we're in the
mountains I can show you short cuts they won't take
with the mule.'

I looked over at the lorry. But she saw my look and
shook her head.

'Too much noise ... opening these big doors. Gerard
has an old Citroën. It's usually parked in a shed round
the back of the barn.'

I said, 'If there isn't time there must be the car Drexel
came in. We've go to take a chance on it.'

But I knew there were other chances as well. The
party up in the hills was probably armed. Certainly
Paviot would have a knife. Even if we could catch up
with them and take them by surprise, the odds were with
them ... I had to have something to bring down the
odds.

'Come on,' I said and grabbed her wrist making for
the small door. I didn't say anything to her but I knew
that if things were quiet outside I was going to go into the
house and see if I could find something ... a rifle, shot-
gun ... something at least to give us a chance. By the
time we did ten miles and found the police, a sleepy,
obtuse gendarme who would be fifteen minutes coming
to his senses and another fifteen getting in touch with
anyone and then the whole palaver of a party getting up
here ... No—there was no help there. Into the farm, I
thought, and God help Sarrasin or whoever got in my
way.

Maybe I prayed too hard that I should come by a rifle
or a revolver. Anyway, my prayer was answered before
I was ready to take it. That's the trouble with prayers
—they usually get answered unexpectedly.

We were within four feet of the little door when it
opened and George Sarrasin stepped into the barn. He
was dressed in 'fancy costume'. Black sweater, the belt
with the silver buckle, and tight breeches. In the pale
light his face was large and ashen, a brooding, forceful

head and some trick of shadows on it made me think
of Nero ... all he needed was a bayleaf crown. That was
the mind, like a snipe never flying straight, but my body
was already moving directly towards him. I saw his hand
swinging towards the back pocket of his breeches and
I knew he was getting my revolver for me. I hit him as
he pulled it out. I hit him with my right shoulder and
low down in the dirtiest tackle of my life—which for a
Scot is saying something.

I heard the breath go from him with an anguished
sough. He crashed back against the barn doors so that
the elbow of the arm that was holding the revolver was
jerked forward. We fell together, and I saw the weapon
fly across in front of me. As I hit the ground, I shouted to
Sophie. The shout was shortened in me as Sarrasin's foot
came out and kicked me in the face.

CHAPTER EIGHTEEN

We came up together and it was as though we moved in slow motion, as though the atmosphere itself had become glutinous and was seeking to hamper our actions. I felt the blood from my injured lips wet and warm over my cheek. He opened his mouth to shout and I dived forward, my hands outspread to catch his neck. His fist came up in a long swing and took me in the chest but my momentum carried me on, crushing down on him, and no sound came from his throat but a short grunt of pain.

We went down, rolling and rolling and striking one another, and we might have been tumbling on a cloud bank and we ourselves made of some insubstantial stuff into which fist and feet sank and then, when withdrawn, left our bodies without mark or pain. But dreamlike as the struggle might seem, I knew that what was in me was in him also. I didn't want just to fight and overpower him, I wanted to kill him. I wanted to destroy him because he had become associated in my mind with all the evil that had wrapped itself round me since I had come to France. I knew that in him there was embodied the apotheosis of all the potent desire of evil to flourish. But alongside all this in my mind raced the sharp, gutter-wisdom that all Scots have when it comes to a fight, the thing that is bred from porridge, whisky and mist. I stood by no rules, since none was demanded. I kicked and gouged and bored. Fist, elbow, foot and, if I could have got a hold, I would have used teeth, for we were not men we were animals and in our wild slamming, rolling and pounding, we were watched by animals and over the suck and gasp of our breath I heard the savage, unhappy roar of animal voices, the frenetic chattering, and the beat of pinioned wings against bars.

I saw Sophie hovering round us, revolver in hand. But there was no chance for her to shoot or strike. We were one body. Many things I remember. The moment when we stood face to face and with a bestial chivalry just swung punch after punch at one another, turn and turn about, until my head reeled. I remember my face thrust deep into straw and his hands about my throat and the wet, mouldy smell of the barn floor. His belt came undone and my fingers clawed at his black jersey, ripping it so that the flesh underneath showed through like a great wound.

After that first attempt to shout he never tried again. He accepted the fight, accepted our isolation, and gradually I knew why. He was going to beat me, to kill me. He was stronger, bigger and impelled by an equal hatred. And I knew too that I didn't care who won ... Maybe I was a little drunk with the frenzy in me. I asked for no more than to go on fighting, win or lose, satisfied that the real consummation of the dark passion between us lay in struggle, not an end to the struggle. But even so there was still the little figure of my common sense, perched somewhere above us, that marked and feared and calculated. The animals were making such a noise that attention must soon be attracted from the house; Sarrasin himself, I was sure, had come because of the noise made by the unusually restless animals.

We slewed round on the ground and his foot slid out wildly and struck the packing case. I heard the hurricane lamp go over and a cry from Sophie. As I twisted sideways from under him, I saw the gloom shot with points of flame. Against the pale grey which filled the far doorway I saw Sophie stamping her feet on tiny spurts and points of flame that ran like animated decorations up the side of a straw bale and among the loose straw on the floor. Then I saw no more of her for Sarrasin was astride of me and his enormous hands clamped themselves on my throat and I had only the vision of his great, overhanging face, lips drawn tightly back and his eyes dark with angry pleasure as he slowly throttled the life from me and held my leaping, straining body down with his weight.

From somewhere behind me the flames from the straw leapt higher and now his face was shadowed and lit with a constant movement. The roar of the blood in my own ears was mixed with the wild din the animals were making. His was the face of Nero over me, brutal with ecstasy as he watched me sink, a face that was pink, gold, black and white; the eyes shutting with a tiny movement each time he breathed and strained his hands against my neck.

Then blackness hit me. I went into the tunnel and suddenly the lights went out. Just the jostling and roaring and pounding of the wheels over the breaks in the rails. In a London tube when it happens the heart leaps sometimes and you say 'I've gone blind'. Dimly I heard myself say, 'This is death'.

When I came round Sophie was kneeling by me shaking my shoulders. I forced myself up a little on my elbows and she called urgently, 'David. Oh, David. Quick, quick. I can hear them coming.'

There was a brisk, crackling sound in the barn and a pink and yellow glow was flickering over the walls. I saw that the fire had spread through the straw on the floor and across to the lorry. It was leaping around the wheels. Sarrasin lay a few feet from me, groaning.

Sophie put an arm under me and helped me up.

I said stupidly, 'What happened to him?'

'I hit him with the revolver.'

I swayed a bit and she held me and slowly my head cleared. I sucked at the air and it was like breathing burnt paper. I choked with the smoke. We stumbled towards the small door. Outside I heard voices calling and then through the open door I could see them. Three figures were running towards the barn and I recognized Gerard, and Fargette, but not the other.

There was no time for us to get out, so I pulled Sophie aside with me, pressing against the big door and behind the shelter of the open small door. With luck they would come dashing in and past us. Not far away was Sarrasin on the floor and a ragged tail of flames curved part of the way round the lorry. If they were quick, I thought, they could get the big doors open and run the lorry out. The lorry was the real danger, for the building was of corrugated iron. I saw Sarrasin stir and then lever himself groggily to his feet. He didn't look our way. He stood for a moment with his hands against his forehead and then with a clumsy urgency he staggered towards the lorry.

Gerard and the others swept in through the door past us. I heard Gerard's alarmed call like the sudden yaffling of a woodpecker and he went, with arms upstretched like a prophet of despair, towards the flames and began to dance and stamp on them.

Sophie and I stayed for no more. We slipped around the edge of the small door and were outside. She took my hand and we began to run.

There was confusion in my mind. Nothing seemed clear and orderly. Life and time seemed to have reduced itself to a postcard album that I was watching over someone's shoulder. They were flipping the pages over too quickly for me to get any lasting picture; only now and then a page stuck and I did see clearly.

There was the morning, a pearl stretch of sky. A row of poplars like angry cat's tails. And the spread of the lake, dull, tarnished tin-plate with a cold eddy of mist on its surface. A shed against the barn and a dust-powdered Citroën with its windshield wet with dew across which I drew my sleeve. The self-starter which complained and complained, whining under my foot.

There was the yard with a few early hens with fluffy feathers round their feet, as though their pants had slipped, pecking away at the dirt and then scattering as we came down upon them, the engine missing and coughing against the damp and cold. There was an open gateway and myself shouting suddenly to Sophie—

'Right or left?'

And hearing but not hearing her reply and turning right on to a rutted track.

The car kicked and bucked and something at the back went *bang*, *bang*, and further behind there were voices, shouting, angry, and then the sound of a shot. Suddenly, I was exhilarated and happy as though I had discovered the right way to live, in a postcard album with quickly turning pages, and I looked down and found Sophie's hand in the crook of my arm and I took my hand from the wheel and touched it.

Then slowly the pages stopped flipping and there was only one page, one postcard, and I drove into it, giving the car hell and not caring. A long stretch of dusty, bumpy lake-side track. The water a few yards away on our right was fringed by tall tufted reeds and enamelled here and there by green lily-pads.

To the left a slope went up gently through patches of grass and whitebroom and long slides of chipped rock into which pines had been stuck at careless angles, and ahead of us, far away round the lake, was the steep black side of a mountain, patterned with shadow as far as the tree line and then suddenly gleaming in the morning light and with a scalloping of snow along a smooth shoulder that ran to a pimpled peak.

Sophie said, 'We keep along this track until we come to a quarry on the left. Then we must go up the valley.'

'Track for the car?'

'For a little way. This is the road they used to bring the stone down.'

I nodded. It was the kind of nod you give to a mildly interesting piece of information at a lecture, knowing you aren't going to remember it for long. Already my mind was ahead, beyond the quarry and up the valley. Somewhere up there, an hour ahead of us was Jabal on his way back to Ramaut ... The cold morning air would have brought him round. He would know what was happening to him. Jabal who played *Smoke Gets in your Eyes* and *Frim-Fram Sauce* and whose father had fought with Lawrence of Arabia. I thought of Saraj, noisy, dusty, sun-drenched, and the meat stalls on the quay with the long skewers turning over the charcoal braziers and the dark-eyed friendly boys who stole anything that was left around.

Out on the right a fish jumped and the ripples gave colour and movement to the dirty leaden surface. And I remembered Sophie talking about Fargette ... I looked across at her and she smiled at me. The sun lifted over a hill shoulder and the morning miraculously became tinged with gold and red and blue.

The car lurched madly over a hole in the track and Sophie was thrown against me. As she drew away, grasping the dashboard to steady herself, she said:

'I've put the revolver in your pocket. It's got a full chamber.'

I'd got her, I'd got a revolver, and I'd taken up the chase. All I wanted for complete happiness was a pair of wings.

A stream came down the hillside and crossed the track to the lake. We went through it at speed and great sheets of spray rose like wings on either side of us, and I laughed because my prayer had been answered. A twist in the conformation of the lakeside brought us for a while into a position where just over my right shoulder I could look back and see the farm. It was small now and stood out on a flat promontory. From behind the barn, the open space hidden from our sight, a grey and tawny trail of smoke looped and swayed up into the sky. I guessed they'd got the lorry out. I wondered what they would do. Come after us or abandon ship? I didn't bother to think it out for them. That was their problem.

We reached the quarry. Running up from it was a valley, more a gorge than a valley, with a noisy, frothy, boulder-strewn torrent coming down full-pelt to the lake. Oaks and scrub reached down almost to the stream-banks. A narrow track twisted between the trees. I put the Citroën at the track, bounding and slewing in my seat and holding myself by the wheel. The outside mirror snapped off against a tree a boulder took a long score down one side of the body, something snapped underneath but she kept going. We must have made nearly three miles before the end came. We topped a small rise and on the far side the track dipped away obliquely. The car slewed sideways and then, skidding back to the track, hugging it like a lover, jumped a rocky step and was suddenly foundered in the stony bed of a small stream whose far bank was studded with young larch.

We got out. Without a farewell to the car Sophie and I plunged into the larches, following a thread of path. She pointed once and I saw the marks of the mule's hooves in the soft ground.

The birds began to sing. Maybe they started because we brought them company and an audience made it worth their while. Behind us the sun slipped above some spur and the wood was full of green and gold haze. After a time the path steepened so that we were using our hands and I could see where the mule had been forced to take the slope on a zig-zag course. I followed Sophie, part of me taking pleasure in watching the strong, easy way she set herself at the climb, and another part of me worrying now about Jabal and the others. They had a long start on us and there was no guarantee that we should catch up with them. I kept that thought out of my mind. We had to catch them. My luck was running well so far ... I didn't care that in the past it had let me down ... this time I was sitting it tight, ready for the sudden buck, the quick slip.

We came out of the trees and were under a broken shoulder of rock rising like a cliff from some Hieronymus Bosch landscape through dark shadows to the pale blue sky touched with cloud-like wisps of morning sleep still waiting to be rubbed away. A nice simile, I thought; but as an Eng. Lit. master I would have slated any boy who had used it. However, this was hurried composition, and there was no self-criticism in me ... just a mixture of happiness and racing anxiety to get ahead. And I knew what was happening to me; any climber would have recognized it. You put your body at a task and your mind swings free, like a ship at slack cable length, and half the joy of effort is the comforting, easy fantasy of thoughts.

The mule track ran away around the right of the buttress.

Sophie said, 'If we go straight up over we shall save a mile.'

We went straight up over. It was like going up the Milestone Buttress on Tryfan, only four times as long and not quite as hard; no need for a rope, but every need for eye, hand and feet.

There were long loose patches of weathered stuff into which our feet sank deep and then a sheer rise in creviced and crannied steps, which I liked better because we made faster time. Once, waiting for Sophie to find the lead, I looked back and down. The lake was a long way below us and the sun had polished it now. There was still a plume of smoke coming up from the farm, and I could see that it came from the lorry which had been run out into the open yard. The animals were safe ... I thought of Sarrasin getting groggily to his feet and forgetting us as he went towards the lorry. Animals meant something to him. He was happy and at home with them. Tarzan of the *Grand Cirque Pyrénéen*. But it was not a sneer. It was admiration ... and because it was there I knew the bad blood was purged from me and old Father Compassion was back, smoking that pipe of his and being so damned wise and considerate that it was hard to make up my mind to kick him in the bottom and to remember all that had happened in the last weeks. You tell me, I said to the old boy, as I grasped at rocks and hauled myself after Sophie, what it is that makes us find something to like in the people we hate most. Perhaps it's gratitude for giving us a mark for a rare emotion ... for hatred is vintage stuff and should be decanted slowly. Friendship—I followed the fancy, with Drexel in mind, as I squeezed behind Sophie up a narrow funnel—isn't even chateau bottled. I was going to suspect it for a long time and stick to hatred and love.

When we got to the top we ran along the edge of a
plateau and then could look down into the twisting valley
that snaked around the great mountain plug we had just
climbed. We stood watching the break in the trees and
rocks where the trail came into view. But there was no
sign of Drexel and his party.

'They must still be ahead,' I said. 'How far is the
border?'

Sophie pointed. Facing us was a long, broken line of
crests cut with valleys whose lower cheeks held a faint
stubble of trees. There's something about hills to be
crossed which can depress you. They sprawl grandly
across the edge of the sky, big, still insolent creatures, and
if you worry about them they only irritate and exhaust
you. The thing to do is to put your head down, keep your
eyes no more than ten feet ahead and go on.

We started forward over the plateau at a gentle jog
trot. After twenty minutes there was nothing gentle
about it. But we kept on, Sophie and I, plugging forward
and I was glad that she was ahead of me, for I loved
every inch of her and every movement in her. She looked
small and not up to it, but she had a strength inside her
which I would never have suspected. She was no drooping
princess over a pond now. The wind took her black hair
and filled her blouse, wickering at it, and there were few
words between us, but many a look and we both knew
what was in one another's thoughts.

I don't know how long we were going. It may have
been half a lifetime; but it seemed longer than that. I
know I had time to get a new job, furnish a house and
raise a family. I had trouble with the boys' names. The
girls I left to Sophie, and I was old and inclined to bore
my grandchildren with the tale of how I first met their
grandmother. We splashed up the course of a stream
that was as cold as all charity. I felt the sole of my right
shoe flapping loose and a bunch of flies began to treat
my cut lips as quick-lunch counters.

The head of the stream ended in a waterfall, a dark,

slimy spout thick with moss and ferns. We stopped, our feet on the gravel bed of the pool into which the fall thundered, the water lapping above our ankles.

'Up there?' I said.

'That or around the slope which will lose us time.'

'All right,' I said, but I didn't like it. It was a wet, slippery, dangerous climb with a notch of blue sky two hundred feet above us.

Sophie made a move forward but this time I held her back. A quick glance had showed me that there were a few overhangs and ledges where she would need a hand coming down to her. I had more height and strength than she. I put a hand on her shoulder and pulled her back towards me. Her face came up to mine. God knows we had no time for it when every second counted, but I didn't like the look of that wall-face and my imagination painted a hundred ugly pictures. We kissed and for a moment there was warmth and tenderness and a velvet smooth oblivion about us. She had her hands on my back, gripping me, and her mouth against mine had a life of its own, drawing me into her. He eyes were open and I saw the fine sheen of sweat on her eyelids, and her eyes weren't black but a dark steel-blue and their brilliance mirrored my face and also the changing colours of the small rainbows that salaamed above the white spume at the foot of the fall. The water could have risen six feet to our heads and I wouldn't have felt it.

I wasn't aware of beginning to climb with her behind me. A miracle must have separated us. It was like going up a cliff covered with wet sealskin. I dug my fingers and feet into the thick moss, tore it away and broke my nails uncovering the hard rock to give her firm holds. Once I slipped and came down three feet with a crack that should have smashed my ribs. The V-notch got wider and wider. The falling water drew away to our right and its spray was now only faint on our faces. We were soaked through and cold. Ten feet from the top I reached down for her.

I began to pull her up, but suddenly she slipped and her hand, wet and slimy with moss, was jerked from mine by her weight.

My heart turned over like a dolphin diving. I saw her falling and below her the long black drop with its ragged white ribbon of water smashing down to the pool at the foot of the cliff. She slid three yards down the rock face and then her outflung hands grabbed at a stone. I jumped, marking a ridge below me, and went down the rock with my heels dug in. I hit the ledge with a jolt and grabbed her as she hung there, lying half over the edge. I pulled her up and clasped her to me. She was making a weird crying noise from shock. I could have killed the whole world in revenge for the fear that was still pounding in me.

I didn't care a damn about Jabal or anything then except her. I kept her there until the terror was gone from her body. I talked to her, not knowing what I said. And, sooner than I thought she would, she came out of it, and I loved her for her courage.

At the head of the fall we were on some kind of watershed; a long stretch of boggy grass that sang with hidden water as we started across it towards a patch of firs. Beyond the firs I could see another ridge rising and drifts of snow hanging in the lee of its spurs. We had only gone a few yards when I saw a movement against the far line of trees. There was the white flash of two faces turning towards us. Distantly I heard someone shout. I began to run squelching across the wet, cushiony ground, and as I went I pulled out my revolver. Behind me I could hear Sophie following closely.

Dunwoody must have been leading the mule and was already lost in the trees, but Drexel and Paviot were behind, standing at the edge of the trees. I had a feeling that somewhere on our climb they must have looked back from some vantage point and seen us.

To my surprise they did not wait for us or try to hold

us off. They turned and ran into the trees, and we went after them. I had my revolver out and I was eager to get after them. But I was not so reckless that I was going to run into an ambush. I waved Sophie back and stopped when I was some way into the trees. Then I called her on, and I went forward another jump, watching every clump of scrub, every tree trunk. They were young trees and the trunks gave no cover. But there was no sign of Drexel and the others. Then I heard them ahead of me. One of them was shouting and I thought I caught the *clop, clop* of the mule's hooves, and the sound was oddly echoing and hollow.

I knew why a few moments later.

We came to the edge of the trees and before us was a stretch of open ground about ten yards wide that abruptly fell away to a long, curving gorge, a great fissure thirty feet across. The ravine stretched along the full length of the foot of the peak that rose on the other side. Across it was a thin, flimsy plank bridge ... But bridge was too fine a word for it, it was just a few slender pine poles and planks and a handrail that was rotten and broken away in places.

It was an ugly looking place, unwanted, barren, as though nature knowing it was a border area, neither France nor Spain, had let the whole thing go. The far hillside was untidy with shale and loose rock, and water from the melting snow patches glistened over it like snail trails. A cold wind came whistling along the edge of the trees and the black crack yawned and grinned like a gigantic shark's mouth with the bridge a toothpick that had got wedged between the upper and lower incisors.

I took a step out of the cover of the trees and went back at once. Dunwoody with Jabal on the mule was halted on the far side of the bridge. Seeing me he raised his revolver and fired. I heard the bullet plug into a trunk not far from me. At that distance it was good shooting.

I pulled Sophie down behind a rock and then peering round the side of it saw what they were doing. Jabal

had had his feet freed now and was sitting the mule upright and looking reasonably recovered, Dunwoody had
the lead rein in one hand and a revolver in the other and
he was watching our rock. At the far end of the bridge
Paviot and Drexel were working. They were kicking
away at the earth and pine pole ends. I saw the turf flying
and then a plank went clattering down into the gorge.
Paviot bent down and got his hands round one of the
long poles and began to heave and strain. And I knew
what was coming. They were going to dislodge the bridge
and then there would be no crossing for us. It would take
us ages to go down the length of the gorge and find a
place across, and by that time they would be up over the
crest and into Spain. On the far side of the crest Sophie
had already told me there was a track good enough
for a car. We'd get there in time to smell their exhaust
fumes.

I got up on my knees and took a shot at Paviot, but it
went wide, striking the ground somewhere near the mule
and making it plunge. Dunwoody fired again at me. I
ducked back into cover, cursing. It was dangerous to
fire at them. I might hit Jabal. Dunwoody could keep
me pinned down easily while the other two worked away.

I was saying 'Hell! Hell! Hell!' to myself stupidly. To
have come so far, to have the whole thing practically in
my hands and now to lose it all . . .

Another plank went and I saw the crazy handrail
sway and partly break away as Drexel now bent to the
other supporting pine pole. The two of them began to
lift the bridge and work it sideways.

And then I knew there was only one thing to do. Not
a thing you think about, but something the body starts
doing without thought. I stood up and began to run
forward, revolver in hand. I sprinted for the bridge and I
was going to cross it before they slid it over into the
gorge.

Dunwoody fired again and shouted, and the bullet
might have gone right through me for all I knew about it.
Drexel and Paviot looked up and across to me. I saw

Paviot's right hand free itself from it's hold on the pole
and slide round to his pocket.

Behind me I heard Sophie shout my name. But I kept
on running and, suddenly, this was another picture postcard, but an animated one; the blue sky, washed on a
little carelessly, and a black splash of a buzzard soaring
somewhere up aloft; the wet snow-water gleams and
the tight clumps of rock-moss; Dunwoody trying to hold
down the head of the restless mule; and Drexel heaving
away at the pole and the end of the bridge now two feet
in the air. And now, seen for the first time, a thin double
strand of wire strung across the mountain flank marking
the border line, and me running in a kind of lurching,
dreamlike fashion, as though I had a whole pack of dogs
about my feet to trip me.

Dunwoody fired again and this time I knew where it
went. The bullet hit the ground a few feet ahead of me
and a splinter of stone came up, whirring like a June bug,
and dug itself into my right cheek, the pain filling me
with fresh anger.

But I never reached the bridge. Paviot's hand came
round full of the blackness of the gun he held in it; but
beyond his hand I saw something else. Paviot became part
of the landscape. I had eyes for no one except Jabal.
Dunwoody shouted and Jabal swung sideways, kicking
out with his foot. The revolver went spinning from Dunwoody's hand. The next moment Jabal had wheeled the
mule round and was riding down on Drexel and Paviot.
It was no wild charge, just an unwilling lumbering movement that proved the mule had no sense of crisis. Jabal
rode down and they heard him coming. It was too late for
them to do anything. He drove the mule straight at
Paviot. I saw the man lurch backwards, heard him yell,
and then he went over the edge of the ravine. Drexel
dropped his pole. The flimsy bridge crashed back and a
cloud of dust went up from its rotten timbers.

I stood there, three feet from my end of the bridge, and
there was no movement in me. Drexel twisted towards
Jabal and tried to grab the lead rein. But Jabal flung

himself off on the far side of the mule from Drexel and the next moment he was on the bridge and running towards me with Drexel after him.

I shouted 'Jabal ...' I would have shouted more to warn him, for the disturbed bridge was as weak as cardboard; but the name Jabal was all I ever got out for at that moment the bridge collapsed with both of them on it.

Behind me I heard Sophie cry agonizingly. The bridge folded up slowly but with an ungodly cracking noise, and I saw white wood splinters fly off into the air like locusts. Jabal flung himself forward, grabbed at a piece of handrail and then slid back towards Drexel and out of my sight as the bridge dropped away.

I moved then, flinging myself to the edge of the gorge, and there the bridge was below me, hanging downwards from my side like a rotten stairway, the transverse planks at all angles like a wrecked xylophone. Twelve feet beneath me I saw Drexel hanging on to a plank with one hand. With the other he had got Jabal beneath the arm and shoulder and was holding him up. The youth's dark face was twisted with pain and there was a cut across his forehead. He was almost out and unable to help himself.

'Quick, David!'

But Sophie was late telling me, I was already on my way down the crazy ladder of the bridge. I hadn't realized until then how deep was the drop in the gorge. It went down like a black and angry wound into the flank of the mountain.

'Hurry, for God's sake!'

I saw Drexel swinging below me as the bridge swayed over the deep drop. Somewhere a timber broke away, hit the side of the gorge and started a clattering fall of rocks and sliding earth. A plume of dust swirled up into my face.

I climbed down, tearing my hands and ripping my clothes and then I could go no further. There was a gap in the planking about three feet long. I hung on to the side pole, not trusting the last transverse plank length and I reached down. I got a hand on Jabal's arm and I began to pull him up. He was coming round a bit and made a feeble effort to help himself. I gripped him and I heaved but with only one arm it was a hell of a strain. Drexel saw this and he helped. His face tensed with the effort to push Jabal up. Slowly he came and then I got a firmer hold on him and his right hand came up and clutched at the plank by my shoulder. But I wasn't looking at Jabal. My face was only a couple of feet from Drexel's and, as I took the strain and Jabal began to help himself more, working up past me, Drexel's face relaxed. Jabal's weight went from him and I saw his freed hand come up towards his other hand to take a hold on the length of broken handrail he was grasping. But he was too late. The rail, rotten with wind and rain and snow, began to pull and crumble free from the clumsy great nails that held it. Drexel looked at me, and he knew he was going. Jabal was past me now, climbing upwards and I could hear Sophie helping him, encouraging him. But they were in another world. There was only Drexel below me, and beyond him the dark gorge with Paviot lying twisted there somewhere far beneath . . . I reached down a hand now to Drexel, shouting to him to take it. He could have taken it easily. But he hung one-handed to the rail and his free hand—though it moved—never went out to take a fresh hold or to grasp mine. His arm came up in a slow gesture, greeting and farewell, and he was smiling, that damned, hard, spit-in-the-eye-of-the-world smile . . . the old Drexel. I couldn't bear to watch it because I knew what he was doing and I didn't want him to do it. I wanted to bring him up, to bring him back, to have it all over and forgotten and things to be the same between us . . . I was the boy who wanted time to go back on itself. But he was a man and he was tired of time and he was wise enough, and big enough, to know that the score chalked up to our friendship could be wiped out now with only one payment.

He just said, 'David.' My name, his voice, his eyes on

me, and everything the same between us, and the payment made. When I grabbed at him the rail went, or, maybe, he let go of it a second before it pulled away. I don't know. I only know that I shut my eyes. Not wanting to see his black silhouette turning over and over and dropping to join Paviot and the blackness below. I shut my eyes but his face was clear in my mind ... and it was the face that had come back to me long ago when I had lain in the sand with the vultures up above and the flies bunching indecently about the wound in my leg. His face and that last valedictory movement of his hand which, had he raised it another three inches, could have grasped mine. And I knew then which was the true nature of Minerva, knew the truth about myself and Drexel, and the truth about the love in our friendship. ... Nothing matters if you love. Nothing. Once it's there, it's there for good.

Dunwoody got away and I never saw him again. He went up the mountain on the mule, plump-bodied and, I'll bet, beaming even in disappointment. I fired the rest of my rounds after him hoping to wake some frontier guard and get him picked up. But it didn't work.

It took us a long time to get back to the farm and when we did we found Didier there with a party of gendarmes. Jean Cagou had recognized me in the circus, recognized, too, that I was no part of the clown act, but it had taken them all a long time, too long, to get round to the farm. Gerard they got, but not Sarrasin. He disappeared into some other jungle; and Fargette—and I couldn't help being glad about this—went with him, or maybe alone. Maybe, somewhere, he still wears a red nose, a large white collar and baggy checks and sets the children's voices shouting with laughter.

The Foreign Office fixed a lot of thing up. What Drexel would have called their 'poops' went to work and the Press never had the full truth. It was all very gentlemanly, except that, a few months later, somewhere along the line Sheik Ahmed ben Fa'id died, probably not peacefully, in his bed. I think Jabal was there when he died. And Anglo-Media's oil concession still stands, renewed for fifty years.

Drexel? He lies on a hill above Banyuls with just his name and two dates cut into marble, and once every spring for certain the flowers against the headstone are fresh ... and afterwards Sophie and I walk down past the Arago Aquarium and along to the *Café aux Bons Enfants* and have a drink. We never talk much over the drink. We just sit there, watching the old women burn the seaweed and after a while her hand comes out and is held by mine.